sonji

Dryzzian Legends—Book 1

ENDORSEMENTS

What an entertaining story. If you like adventure and gentle romance, then *Sonji* is a story for you. Join the excitement as Astra recaptures her stolen magical horse and races this horse across the Great Desert against stiff competition. Travel with Hamal and Astra as they learn the meaning of friendship, love, and forgiveness.
—**Derinda Babcock**, author, A Tale of Three Kingdoms series

Jessica Tanner's rare talent to transport her reader to another universe is well experienced when reading *Sonji*. She spins tales along with magical descriptions using a deft hand born of the story tellers of old. Tanner holds us from beginning to end and leaves us hungry for more.
—**Lynn Moffett**, author, the Incursion series and the Woodbridge trilogy

The story of *Sonji* is charming and compelling. Jessica Tanner's story is tightly executed and full of action. Readers will fall in love with her characters. Tanner has a unique sense of storytelling. Her talent and skill in craft are beyond her age. She brings readers into a believable and riveting fantasy world. Her story is grounded in history and spiritual principles. With intense conflict, but subtle, the readers will move through the story plot satisfied to the end. Enjoy a trip into another world where good triumphs over evil.
— **Betty J. Slade**, columnist for *Pagosa SUN* newspaper and author, *Taming Wild Hearts*

This story is a wonderful blend of *The Black Stallion* and *Hidalgo*, laced with the magical wonder of fantasy greats such as the Narnia series. I love the allegory that unfolds in this story, and the way the Creator reveals such things as speaking to His different children in different ways.

This truly spellbinding story will speak to lovers of horses, adventure and love as much as it will to those looking for the next fantasy read. I can't wait to see what Ms. Tanner will bring in her next book!

—T.E. Bradford, author of Selah Award finalist Divide Series books, and Writers of the Future, Realm, and Golden Scroll award-winning *Awakened*.

I liked it. Mystical, magical. It kept me intrigued. Looking for what's next.

—Brent Tanner

sonji

Dryzzian Legends—Book 1

Jessica A. Tanner

A Christian Company
ElkLakePublishingInc.com

COPYRIGHT NOTICE

Cover and Interior Design: Derinda Babcock, Jeff Gifford, Deb Haggerty
Editor(s): Mel Hughes, Deb Haggerty

PUBLISHED BY: Elk Lake Publishing, Inc., 35 Dogwood Drive, Plymouth, MA 02360, 2023

Library Cataloging Data
Names: Tanner, Jessica A. (Jessica A. Tanner)
Sonji / Jessica A. Tanner

408 p. 23cm × 15cm (9in × 6 in.)
ISBN-13: 978-1-64949-908-0 (paperback) | 978-1-64949-909-7 (trade hardcover) | 978-1-64949-910-3 (trade paperback) | 978-1-64949-911-0 (e-book)
Key Words: Christian fiction; young adult; fantasy; adventure; family; horses; young romance.

Library of Congress Control Number: 2023940406 Fiction

DEDICATION

To Mom and Dad

ACKNOWLEDGMENTS

Thank you, Mom and Dad, for your support and letting me write to my heart's content. Little Bro, who's not so little, I'm forever in your debt for your putting up with my need to double check the plausibility of a million ideas. To my grandparents, thank you for sharing your love of stories and reading—and for taking peeks in my writing journals and then commenting on what you found.

Ms. Field, thank you for your endless support and the Creative Writing Club you started, where I could hang out and share stories with fellow writers my age.

Linda Farmer Harris, Betty J. Slade, and the Wolf Creek Christian Writers Network—you rock! I can never thank you enough for the knowledge you've shared, your constant prayers, and the endless supply of great books you've shared with me for learning and more.

Mel Hughes, you are awesome for helping my story go from a lump of coal to a diamond!

Deb Haggerty, thank you for accepting my story about a girl and her magic horse—I'm forever grateful you signed little me. Derinda Babcock, the cover layout and everything you did made *Sonji* an awesome-looking novel! Jeff Gifford, thank you for my cover design. And Elk Lake Publishing, Inc., thank you *so* much for your warm welcome to the family!

Last, but not least, I thank you, God, for leading me and blessing my work with the people I encounter.

PROLOGUE

In the days of old, the leader of the Destroyers, the Deceiver, tricked many into following him instead of their Creator. A great war between the Creator of All and the Deceiver ravaged the land for many years. To stop the war and to protect us, the Creator made a Veil—but the Deceiver did not take his loss well. He whispered in the ears of the weak of heart, guided them to the machines powering the Veil, and told them how to destroy the machines. So, the Creator summoned the people and tasked them to restore the Veil, but many never returned ... even those helped by his great white mare, Sonji.

That is what many say. But it was all long ago, and no one believes in such things anymore.

CHAPTER 1

Astra Paksim snipped the final thread of her needlework and slid her scissors into her basket on the bench. Princess Gefen, the golden sand, and the prancing horses in her sewn scene glittered like jewels in the afternoon sunshine.

Sonji, the mare she'd rescued two years before, attempted to grab a corner of the needlework with her teeth. Astra had found the milk-white horse in the desert, her lead rope wrapped around the wheel of an abandoned wagon. Her ribs showed and her sticky-dry tongue stuck from her mouth. She had no markings or brands. The commander of the *jundiin* stationed in Astra's village did not recognize Sonji or know of anyone missing a horse. Since no one had claimed the mare after a month, the commander said she could keep the horse.

Astra jerked the needlework away. "Not for you." Sometimes she wished her bench didn't sit in the middle of the animals' yard.

Slender fingers stole her work.

"Can I see?" Her little sister, Ehsan, stood on the bench and held the scene in a patch of sunlight. "Mrs. Zilfel will love this."

Mrs. Zilfel was a respected widow in Sh'vah Nahrot and mother of a well-established trader. Her opinion of Astra's needlework could bring higher paying clients ... or return her work to hobby status.

Sh'vah Nahrot meant "Seven Rivers." Most called the village Nahrot, the full name too much for speedy conversation. And according to legend, the place where seven underground rivers met was the gateway to the trail to the Palace of the Creator. Astra had ridden and explored miles of desert beyond the village but never found a trail leading to a palace.

"Are you sure?" Astra stepped onto the bench.

Twelve-year-old Ehsan nodded. "This is the celebration after Princess Gefen and her horse Sonji rescued the people from the wicked sultan and put her brother on the throne, right?" She tilted the scene. The pinks and oranges in the princess's dress sparkled.

"Yes." Astra bit her lower lip.

"Why'd you use silver in the mane and tail of her Sonji?"

Astra snatched her work from Ehsan, rolled it, and tied a ribbon around it. She grabbed her sewing basket and jumped off the bench. "The silver offset better than adding more gold."

Her mare nuzzled her pocket, so Astra handed over her last dried apple slice.

"True." Ehsan got off the bench. "But I doubt that's the reason you used it instead of more gold."

Astra held her work close. "I ran out of golden thread."

Ehsan attempted to snag back the needlework. "And the thread is expensive."

"Yes." Astra avoided the attempt. If Mrs. Zilfel bought this piece, she'd have the last of the money she needed to sign up for the Great Desert Race of Dryzza. And with Sonji, Astra would win. Winning would bring riches and respect to her family. They'd no longer live a quarter of a mile out of the village and be treated like outcasts—people who didn't look like them—a description Astra fit perfectly because of her freakish brown and green eyes. And, by winning, Astra would no longer feel worthless.

But first steps first.

Ehsan hugged Sonji and slipped her a treat. "Why did you pick the celebration for your needlework this time?"

Astra rubbed the soft face of her mare. "I could envision the scene." And because of her intense dream months before, she'd also felt like she'd been part of the celebration. She entered her family home through the side door, with Ehsan following.

"Ehsan, why did you pick Sonji as the name for the family horse?" Astra hurried by her mother making dinner and into her room. She slid her needlework and basket far under her bed.

"She's your horse, not the family's." Ehsan climbed onto her own bed. "And she looks like the legendary Princess Gefen's Sonji—she's white and pretty and she runs faster than any horse I've ever seen."

Astra rolled her eyes and tried not to giggle. "When have you seen running horses?" Nahrot had no short distance races, and wild herds kept far away from people.

"When the horses broke out of Isaac's corral." Ehsan picked up her doll, a gift made by Astra for her birthday four years prior.

Isaac Zilfel was Mrs. Zilfel's son and the owner of the trading post. People from all over Dryzza worked with him because he had a sharp eye for stock—both animals and materials.

"I thought you were home when that happened." Astra changed from her skirt to her pants before she grabbed her riding boots from behind her bed.

"Are you going riding again today?" Her sister braided her doll's hair, multicolored pieces of leftover thread.

"Sort of." Astra ignored an uncomfortable heat rushing from her chest to her cheeks.

"You're going to meet Hamal then." Her sister grinned, a mischievous glint in her golden brown eyes.

"He's my friend. Quit with the romantic notions." The heat intensified, and she turned away from her sister to face the mirror.

"I didn't say anything." Ehsan tied off the end of her doll's woven hair before she set the doll on top of her pillow.

Astra adjusted the ties of her *sinar* around her head of raven-black hair. "Your expression talks for you."

"Tomorrow's Shabbos." Ehsan slipped off of her bed and bounced on the balls of her feet.

"I know. I'll be back before sunset." Astra breezed by her sister. She couldn't take any more questions or sharp observations without warming further, and besides, she was running late.

CHAPTER 2

Astra knocked at the back door of the blacksmith shop. Sonji, reins looped over her neck, stood behind her.

David Vassar stepped out, something black smeared on his forehead. He tucked a stained rag in his pocket. "Astra. Pleasant surprise."

She shifted to her left and tried to look behind the man without being obvious. "Hello, David, sir." The inside of the shop, despite the shutters and the double doors being open, seemed darker than a cave.

He chuckled. "You don't need to call me 'sir.' And Hamal has already headed home for the day."

"Oh." Astra reached a hand in her pocket, her fingers curling around the well-worn handle of her bell. Hamal would never forget her.

"He said he wanted to clean up before meeting you." He leaned against the doorframe of his shop, a twinkle in his eye much like the one Ehsan had earlier. "Our attempt to clean the forge made an awful mess."

"Thank you, David." She walked by his corralled donkey and up the street with Sonji following.

They passed Wisewoman Yasif's on the way to Hamal Nuru's home. The curtain for the front window lifted and fell. The medicine woman didn't live up to her title like Astra's grandmother had. Always snooping, always gossiping.

Astra's heart ached. Almost four years ago, her grandmother had moved in with her family, leaving her little house to the new village wisewoman. Astra's parents used the spare room in her father's furniture-making shop as their bedroom and let Grandma have their room in the house. Astra and Ehsan helped clean, feed, and dress their grandmother after she'd suffered whatever stole her speech and most of the mobility in her left side. Mama read and read from Grandma's journals and medicine books but could never figure out what caused her mother's sudden decline. And Wisewoman Yasif was as clueless as Mama.

Right after she turned thirteen, Astra had begun her apprenticeship under Grandma. She'd been so excited. Learned everything she could about raising healing herbs and what each one did and how to combine them for the best salves. She even had the chance to assist with the delivery of Isaac and Peridot's first baby. She'd heard they were expecting a second now.

A year after moving in, Grandma died.

Grandma's dying hurt worse than any physical wound Astra had encountered. She could have helped Mama search the journals and books. Could have helped find an answer. Instead, she pushed away her chance at becoming the next wisewoman. Pushed away what she'd done with Grandma. Pushed because practicing at being a wisewoman reminded her too much of what she'd lost.

She took an apprenticeship under her mother for embroidery and seamstress work. A few days later, Astra found Sonji.

Astra shook away her thoughts. Now was no time to relive the past and allow her buried tears to surface.

Sonji stopped, her ears flicked, and she faced a simple wooden door.

Seventeen-year-old Hamal emerged from his home and offered Sonji a carrot.

The mare accepted, the carrot vanishing in a single, crunchy bite.

Astra smiled. "Ham." He smelled like mint soap with a hint of metal and his turban sat on his head with a defiant tilt.

"Astra. What's your plan today?" He grinned and pulled a silver ball from his pocket.

"You'll see." The same warmth she'd felt when her sister bothered her rose from her chest and into her cheeks.

CHAPTER 3

Late that night, Hamal watched his silver gizmo, named Mo by Ehsan, roll around him on his bed. He should extinguish his oil lamp—wasting oil bothered his mother—but he couldn't bring himself to snuff the flame just yet.

"Someday I'm going to figure out how you work." Hamal had made Mo from gears he specially crafted and various pieces of scrap metal. He'd planned a twist-and-crank apparatus for the thing's different appendages, but Mo had seemed to come alive and worked without any obvious power source.

Mo rolled over his chest and down his right side, heading for his feet. The movement left a faint track in the blanket, kind of like a snake slithering across the sand.

Hamal had observed trains powered by steam and coal. He'd helped build pulley systems powered by an animal or person pulling on a rope. He'd wound clocks to keep them on time. How was Mo powered? Magic? Impossible … right? Right.

Hamal folded his hands behind his head. He and Astra had discussed her hopes of winning the race. He marveled at her dreams, despite her lack of money for registering for the race. And her connection with Sonji—incredible. Every ring of the bell he'd gifted her for her fourteenth birthday brought the horse running from wherever she and Mo would wander off to play.

Why did Sonji not fear Mo? Other animals did. Instead, Sonji played with Mo like it was her best friend.

He caught his gizmo and unleashed the wings. It zipped around the ceiling like a little bird, performing flips and quick turns. Its flapping created a soft *click-click* sound. The flight was a feat that according to Hamal's calculations should be impossible and yet was happening before his eyes.

Hamal whistled, and Mo sailed across the room. A second whistle, and it dropped into his hand. Amazing. He twisted once more, and the wings folded into the silver sphere—not even a seam to reveal where they came from.

The sharp ring of a bell broke through the nighttime quiet.

Hamal pocketed Mo and leaped from his bed. He ran into the main room, his heart beating faster than a train on the tracks.

Mother, in her nightgown and cloak, threw open the window and pushed aside the shutters as Hamal's mentor, David, raced by.

"David, what's wrong?" she yelled.

"The Paksims' furniture shop is on fire." He ran toward the southern part of town.

Hamal burst through the front door and onto the street. Astra's father's shop made up part of the fence around their house. If the fence went, the barn and house could too.

"Hamal, Hamal," his mother hollered from the window. "Be careful."

"I will," he yelled over his shoulder. He inhaled the scent of burning wood and watched dark smoke hide the stars.

Candles and oil lamps glowed yellow in his neighbors windows and doors swung out onto the street. Men and women raced from town and up the quarter-mile-trail to the Paksims'.

"Start a bucket line." The mayor, an aging, portly man, organized the villagers. The front gate for the fence around the Paksims' home was thrown open.

People doused the fence with buckets of water. Others threw water on the shop. The flames, while not huge, were still hot and cast dark shadows over everything.

Hamal joined the bucket line from the Paksims' well. He wished he could see Astra or Ehsan or their parents. Despite the mayor's efforts, the scene was chaotic, and soot covered most of the villagers, making identification harder.

Night marked the beginning of a new day, of Shabbos, the day of rest, but this one promised much work and no rest.

CHAPTER 4

The eastern horizon shifted from a black sky covered in stars to a faint gray. The fire had shrunk to a few embers that refused to cool. And the Paksims' well was dry. But the house and barn stood untouched, and the back wall of the furniture shop held true.

A fellow villager approached. "My turn for fire watch, Nuru." He seemed awake, freshly shaved and clean clothed.

Hamal nodded and forced back a yawn. "The embers are almost out, sir."

He walked the trail to the village, ready for home and some sleep. The gray sky lightened further as he tugged at the corner of his wrinkled, smoke-scented shirt and rubbed his stubble-covered chin.

Astra, covered in soot, slammed into him on the outskirts of Nahrot. They landed in the cool sand. A faint hint of vanilla and cinnamon combatted the wood smoke. She scampered off him before yanking him to his feet.

"Ham"—she grabbed his arm—"Sonji is gone. I took her and the chickens to Isaac's to keep them safe, and now she's gone!" She dragged him in the direction she'd come from.

She stumbled to a stop beside the barn and corrals behind the trading post. "I put Sonji in this corral. She was the only white horse here. I tried my bell and heard a faint whinny—but she never came." She paced by the doors to the barn, skirt flaring around her boots like an upside down blossom agitated by the wind.

He caught her by the shoulders and forced her to meet his gaze. "Let's try ringing the bell. Maybe she'll answer again."

"I've tried ... and tried ..." She sighed. "But I can try again." She reached in her pocket, pulled out her brass bell, and swung the handle.

A beautiful chime echoed through the village and beyond. A more cherished sound than the shrill cry of the bell by the House of Citizens.

Nothing.

Isaac's horses, a mixture of browns, blacks, and reds, shied and pushed against each other on the far side of the corral.

She swung again. Another chime.

Still no answer.

A memory of men passing drinks after a successful theft surfaced. A man he'd once called uncle sang a tale about a white horse ridden by a legendary princess, a horse symbolizing the success of a revolution, of a people freed from a tyrant. And she doubled as a key to the treasury of the Palace of the Creator, home of the biggest pile of loot ever known.

He cleared his throat. Paranoia would get him nowhere. He needed to put the past behind him and focus on the present.

Astra turned from the open desert, gripping her bell with white knuckles. Early morning sunlight glinted in her gold and emerald-green irises and drew out the deep blue and green hues of her ebony hair.

Hamal pointed. "How about you check the barn? Make sure the chickens are still all right, and see if there's any sign of Sonji in there."

She nodded. "Sure." She stuck the bell in her pocket and walked inside the barn.

Hamal checked the corral. Everyone had been distracted by the fire and left Sonji unwatched. But most of the footprints by the gate appeared to be Astra's, and so his hope for a clue to the thief's identity coming from his footwear or shoe size evaporated. He felt along the wooden gate and the support posts. No fibers. At the base of one post, he found a chip of wood, the image of a running horse carved into one side.

The calling card for his father's thefts.

He gripped the chip tight enough that the carving pressed into his palm to the point it could cut him.

Astra emerged from the barn and raised her hand to shield her eyes from the rising sun. "The chickens are fine. I didn't see any sign of Sonji in there."

"Which direction did you hear the whinny from?" He snuck his clue into his pocket.

Astra pointed to the south, nibbling at her lower lip.

She stopped, faced him. "Sonji has never wandered off before—someone has to have stolen her. I think we should go after her and the thief."

"I do too, but we need to go prepared." Prepared because the greatest thief of Dryzza never went anywhere without henchmen and his sword. Hamal knew this from past experience, experience he'd rather forget.

"I agree." She twisted the ends of her hair around her finger, her gaze distant like she was creating a mental list.

"And we're going to need help catching up." He rubbed the back of his neck. "How well do you like donkeys?"

Her forehead wrinkled. "I like them fine. Why?"

"Go get ready, and you'll see. We need to leave soon if we're to have any hope of catching up." His father's men could cover ground better than a steamed-up train on open track.

She ran off, her skirt flapping around her and a cloud of sand kicking up with each step.

He went home and washed off what he could of the soot before he collected supplies and borrowed David's donkey.

An hour later, as the villagers headed for Shabbos gathering, Hamal, Astra, and David's donkey trekked into the desert.

CHAPTER 5

Her breath caught at the sight of the white horse. Silently, she thanked the Creator.

Astra had found her stolen mare.

From behind her, Hamal said, "See her?"

She bobbed her head once. Their half-a-day trek on the faintest of trails had led right to Sonji. Her mare and three other horses were tied to a rope stretched between a pair of palm trees. Four camels were tethered to some other trees. Tents and crates spread under the cluster of palms like a makeshift corral. A woman knelt by the edge of a spring and filled a water skin while three men and a couple of dogs wondered through the camp.

Astra scooted away from the edge of the sand dune and the stink of dirty men and animals wafting on a hot breeze.

Hamal grinned. "Time to act?" His brown eyes glittered with mischief despite the purple crescents beneath them hinting at his exhaustion.

"No. I think we should wait until dark to steal her back." She opened the cuffs of her tan sleeves and shook out handfuls of scratchy sand.

Hamal cocked an ebony eyebrow. "She's white. She'll stand out in the dark."

"They'll be tired and drinking then." She refastened her cuffs, and wished she'd thought through how she'd steal back her horse before finding her.

"That doesn't mean they'll be blind."

She groaned. "Why release Mo now?" She couldn't believe she was considering his far-flung plan, but she'd come up empty on ideas.

"They'll be less inclined to follow us in the midday heat." He used the edge of the turban wound around the top of his head to wipe his forehead.

She shrugged. "They stole my Sonji-girl in the middle of the night."

"And they started a fire to keep us distracted." He wiggled both of his eyebrows like they helped demonstrate his brilliance.

"Maybe you're right." She tried not to laugh at her friend's antics.

Hamal nodded and pulled his gizmo from his pants pocket. He twisted Mo. Strange whirring noises echoed from inside.

"I don't know, Ham." She covered her face with her hands but peered between her fingers.

"Mo has never failed us before." The mischievous gleam in his gaze deepened.

Silver wings clicked from Mo's sides.

She bit her lower lip and dropped her hands to her lap. None of the thieves' animals would know what to do with the gizmo. Many would freak, and people could be trampled.

But she needed Sonji.

She released her lip. "Send in Mo."

He whistled. The winged ball zoomed toward the camp. Moments later, shrieks from terrified horses and the grunts of startled camels filled the air. Shouts from people joined the chaos, along with the barks of dogs.

Hamal grabbed her arm. They scrambled to their feet and slid down and around the dune to the base, where they stumbled to a halt.

SONJI

Hamal leaped on David's gray donkey.

Mo slashed a wing across the ropes securing the horses.

Astra pulled from her pocket and rang her small bell.

Sonji ran toward them ... followed by a cussing, one-eyed thief.

CHAPTER 6

Sonji skidded to a stop beside Astra and Hamal. Astra stuck the bell in her pocket and grabbed the severed rope dangling from her mare's halter. She sprang onto the sturdy horse and wove her fingers through Sonji's thick mane.

Hamal whistled and held out his hand. Mo flew to him. He twisted his gizmo and the wings snapped in with a click before he slid it into his pocket.

Astra tapped Sonji's sides with the heels of her boots and the sand flew beneath her. This was where she belonged.

A shout and a donkey bray echoed behind her.

She glanced over her shoulder, the wind whipping loose strands of her hair into her face.

Hamal and the donkey cantered several strides behind.

The one-eyed man stopped chasing and shook his fist. He shouted, his voice accented and full of rage.

Nothing else stirred. No one else attempted to follow.

A while later, she adjusted her position on her mare, urging the horse to slow and preserve energy. Astra smiled. Even going slower than a canter filled her with giddy tingles.

Hamal and the donkey caught up. He pushed his dirty turban away from his eyes and leaned close to Astra. "I don't see anyone pursuing."

"Good." Astra patted Sonji's shoulder and lifted her face to a cool breeze defying the desert afternoon.

Not a drop of sweat coated Sonji's fine body. The old donkey, on the other hand, had a bit of a sheen to his gray hide. Astra hoped the sweat would dry soon. She didn't want the old boy to get sick.

Hamal asked, "Do your parents know about this?"

"No." Astra shook her head, her sinar loosening and slipping back. "I told them about the theft, but not about us going after her."

"Why not?" Hamal lifted an eyebrow and swayed with the donkey's bumpy gate.

"I was afraid they might tell me not to." She rubbed her mare's neck. Sonji was the first horse her family had ever owned, since buying even a good one—much less one as fine as Sonji—cost more than they made in a year. Astra had traded her sewing projects for feed and tack.

"I doubt they would have told you no." Hamal sipped from his water skin, some of the liquid dripping onto his wrinkled shirt.

The sun continued to descend, and the mare and the donkey slowed. Astra and Hamal slipped from their mounts' backs and walked alongside.

The sweat had dried on the donkey. Sonji bore no new bruises or visible wounds on her body.

Astra patted her mare's side. When they reached a safe place for the night, she'd pull food and water. Sonji and the donkey deserved a good meal. Apparently the donkey agreed, as he nuzzled Hamal's pack.

Hamal patted the animal's muzzle and nodded to the dune ahead of them. "There's shelter ahead."

Astra shivered. "I don't like sleeping in that abandoned place."

He nodded. "I know. But it's better than resting in the open."

"I know." She stepped closer to Sonji and touched her shoulder, the warmth and feeling of movement calming her, pushing back her discomfort.

The foursome rounded the dune, and the abandoned homestead spread before them. A broken-down fence and shed sat to the left of a sand-filled well. Behind the water source was a one-room house. To the right of the house sat an outhouse. Nothing stirred.

Rumor said the master of the house killed his wife in a drunken fury when he thought she'd been sneaking out with a neighbor. After he sobered, he realized what he had done and put a gun to his head. They'd never had children. A neighbor had come to trade for some goods and found them.

The mare nuzzled Astra's shoulder. Astra ran her hand along the smooth face. The soulful brown eyes in the late-afternoon light stole her breath away. There was more to this horse than any she'd been privileged to get near.

Hamal led the group to the well. "We can rest until early morning and keep ahead of any trackers." He scanned their surroundings.

"All right." She took the pack from him and removed a bowl and water skin. She filled the bowl and offered it to Sonji. The mare slurped up the drink. Astra did the same for the donkey, and he emptied the bowl.

Astra removed a couple of handfuls of dried grass from the pack and fed her horse and the donkey.

Someone sneezed.

Astra turned, reaching for the throwing knife strapped to her belt.

The donkey kept eating.

A girl about Astra's age rode a dark horse with a crescent-shaped forehead marking around the house. The stranger lowered the scarf from her face and pointed to the well.

"Can I have some water? I'll trade you whatever you want." Her accent was crisp, almost sharp, against the Dryzzian language.

Hamal stood tensely beside Astra, blocking the well. "Who are you?"

"Vivian Rose." She reined her horse to a stop a few feet from the foursome. "Can I have some water?"

"The well is dry." Hamal didn't move from Astra's side. He served better as a wall than a shield. "What are you doing here?"

"Stopping for water." Vivian scowled. "Why are you being so protective of an empty well? And if it is empty, why are you here?"

"We needed a moment to rest." Astra pushed Hamal back and handed him the lead rope for her mare before she held her water skin out to Vivian. "Here."

"Thank you for the offer, but I have enough pouched water. I was hoping for a fresh drink." Vivian tipped her head, and some of her golden hair peeked from beneath her sinar. "I hope you and your escort have safe travels." She tapped her horse's sides with her heels and clicked her tongue.

The dark mount trotted south, away from them and away from Nahrot.

Astra turned to her friend, hands firmly planted on her hips and an edge to her voice. "Why were you so sharp with her?"

He averted his eyes. "Why does it matter?" He led Sonji and the gray donkey toward the abandoned house. "We should get some rest."

Astra sighed heavily, lowered her hands from her hips, and followed Hamal. They did need to rest before crossing the last stretch of desert for home under the cover of night.

But what if Vivian and the bandits crossed paths? What if they asked her about a white horse? And what if she pointed them in the right direction?

There was no safe way to sleep the night at the creepy shelter. They needed to return home. She shivered at the idea of losing her Sonji-girl again.

CHAPTER 7

Hamal couldn't sleep. His restlessness had little to do with the sun not down yet or the incredible heat permeating the old shack or even his lack of sleep from the previous night. His gaze flicked to Astra, sprawled out and asleep. She looked like an angel, no worry lines creasing her light brown complexion, and her raven-black hair escaping the sinar to frame her face. Even though she regularly wore men's clothes, she always looked feminine and beautiful.

The horse snorted, and he peeked back at her. The rope halter her captors had placed on her face was rubbing some areas raw. It must have been on tight, and the thieves had to fight often with her.

He abandoned his place by the empty doorframe and went to the mare. She sniffed his hand before allowing him access to the halter. He tested the knots, found them too tight to loosen, and lowered his hand to her neck. He could pull his knife from his boot and slice a section of the rope to free Sonji, but doing so without Astra's consent could get him in trouble.

"I'll ask Astra if I can cut it off when she wakes," he whispered in the horse's slender, flickering ears.

The donkey, his eyes half-closed, grunted from where he lay in the corner.

Outside, the sun touched the western horizon, and the heat of the day was fading. Soon they'd leave the abandoned house and head for their village. After the way he had treated Vivian Rose, he doubted Astra would let them spend the night. He knew her suspicious mind—and besides, being away from home was hard on her.

He leaned against the doorframe and stared hard at the lengthening shadows. Seeing his father's brother and right hand man, Willard, amongst the thieves unnerved him. The eyepatch had thrown him, but the accented shouts cinched his identity and had nearly froze Hamal.

Then there was Vivian, the girl from the northern country, the girl from a past he wished to forget. The last time he'd seen her had been three years ago. Her sky-blue eyes, freckled nose, and peach-colored skin were still as pretty as he remembered. And her colt had grown into a sound animal. But her arrival in the desert was a bad omen. He could feel it in his gut.

He jerked around. Something disturbed Astra's steady breathing—yet she still slept. Had the sound come from outside?

Again, he searched the shadows, the long, black scars stretching toward night and able to hide anything.

Nothing appeared.

He suspected Vivian had recognized him, but perhaps he'd been lucky. Doubtful—but as Astra liked to say, "Sometimes the sand tiger doesn't bite." Too bad her turn of phrase didn't normally work out, because the sand tiger seemed to like to bite more often than not.

Something dark moved in the shadows.

Hamal reached into the pocket of his billowy pants and his fingers wrapped around the familiar mechanical ball. Whatever lurked out there would soon be sorry.

Nothing emerged. A bird called overhead. Hamal

removed his hand from his pocket.

"Are you ready to go?" Astra's musical voice tickled his ear.

"Night isn't here yet." He kept one eye on the desert as he turned toward her.

"It will be soon enough. Are you ready to move on?" Her brown eyes with their intermixed gold and emerald-green were startling and intriguing as they flitted over the land. Fatima Paksim, Astra's mother, was not afraid to admit the family had mixed blood. It was part of what made them who they were.

"Yes." He was more than ready to leave the desert and its surprises.

Astra nodded before disappearing inside.

Hamal checked the encroaching night once more before returning to the interior of the dilapidated house. Astra held the cut rope halter of her horse while she applied some sort of cream to the abrasions. She whispered to the mare as if the creature understood every word. He smirked. Perhaps the horse did understand Astra. The two had a strange relationship.

Astra shoved the torn rope into the bottom of her daypack and pulled out a worn leather bridle. The mare slipped her head into the device. Astra fastened the throatlatch and led the way out.

Hamal and the donkey trailed after them. Barely a wisp of sunlight decorated the tops of the sand to the west. A black sky speckled in diamond-bright stars stretched from the east, ready to eat the last of the daylight. A quarter moon, its minimal light enough to help his father's thieves track their lost prize, peeked over the far horizon.

Astra vaulted onto the back of her beautiful mare. She adjusted her sinar and hid her hair from view. "Ready?"

"Of course." He mounted the donkey, and the beast

grunted beneath him.

The horse, sure-footed and white as the moon, led them toward home.

But with each step, Hamal's stomach knotted. What if Astra's mare was the one from the old legend his father and uncle obsessed over? The one who could unlock an unbelievable hidden treasure?

CHAPTER 8

The two friends reined in their mounts by the fence surrounding Astra's home. Hamal dismounted from the donkey and opened the broken back gate.

Astra stood beside her mare. "Can I trust you not to scare your mother if I don't escort you home tonight?"

"No." Hamal grinned. "I have more fun scaring the life out of her without help."

Astra smacked him in the arm. "You should be nicer to her."

"That would be too easy." The smack hurt, but he refused the urge to wince and rub his arm.

A candle was lit near the back of Astra's house, and her sister softly called.

"I'll see you tomorrow, Ham." Astra dropped a small kiss on his cheek before entering the yard with her horse and closing the gate.

Hamal couldn't move from his spot. Even though the kiss was no more than custom and quicker than a flash of lightning, it affected him. Every time she touched him lately, his insides stirred with unfamiliar feelings. At times like this, he wished to have someone to help him understand the emotions—and then he remembered his journey to find his father. The yearning vanished. He'd rather never have learned about his father. Allowing his mind to play with wonderful possibilities like a child would have been better than learning the truth.

The warm feelings from Astra's kiss died.

Hamal and the donkey crossed the quarter mile of open sand to Nahrot and snuck between the homes to David's. The windows of both home and blacksmith shop were dark.

Hamal untacked the donkey and fed him in his corral before stowing the bridle and saddle in a shed.

A shape emerged from the shadows. "Enjoy your latest adventure, lad?"

Hamal froze by the entrance to the blacksmith shop. "David."

An oil lamp lit, revealing the bearded owner in its soft light. "Hamal. Enjoy your adventure?" He smiled, nothing in his countenance reading angry or upset.

"I guess." Hamal pulled off his turban and fussed with the dirtied fabric.

"How are the Paksims?" David settled the lamp on a hook and sat on a stool by a workbench.

"Fine." Hamal's heart hammered against his ribs. Shouldn't his mentor be mad he borrowed the donkey without asking?

"I bet they're glad to have their daughter and horse safely returned." David, his dark eyes twinkling, crossed his arms. "Have you mentioned to the girl how you feel yet?"

Hamal's heart froze before hammering again. "Feel?" His voice cracked and he cleared his throat. "I don't know what you're talking about, sir." *Stupid rumors.* Why did the old wisewoman have to circulate them to everyone?

His mentor smiled. "I'll see you in the morning, lad. Best let your mother know you're home."

"Yes, sir." Hamal returned his turban to his head and exited the shop.

He climbed to the top of the fence for the donkey and jumped as lithely as a sand tiger to the flat roof of the blacksmith shop. His soft, sure-soled shoes never made a sound. He bounded from one wood-planked roof to another until he dropped into the tiny backyard of his mother's home and slipped through the back door.

A candle lit. "Where have you been? Off with Astra?" The tiredness in the familiar voice sent pangs of guilt through Hamal's heart.

"Hello, Mother." His feet felt glued to the floor by the door.

"Son." Her fingers tapped the scratched surface of their lone table. "Where have you been?"

"Astra's horse was stolen, and I helped her get it back." He slipped a hand in his pocket, his fingers brushing the woodchip bearing the carving of the running horse.

"Is that all?" Her coffee-brown eyes held no fury. Instead, exhaustion etched her every movement. She'd worried over him the long day he'd been gone.

"Yes, I promise." He didn't have the guts to tell her about Vivian Rose or the woodchip. After his trip to find his father, he'd come to love and respect his mother more than he ever had. But he couldn't bring himself to tell her about his journey. Things would drop from his lips unplanned at times—but never the whole story.

"The hour is late." She rose from her creaky chair and a piece of paper dropped from her lap. "Perhaps we should catch some shut-eye before the sun rises?"

"We should." His feet refused to move.

His mother wet her thumb and forefinger with a lick of her tongue, using them to extinguish the flame of her candle. Her shoes scuffed the sandy floor of their home in the direction of the small bedrooms.

Hamal waited several seconds before he picked up the dropped paper and went to his room. He never liked causing Mother to fuss over him. The symptoms of her degenerative disease seemed to worsen when she stressed.

He lit a stub of a candle. The paper crinkled as he unfolded it and faded silvery words reflected in the candlelight: *You are summoned*.

CHAPTER 9

An oil lamp glowed on the kitchen table, and Astra debated blowing it out and sneaking off to bed. Instead, she tiptoed to her mother's side.

Mama, her eyes closed, lay on a bench, back against the wall. Her chest rose and fell in a steady rhythm.

Astra, fingers trembling, gently shook her mother.

Mama gasped and her eyes fluttered open. "Astra." She yawned as she shifted to a sitting position.

Astra sat beside her mother. "My mare is home." She couldn't bring herself to meet Mama's gaze, so she stared at her lap.

Mama wrapped her in loving arms and rested her chin on Astra's head. "I'm thankful you're home."

"I'm sorry I worried you and Papa." She melted into her mother.

"You left to tend the animals at first light and never came back." Mama pulled back and brushed a stray hair from Astra's face. "We understand you are growing up and need room to live your own life, but you still live under our roof."

"I know." She dropped her gaze from her mother's and again stared at her lap.

Mama planted a kiss on her forehead. "We'd best get some rest while we can." She leaned over the table and blew out the lamp. "Good night, my blessing."

"Sweet dreams, Mama." Astra stayed in the dark. Mama's scent, fresh bread and honey, lingered, and her gentleness deepened Astra's guilt. She should have told her parents.

The glow beneath her bedroom door revealed her little sister waiting for her. She cringed. Racing off with Hamal to steal back Sonji wouldn't teach Ehsan how to behave.

The door inched open, and Ehsan stuck her head out. "Astra?"

"Here." Astra left the bench and slipped by her sister into their shared bedroom.

Ehsan closed the door with a soft thump, jumped on her bed, and patted the space beside her. Her brown eyes sparkled with hints of gold in the flame of the candle on the nightstand. "How did you and Hamal rescue your mare?"

Instead of taking the offered place beside her sister, Astra crawled atop her own bed. "Well ..." The story spilled from her lips even as her worry gnawed at the back of her mind.

Ehsan, grinning, her eyes wide, wrapped her arms around a pillow, and leaned toward her. But by the end of the story, her eyelids drooped and she propped her head on her upturned hands. Beside her sat her squished pillow. "Your adventures remind me of the stories about Princess Gefen."

"Why?" Astra, head buzzing with exhaustion, pulled her nightclothes from beneath her pillow and laid them on the bed. She ensured the window shutters were tightly closed.

"You get to see the desert, the world." Ehsan rested her head against her pillow, and her arms curled around her favorite doll, its multicolored hair still in a braid.

"I guess." Astra blew out the candle and changed clothes before she snuggled under her covers, grateful the thin mattress was not part of her sister's bed and her movements wouldn't wake her. Exhaustion attempted to keep her mind active until she counted Ehsan's even snores.

A beautiful, female voice sang into the late night— probably Isaac Zilfel's wife, Peridot, soothing her little one.

CHAPTER 10

Thump. Astra groaned and her bed rattled. *Thump.* She snagged Ehsan's hands to keep her from thumping her bed with them again and squinted against the blindingly bright sun. "What time does the clock say?"

"About ten in the morning." Ehsan wiggled free, happy energy oozing from her.

"I need to feed my mare and the chickens." Astra yawned and covered her mouth to keep her sister from looking down her throat.

"Papa and I brought the chickens home and fed the animals this morning." Ehsan hopped on the bed, her sinar sliding off her head and the bed bouncing beneath her.

"Thank you." Astra shifted into a sitting position and wiped sleep sand from her eyes.

"You're welcome." Ehsan puffed her chest like a proud rooster. "Mama said Mrs. Zilfel should be here soon."

Astra pulled her legs under her and tried to stifle another yawn. "Good to know."

Her little sister's light brown eyes sparkled. "Are you excited to sell her the needlepoint of Princess Gefen and the horses?"

"Yes." How could her sister be so full of energy after a late night and an early morning? Astra guessed excitement pushed aside the need for sleep, at least for the moment.

The door creaked open, and Mama entered with a smile and her green-brown eyes bright. "Good morning, my blessings."

Ehsan jumped off the bed, her shoes thudding against the floor Papa'd made from scrap wood. "Is Mrs. Zilfel here?" She adjusted her sinar and straightened her skirt.

"She is." Mama gestured toward the main room.

Ehsan grabbed the rolled needlework from beneath Astra's bed and ran from the bedroom.

"Ehsan." Astra struggled with her tangled bedsheets and finally freed herself as Mama closed the door.

Astra paused, feet dangling over the side of her bed, and fiddled with a snarled strand of her hair. Should she wait for Mama to speak or grab her hairbrush off the bedside table and try to get ready?

Mama perched on the edge of the bed and wove their fingers together. "Despite your most recent ... adventure ... I've managed to convince your father to allow you to enter the race."

"Papa agreed?" Astra straightened and her nerves zinged.

"Yes. But ..." Her mother sighed and settled a hand on her knee.

She forced her excitement down. "But?"

"You have to be open with us. No taking off." Mama didn't let Astra avoid her gaze.

"I won't. After dinner, I'll bring out my map and explain every detail of my plans to you." Astra flung her arms around her mother and squeezed.

Mama hugged her back and kissed the top of her head. "My baby girl is so grown up."

For a long moment, she stayed in the warm embrace. She didn't feel grown up. She hardly felt prepared to take on the race of her dreams, despite years of planning.

Her mother pulled away and cupped her cheek. "I'll let Mrs. Zilfel know you'll be out in a minute."

The door thumped, like the chime of a clock announcing the arrival of a fateful hour.

Astra slid off her bed and crossed to her bureau. She opened the top drawer and pulled out her favorite blouse. The sleeves of her shirt reached to her elbows, flowers embroidered by her mother lined the collar, and the material, though washed, still felt soft as flower petals. She pressed her face into the fabric. Her mouth dried and sweat slicked her hands.

Please, Creator, let Mrs. Zilfel like my work.

CHAPTER 11

Hamal rolled out of bed not long after the sun peeked above the horizon. He shaved, changed from his adventure clothes, and braced himself as he stepped into the main room.

The door to his mother's sleeping quarters was shut, and her kitchen supplies lined the counter in an orderly fashion. His return must have eased her worry enough for her to sleep soundly.

He exited his home for the street and the cool morning air carrying the sweet scent of honey bread fresh from the oven. His stomach growled and his mouth watered. He followed the smell to the bakery near the market square.

A woman entered the bakery ahead of him. Her cream-colored clothes, a sure sign of someone from out of town with money, and her turned-away face intrigued him. Her movements, smooth and purposeful, were strangely familiar.

He feigned looking at items cooling on the shelves around the inside of the shop as well as what was placed in the window display.

She picked up a small loaf of bread and a fruit-filled pastry before approaching the payment counter. She set her selection on the counter and removed from her purse the winklls the baker's son requested. The boy accepted the payment, and the woman left.

Hamal quickly bought a honey bun and returned to the street. But the woman was gone. Who was she? He nibbled on his bun and reviewed those he knew or even sort of knew from over the years. None fit the woman. If only he'd been able to see her face—even a glimpse would have helped. He licked his fingers clean and hoped for another chance to see her.

The streets filled with people as the sun rose higher. Some worked while others clustered in small groups to chat. Children wove among the legs of adults and work animals. Dogs barked and cats kept away from hurried feet.

Tariq Ke'ev, the local spiritual leader, or *tollarb*, approached Hamal. "Good morning. You're Omaira Nuru's son, right?"

"Yes, sir." Hamal tried not to squirm, knowing the man would call him on his lack of attendance for Shabbos gathering.

"I have a few pieces needing mending. Can I drop them off this afternoon?" *Tollarb* Ke'ev tipped his turban toward someone and waved to a group of children kicking around a ball.

"Yes." Hamal disliked meeting the *tollarb* in the street and hoped not to be home when the man delivered his mending. "Why do you ask?"

Tollarb Ke'ev shrugged. "Your mother is a busy woman, and I don't want to cause problems." He took a step away and paused. "Please, let her know I'll be by." The tall man wandered off, calling to various people he passed.

Maybe *Tollarb* Ke'ev would forget to drop by—like how he forgot to ask about his lack of attendance for Shabbos gathering—Hamal hoped. He returned home.

"Hello, my son." Mother sat at the table and sewed a pair of torn trousers. "Where have you been?" Piles of laundry filled the only other chair and the bench by the door.

Guilt riddled him. "I went to the baker's." Why hadn't he grabbed an extra bun for her?

"Find anything interesting to try?" Her fingers shook a little as she pushed the needle through a thick seam.

"No." The truth was he'd not inspected the baker's tray of new recipes—instead he'd inspected something else. "I saw a woman."

"Oh?" She lifted a slender, dark eyebrow and never paused in her sewing.

"She wore cream-white clothes as nice as Mrs. Zilfel's, but she was shorter and more slender." He filled a cup with water from a pitcher on the counter. "I never saw her face, but the way she moved reminded me of someone—I just can't remember who."

"Maybe you'll see her again, and she'll let you see her face." She chuckled. "Be careful you aren't near Astra when you find your stranger."

"Mother, what are you talking about?" He spilled some of his water on his shirt and wiped it away with his sleeve.

"The two of you are adorable. Neither has yet realized the other's shifting feelings, blushing anytime anyone mentions something." She tied off her stitching and clipped the thread. "You remind me of my youth."

He finished his water, set the cup down, and moved toward the door. "I promised David I'd work for him today. I'll be back in time for supper."

She shook her head. "Always quick to squirm, my boy." She smiled. "Have a good day, and stay out of trouble."

"I will. Love you, Mother." Her smile filled him with warmth and he forgot about the *tollarb*'s request.

He headed for the blacksmith's workshop, his gaze roving the crowds and alleyways. No sign of the stranger from the bakery. Who was she? Was she Vivian? And if so, why was she here?

CHAPTER 12

No sign of the mystery woman or Vivian's dark-colored horse. A sharp bray drew him from his search, and Hamal paused by the fence by the blacksmith shop. He scratched the donkey between his long ears. "Hello, old friend."

David stepped from the shop. "Hamal, my boy, glad you came. We've a full day's work ahead of us."

Hamal pasted on a smile. "Good." An apprenticeship with the village blacksmith was an honor many boys sought. He'd been lucky David saw potential in him and took him under his tutelage ... but sometimes, he yearned to tinker instead of work.

David turned and headed inside, his impressive bulk shaded by the workshop.

Hamal patted the donkey before sliding his hand in his pocket. He'd find time in the midst of his work to tinker with Mo. He had to, because Mo cutting the ropes of the bandits' horses was even more unnatural than its flying and answering to whistled commands. So, how did his little gizmo operate? He'd never crafted a power source, only fitted together gears and scrap pieces of metal.

He entered the blacksmith shop, and the strong scent of smoke, boiling water, and hot metal enveloped him. A comforting and stinging smell for sure. He stood in the doorway a moment, so his eyes could adjust to the shaded interior.

David, work goggles in place, hammered away on a piece of heated metal, probably the beginning of a recently ordered candelabra. The recent invention of electric lighting had not yet reached Nahrot, but Hamal had seen it work once. Fascinating.

"What do you need me to do, sir?" He tied on his work apron and put on his goggles.

"I placed a list on your bench." His mentor paused in his hammering and wiped his brow with the back of his glove.

Hamal opened the shutters above his workbench. A cool morning breeze tickled a corner of the list. Everyday items were requested: a hammer, a pair of pliers, screws, and a shovel. He selected what he needed from the scrap pile in the corner and set to work.

Midday break. Hamal dribbled water from his pitcher over one of the wisewoman's raised garden beds to soften the ground. He dug out weeds and laid them on a board to dry. Once dry, they were easier to burn.

Lounging on the top of the garden fence was a gray cat, licking its paws and twitching its tail to some unheard rhythm.

Mo imitated a butterfly. There wasn't a need for the winged sphere to work the garden because a neighbor's honeybees always visited, but Mo behaved better after a bit of exercise.

"Eh-hem." Sinar pulled forward to shade her eyes, the owner of the garden tapped the outside of a raised bed with her walking stick.

Hamal dropped his handful of weeds and stood, his back protesting the sudden move. "Wisewoman Yasif."

She rubbed her fingers against a Dryzzian mint plant. "Hamal, the garden is looking well."

The strong, sweet-mint scent of the plant tickled his nose, and he suppressed a sneeze. Astra told him once how special Dryzzian mint was—how it kept away infection, and when chewed or drunk, it helped suppress pain.

"Thank you, ma'am." He picked up the scattered weeds and set them on his board. "Do you need something?"

"What do you know of the Creator's affairs with the Paksim family?" Her eyes gleamed as she plucked a mint leaf and chewed on it.

He raised an eyebrow, curiosity and confusion filling him. "The Creator's affairs with the Paksims?"

"I've seen you and the elder daughter off on adventures." She leaned toward him, her eyebrows reaching into her sinar. "So surely you know something of the goings-on in the family."

Heat flooded his face. "I know nothing about the Creator's affairs with the Paksims."

"Too bad." She turned from him and shuffled toward the house. "A messenger rode to their home, and Mrs. Paksim slammed the door in the man's face."

He turned back to the garden bed. Why had the Paksims been visited by a messenger of the Creator? How could they be? Perhaps the wisewoman meant a messenger from the sultan. But the Paksims were a simple family from a tiny village many miles from the palace.

The cat leaped from the fence to the top of a garden box and batted at Mo. The flying sphere whirred, and claws popped from its sides before it charged in retaliation. The cat yowled and ran between the legs of the old woman.

"Hamal!" Wisewoman Yasif wobbled and clutched at the side of her gardening shed by the house. "What have I said about that thing of yours?"

"I'm sorry, ma'am." He whistled, and Mo pulled up short of grabbing the cat's tail before flying to him. Hamal held out his hand, and it landed in his palm.

"You're not supposed to attack the cat." He tapped the top of the sphere, and its appendages tucked in. "I'm sorry, buddy." He slipped his gizmo in his pocket and hoped its antics hadn't delayed his payment for his work—a vial of medicine for his mother to curb the pain and discomfort of her disease.

He grabbed a weed, wiggled it, and pulled. The plant refused to move, Hamal pulled again, and the weed came free. Dangling from its roots was a shiny, cog-shaped thing. "Strange." He removed the cog from the roots and slid it in his empty pocket. He pulled the rest of the weeds from the garden box before him and ran his fingers through the dirt at the base of the vegetables and herbs. No other metal pieces revealed themselves.

He checked another bed. Nothing. He'd sifted through every grain of soil when building and planting for Wisewoman Yasif, so how had the cog become entangled in the roots of the weed?

And who was the Paksims' visitor?

CHAPTER 13

Astra, her heart fluttering in her chest like a caged bird, emerged from her room.

Mrs. Zilfel sat at the kitchen table, her rings and bracelets clinking together. She held Astra's sewn scene one way and then another. "The detail in this piece is magnificent. The horses could gallop off this, and the girl dancing amongst them is amazing." She smoothed the needlework across the table. "This reminds me of the celebration after Princess Gefen and her magical mare saved our homeland."

Mama squeezed Astra's shoulder. "My daughter has been blessed with talented fingers and a vivid imagination."

Astra tugged on the edge of her sleeve. "You're too kind, Mrs. Zilfel."

Mrs. Zilfel reached into the folds of her skirt and removed a pouch, the jingling of coins filled the room. She tapped the needlework. "How much?"

Her biggest project so far measured over three feet wide and two feet long. Astra nibbled her lower lip for a moment, the prices of her other pieces flashing through her mind. Most of them were paid for in horse feed or tack, not money. She released her lip from her teeth. "Seven copper winklls."

Mrs. Zilfel shook her head. "You're too cheap." She removed a large gold winkll—a coin featuring a silhouette of the sultan on one side and the palace on the other—from her purse. "The workmanship is incredible."

Astra's jaw dropped. One gold winkll was worth four silver winklls, and a silver winkll was worth ten copper ones. She tried to calculate the difference, but she couldn't with the gold shining in front of her. The sale of her latest needlework more than paid for the entrance fee for the race—the Creator had answered her prayer.

Mama pushed Astra's mouth closed. "Thank you for your generosity."

"It's only fair." Mrs. Zilfel rose from her place by the table and rolled up the sewn picture. "I can hardly wait to see another piece."

Astra's thoughts darted to the half-finished project beneath her bed. It would be smaller than what Mrs. Zilfel had bought. The scene was of Princess Gefen kneeling by a mouse hole and a tiny Sonji on the other side of a wall stealing the key they needed from a sleeping sultan. Perhaps she could buy the thread she needed to finish with the money left over from her entrance fee.

"We can't wait, either." Mama nodded to Mrs. Zilfel. "What little Astra has shown us is very detailed." She walked with the woman to the door. The two chatted softly and laughed before Mrs. Zilfel left.

Astra touched the winkll on the table and ensured she wasn't imaging her luck.

Mama squeezed Astra's shoulder, touched her cheek to hers for a moment. "You deserve it."

Astra shook her head, the tail of her braid swinging. "I've never been paid so much before."

"None of us have—at least not all at once." Mama released her.

Papa entered through the front door. "Fatima, my dear, there is someone here to see you."

"I'll be right there." Mama smiled and cupped Astra's cheek. "My blessing from the Creator." She followed Papa outside.

The side door to the yard burst open revealing Ehsan, breathing heavily with her sinar hanging about her shoulders. "You should come and see." She left the door open and vanished into the yard.

Astra hurried after her sister and closed the door before any animals could get in. No one wanted the chickens roaming the kitchen.

Ehsan stood on a barrel along the tall, wooden fence and peered over.

Astra climbed a crate next to her sister, and for the second time in an hour, her jaw dropped. A fine red horse with a white stripe down his face was held by a man in fine clothes. The horse's tack dripped embroidery of fine silvers and purples. The man's billowy desert clothes and turban were plum-colored, and he looked almost as attractive as his horse.

The man and Mama spoke in hushed tones and close to each other. Papa slipped his arm around Mama's waist.

Astra wished the stranger and Mama would converse in louder voices. She leaned closer, hoping to catch a few words until something gently tugged on her skirt. "Not now," she whispered and pushed her mare's head away from her legs.

Sonji snorted, and again tugged on her skirt.

Ehsan leaned close to Astra while she slipped the mare an apple slice. "Why did you apply cream to her face?"

"She had wounds." Astra turned to her sister briefly, afraid of missing what was happening beyond the fence.

"No, she doesn't." Ehsan crinkled her little nose.

The man handed Mama something before he bowed and mounted his steed. The symbol of the Creator—a flower bearing three petals, sewn in silver thread—glittered on his shoulder.

Ehsan's eyes widened to the size of eggs. "Did you see him bow?"

"I did." But like the winkll sitting on the kitchen table, Astra had a hard time believing the action to be real.

Mama, clutching something to her chest, and Papa, holding her free hand, headed for the house.

Astra hopped off the crate, rubbed her horse's forehead, and whispered in her ear. "How did your face heal so fast?"

Sonji's ears flickered, and she nuzzled Astra's pocket.

"Sorry, girl, I don't have anything for you now. Maybe later. Besides, Papa and Ehsan fed you not too long ago." She kissed her horse's muzzle.

Ehsan sprinted past Astra. "I want to see what the man gave Mama."

"Me too." Astra followed her sister into the house.

Mama, her breathing rapid and her voice shaking, smacked a rolled paper on the table. "I won't go back, Jabir."

The paper sat like a squashed bug, even its purple ribbon ruined. Astra wondered what message it held.

Papa pushed the girls toward the door. "There is much for your mother and me to discuss. Why don't you two shop at the market?" He placed a few winklls in Astra's hand.

Astra thought about refusing, but the pleading in her father's deep brown eyes cut off her idea of going out the door, around the back, and listening from the side door. "Sure, Papa." She wrapped her arm around Ehsan.

Ehsan opened and shut her mouth several times, and dug in her heels like a stubborn donkey.

"Please," Papa said, pleading entering his soft, confident voice.

Ehsan slumped, Astra grabbed her sister's hand, and they traveled the familiar trail into Nahrot.

CHAPTER 14

Astra gripped her sister's hand and wove through the market crowd. Strong scents assailed her nose—turmeric, cumin, and sage mixed with body odor and camel dung. Vendors hollered, "A copper for two apples. A silver for a pair of shoes. The best oranges in all of Dryzza," over barking dogs and bawling goats. She veered away from wares shoved in her face and hurried for the far side of the crowd. A few houses edged the area, and beyond lay the dunes.

The sight of open land relaxed Astra. She loved her people, but not all of them were as kind as Mrs. Zilfel toward outcasts, and in the crush of bodies she feared being swallowed up or smooshed.

"Look." Ehsan waved a beautiful scarf in Astra's face.

"Very pretty." She rubbed the winklls from Papa. Should she spoil her sister or try to buy what she knew they needed?

Ehsan folded the scarf and set it on a merchant's table.

"You no like?" The foreign man behind the table stood, but did not straighten fully since the roof of his booth was not very high.

"I like it." Ehsan smiled and ran her fingers over the flowery print. "I'm not sure about buying it."

The man's forehead filled with wrinkles. "You like—why not buy?"

Astra slipped a winkll in her sister's hand and whispered in her ear. "Papa said we could shop, so I think one new scarf will be all right."

"But what about—"

"We have enough." Her stomach clenched as she calculated the numbers in her head. They'd be tight. She hoped none of the items they needed were scarce, since scare items cost more. And she hoped none of the local vendors would harass her because of her status.

Ehsan twisted her lips and scrunched them tight like a closed flower bud before lifting the scarf. "How much?"

"Five copper." He grinned and held up his open hand.

She shook her head. "Two."

"Three?" He held up fingers to match his number.

"I'll take it." She dropped her winkll in the merchant's hand.

He rifled through a coin purse on his belt and offered her several smaller winklls. "Thank you for purchase." He bowed awkwardly over the table and then returned to his seat.

"You're welcome—and thank you." Her cheeks turned a soft pink and she handed her change to Astra.

Astra put away the winklls, her lips tugging upward, as her sister lowered her old sinar and tied her new one around her dark hair. Then they joined the crowd.

Ehsan eased them into a quiet alleyway. "The merchant bowed to me—like the man with the horse did to Mama."

"Uh-huh." Astra shifted. They still had more shopping to do, and she wanted to get home soon, maybe learn why the stranger's visit upset Mama.

Ehsan tapped her chin, her gaze distant. "The paper the man gave her was the same color as the one Omaira waved in front of Mama after the last Shabbos gathering."

"What?" Two papers of the same color, and Omaira was waving one—why? Astra needed some answers.

"I thought they'd been upset over you and Hamal leaving to rescue Sonji ... but now ... I really wonder what's written on those papers." Ehsan shook her head. "We need to finish shopping, right?"

"We do." Astra had thought that before connecting to her sister's shared information, but now she wouldn't mind skipping the errand.

"Then, let's." Ehsan smiled, showing off her dimples and giving her nose a slight wiggle.

"All right." *And hopefully, when we go home, Mama will be ready to talk.* Astra gripped her sister's hand again.

They marched into the flow of people.

Their first stop was the basket maker's booth, where Astra had delivered a heavy dress a month earlier—a dress that broke Mama's favorite basket. Not long after, the basket maker's wife wore the dress for a festival, tripped on the hem, and ripped it apart at the seams. Thankfully, she wore a slip beneath, but Astra's reputation as a seamstress was ruined. The failed dress was why Astra had worried about Mrs. Zilfel's opinion of her needlework. If she couldn't sew, what would she do as a livelihood? And how would she ever rid herself of being considered a worthless outcast?

Astra guided her sister behind her and slid her quivering hands into her pockets. *Please, Creator, let the old man be nice today.*

A skinny man with crooked teeth and a white beard snickered. "Come to get your mother's basket, huh?"

"Yes, sir." Astra nodded once. Last time she'd come to see about Mama's basket, the man had spit at her, and she didn't want Ehsan experiencing that kind of rudeness.

He rattled off the price for the repair.

She placed the winklls on his table, and inwardly accepted that some purchases would not be made in the market today.

He pulled the basket from beneath the table and handed it to her. "Now get out of here, you worthless freak."

She grabbed Ehsan's hand and dashed into the crowded market. They purchased all they could afford from the other vendors.

After they finished, they walked by the House of Citizens. Seated by the front doors and under the shade of a pair of palm trees was a *jundiin*. Next to him stood a table topped by a quill, an inkwell, and a stack of papers held in place by a rock. A familiar figure dressed in cream-colored clothes signed something—probably race entry forms. Behind her waited a dark horse.

Astra fidgeted with the handle of the repaired basket. Why was the girl at the well—Vivian Rose—here? When they'd met at the haunted shack she'd been riding further south, maybe southwest. Why come back north?

Ehsan tugged her sleeve. "Astra, let's visit Hamal." She bounced on the balls of her feet and glanced ahead like she could see through the buildings to the blacksmith shop.

A peek at the clock embedded in the House of Citizens revealed the time. "He's probably working for the blacksmith."

"Please." She held her hands like she was praying, her bouncing intensifying. "I only want to say hello."

"Hello—and then we head home." Astra watched Vivian a moment longer before she followed her sister up the street. She'd ask Hamal about the freckled girl, because his reaction to her the day before suggested a previous meeting between the two. And she'd ask him if he knew something about their mothers' discussion yesterday.

Ehsan ran past David's small house, slipped the donkey a treat, and disappeared through the open double doors of his large shop

Astra stepped into the shady blacksmith shop behind her sister.

"Mr. David? Hamal?" Ehsan called.

Astra paused by the entrance, the strong scent of metal stinging her nose. "Hello?" Her mind flashed to the kiss she'd left on her friend's stubble-covered face the night before. Heat filled her cheeks.

CHAPTER 15

Something clunked to his left. Hamal looked up from the shovel he was shaping on his anvil. He grinned. "Ehsan, what brings you here?"

Ehsan righted an overturned bucket. "Astra and I wanted to say 'Hello' on our way home from the market."

"Why'd you visit the market?" He tugged off his gloves and leaned his back against his workbench.

Ehsan wiped her hands on her dark brown skirt. "Papa sent us." She snatched Mo off the corner of the bench and rolled it in her hands, twisting until the wings clicked free. "A purple-clothed man on a beautiful red horse visited our home and gave Mama a scroll. She smashed it on the table."

Hamal leaned toward Ehsan. "What do you suppose is written on the scroll?" He thought guiltily of the paper of his mother's that he had sneaked and read but not returned. *You are summoned.*

Ehsan shrugged. "I'm not sure, but maybe when Astra and I get home, Mama will tell us."

Astra stepped from the doorway, a full basket swinging from her arm. "We should be going. I know you have work to finish." She took Mo from Ehsan and set it on the workbench beside the vial from the wisewoman.

Sweat slicked his palms at the sight of his beautiful friend. "Hello, Astra."

She smiled, the limited sunshine highlighting the gold and emerald in her eyes. "Good afternoon, Hamal." She caught her little sister's hand. "Time for us to go."

He nodded, wishing they would stay longer.

Ehsan freed herself and removed a dagger from a rack. "This is more impressive than the one I saw last time."

Hamal chuckled and wiped his wet hands on a rag. "Last time was my handiwork. David crafted that one."

"An *amir* ordered it. Said he'd be over this way because of the race." David sat on a stool, his goggles dangled from a leather cord around his neck.

"The *amir* has good taste." She returned the dagger to the rack and grabbed the basket from Astra. "Papa gave us some extra winklls today, so I bought a new sinar for Shabbos gathering." She stepped into the sunlight streaming through the doorway and held a silky piece of material by the top corners. Pink, white, and yellow flowers with green vines wove their way across a royal blue background.

"Very pretty," Hamal said. And better to focus on than Astra.

"Thank you." Red dotted Ehsan's young cheeks. She folded her sinar and tucked it into the basket.

"Ehsan," said Astra, "would you wait here a moment?" She inched toward the outdoors, her green skirt swishing about her.

"But you said we had to go." Ehsan tipped her head in the direction of their home.

"We do." Astra tucked her hair inside her sinar.

How soft was her hair? Hamal shoved the thought aside and stuffed his hands in his pockets.

Ehsan crossed her arms. "If you're going to tell him Mrs. Zilfel's payment for your needlework is more than enough for you to enter the race, there's no need to send me out of earshot."

David laughed, the sound loud and warm.

Hamal tried to suppress a smirk but couldn't keep his lips from turning up.

Astra glared at her sister before grabbing his arm and leading him outside. "The race is one of the reasons I wanted to talk with you, but there's something else."

"Oh?" He watched her release him.

"Vivian Rose, the young woman we met at the haunted shack ... I saw her registering for the race." She nibbled her lower lip a moment. "How do you know her?"

Hamal's heart froze in his chest before smashing against his ribs. "I don't." He pushed his work goggles from their perch on his nose to the top of his head.

"I saw the way you looked at her, Ham."

His soul twisted under her intense gaze. If he told her the truth, what would happen to their friendship? He couldn't lose her. "Could we meet after dinner tonight?"

"Are you promising me an explanation?" She lifted a fine, dark eyebrow.

"Yes." Even though such a promise pained him.

Ehsan emerged from the shop with Mo. "Did you know this has claws?"

The two-fingered hands clicked together.

Astra took Mo from her sister and placed it in his hands. "Time to leave." She met his gaze. "Tonight, after dinner, don't forget." She pulled Ehsan toward their home.

"What's tonight?" said Ehsan, the basket swinging on her arm.

Astra grunted and never turned back.

A shadow passed over Hamal. He shivered and glanced up to find a bird flying overhead. *Not a Destroyer.* He slid his hand in his pocket. He still needed to return his mother's note. The longer it stayed with him, the more his mind drifted to the stories Mother had whispered in his ear when he was a child.

CHAPTER 16

Hamal walked the dusty streets of his village for home. Beside him flew his gizmo.

A young woman, dressed the same as the one from the bakery that morning, and her dark horse stepped from an alleyway and blocked his path.

"Hamal Nuru." She tipped her head toward him, loose strands of frizzy blonde hair dancing about her face in a late afternoon breeze. Her sinar hung about her neck. She held the reins of her horse, the docile animal standing behind her.

"Vivian. What are you doing here?" Heat drained from his face to his feet, and he cringed as soon as the words left his mouth.

"I could ask the same of you." She crossed her arms, a frown marring her pretty face.

Tension slithered along every muscle of his body. "I ... um ..." What to say? He lived here?

"You left in a rush all those years ago. Why?"

He scanned the streets. Empty. He looped an arm through hers and strode toward the edge of Nahrot.

Vivian pulled free. "I want answers." Her horse flicked his ears.

"And I'll give them." He didn't want to. He yearned for his past to stay in the past, to disappear.

Her blue eyes narrowed. "Is there a reason we cannot exchange information here?"

"Gossip travels faster than a sandstorm." He scanned the streets again.

No one seemed to be looking their direction. A boy and his dog disappeared in an alleyway while a little girl trailed her mother into a house. Men argued over a load a donkey pulled, and a cat lounged on a windowsill.

Vivian scoffed. "So why loop your arm with mine?"

Hamal scowled at her. "Do you want answers or not?"

The right side of her mouth twitched up. "So, you're willing to speak with me?"

He pointed to the dunes. "I'll tell you whatever you want to know, so long as we can do it away from prying eyes."

"Lead the way." She and her steed followed him into the towering dunes.

Once out of sight of the last house, he relaxed slightly. "What do you want to know?"

"Why you left—because I'd thought we were getting along grandly—and Father was impressed with your horsemanship." She ran her fingers along the forelock of her dark bay.

Memories of the past crashed over him. He shoved his way through the mess, recalling the day he left the Roses' estate. "This is my home."

"And ...?"

"And my father is Kaseem Nuru. He discovered I was working at your family's estate ... and he wanted me to help him rob you. I told you you were broke because of your mother's treatments, but he didn't believe me. His greed made me sick, and I couldn't stay." He kept his answer simple. Giving her the whole, complicated truth before he spoke with Astra felt like a betrayal. Perhaps he should have tried to put Vivian off for a few hours.

She lifted a blonde eyebrow, reminding him of Astra. "Is that all?"

"Why do you want to rehash the past?" His guilt gnawed at him like a hungry sand tiger with a fresh kill.

"I thought we could be friends again." She mounted her horse and trotted away.

Hamal shoved off his turban and ran his hands through his hair. His head spun with each memory jerked forth by seeing Vivian and her colt. Their arrival meant Willard and the others would soon ride over the horizon again. He never should have sought his father.

CHAPTER 17

Astra slid her mother's heavy basket onto the kitchen table. Her mind buzzed. What would Hamal tell her this evening? Did he know about the note his mother waved at hers?

"Mama, Papa, we're home." She pulled items from the market out of the basket and laid them on the table.

No response.

"Mama, Papa." Ehsan pushed the door open to their parents' room—but no one was there. Mama and Papa had moved back into the house after Grandma died, her things stored in a trunk in the corner.

Ehsan opened the door to her and Astra's room. Again, no one. She crossed the main room to the side door, paused, turned, and said, "Do you think they'll be out there?"

"I don't know." Astra shrugged.

Ehsan led the way to the barn, then the burned shop—and still no parents.

The sight of their father's ruined projects and the scent of burnt wood made Astra ill. How were their parents going to pay for fixing this? *The gold winkll from Mrs. Zilfell.* Astra's stomach lurched. Her plans for racing were vanishing before her eyes. She had to do something.

She and her sister reentered the house and checked every room again. No one was inside. So the two sisters sat at the kitchen table, neither saying anything for a long time.

After a while, Ehsan fiddled with several new spools of thread. "Where's the scroll Mama squished?"

Astra put away their purchases. "I don't know." Without her mother's cooking, the house smelled of sand, and her hunger since missing breakfast died.

"Our village isn't very large. Shouldn't we have seen them on our way home or while we were at the market?" Ehsan rolled a spool across the table and over the edge.

Astra retrieved the thread from the floor. "We did return the long way from the market. They may have gone the short way or taken a walk through the dunes." Nerves filled her stomach and shivered her hands. There should be a note, but she had yet to find one.

"Maybe." Ehsan stacked the other spools.

Astra stepped toward Mama's sewing supplies in the corner. *Clink.* She looked down, her payment from Mrs. Zilfel glittering from under the toe of her shoe. She picked up the gold winkll. Mama said Papa was all right with her entering the race. Her fingers curled around the winkll. "Do you mind staying home without me for a while?" Guilt gnawed at her.

"I do." Her sister stood, knocking over her stack of thread. "Where are you going?"

"To the House of Citizens." Astra set the original spool on the table. Should she be pursuing the race? Papa's shop was in ruins after the fire, a fire set so thieves could steal her horse.

"You're going to sign up for the race, aren't you?" Wrinkles marred Ehsan's forehead, and Astra hated seeing them.

"Yes." *And maybe speak with Vivian.* "And I'm taking Sonji with me."

"Why?" The wrinkles deepened.

"I'm hoping to train for a while before nightfall." *And I need some alone time after everything.*

"Can I go with you for race sign-up, please?" Ehsan stood and grabbed a large jar. "I can collect our share of water for today."

The fire had cost more than Papa's furniture-making shop and his projects. The family well had run dry in their effort to quench the flames. Until rain season came, only a few drops of water lived at the bottom of the well.

Astra sighed, even as her grip tightened on her winkll. "You can come." She changed into her pants and tossed her old pair to her sister. "Wear these under your skirt."

"You're letting me ride?" The wrinkles vanished and her eyes widened, shining like stars.

"Yes." Astra adjusted her sinar, headed out the door, and clicked her tongue. "Sonji."

CHAPTER 18

The House of Citizens marked the north side of the village square. A foot below the flat roof, posts stuck out like evenly placed pins in a pincushion. Windows dotted the two stories of the House at appropriate intervals. The faint outlines of colorful murals covered the tan plaster walls. The two eight-foot doors made of wood from the forests of the far north were closed, and a smaller door built into the large ones stood ajar.

Astra left Ehsan in the middle of the square to collect water from the village well, the place where seven rivers met. Sh'vah Nahrot. Seven Rivers. The gateway to the trail for the Palace of the Creator.

The Creator—the one who had fashioned her as an outcast.

Yet, her mama always prayed to him and had ingrained the habit in Astra, so she whispered a prayer on a hot breeze and led Sonji to the sign-in table by the House.

A *jundiin* straightened in his seat in the shade and brushed dust from the front of his gold and off-white uniform. "How may I help you, Miss?"

"I'm here to sign up for the race." She forced her voice to stay steady, forced herself not to quiver, not to reveal her sudden nerves.

The *jundiin* walked around the table. "I need you to unsaddle your mount."

"Why?" She shifted closer to her horse.

"New rule this year. You can't register without an inspection of your mount."

She wrapped Sonji's reins around a hitching post and removed her saddle. "Why the new rule?"

"Don't know." He ran his hands over Sonji's limbs, middle, and neck. "This mark on her shoulder ..."

"She's had it a while. Never seems to bother her." But Astra had no clue where it came from.

"Hmmm." He asked Astra to trot her mare to the well and back.

Ehsan waved to them from where she sat in the shadow of the well, a full water jar in her lap.

Astra tipped her head to her sister before returning to the *jundiin*.

"Good." He checked Sonji's pulse, ears, mouth, and eyes. "Very good. What's your name?"

"Astra Paksim." She again fastened Sonji's reins to the hitching post before saddling her.

He ran a calloused finger along the edge of a sheet of paper on the table. "You must be a first-year racer. I don't see anything showing you've received papers and sent them in." He slid a form and quill across the table.

"Received papers?" *Please don't comment on my eyes. Don't treat me different when you look up.* Her heart fluttered. Rumors danced in her head—outcasts being disqualified for no other reason than being an outcast.

The young *jundiin* never met her gaze. He returned to his seat and propped his feet on a corner of the table. "The sultan sent all previous racers copies of the entry forms and the new rules this year because everyone, even the council, are tired of their race posters being ripped off the walls by the wind."

"Uh-huh." Her hand trembled as she filled in the form.

"Put the form at the bottom of the pile when you're finished, and don't forget the rock on top."

"Uh-huh." Her throat and tongue felt drier than the desert air. She filled out her form and slid her payment—her gold winkll—onto the table. The gold vanished, replaced by a silver winkll. She stuck the silver deep in her pocket, and silently promised she'd use her winnings to pay for the repairs to Papa's shop.

She turned, more than ready to leave, when a spotted sand snake darted in front of her and Sonji. Her heart raced. A snake, no matter the kind, crossing one's path meant trouble on the journey ahead. *Please, Creator, let the old wives' tale mean nothing.*

Astra hurried to the well, where she loaded her sister and a jar of water on Sonji before heading toward home. As they passed Wisewoman Yasif's, a curtain stirred. Astra tried to ignore the pang that stole through her.

CHAPTER 19

I shouldn't have been so abrupt with Vivian. I should have heard her out. Hamal forced his breathing to slow before he entered his home.

His gizmo buried itself in the basket of folded and mended clothes by the door. A muffled whir died off to silence.

The smell of vegetable stew and freshly made flatbread had his mouth watering. He crossed the room and glanced in his mother's pot. Bits of orange, probably carrots, floated beside beans, lentils, onion, stewing cabbage, and more. "How long until I can eat?"

"You can eat now if you get yourself a bowl." Mother stirred her pot hanging over the open stove. "I think this stew is better than my last."

He grabbed two wooden bowls off the counter and held them near her pot.

"How was Wisewoman Yasif today?" She filled the bowls before she removed the stew from the flame and set it on a woven cloth on the counter.

"Her usual self." He set the bowls on their table.

"Good." She laughed and brought over the plated bread, two spoons, and a knife before she took her place. "And David?"

"Same as ever." He joined her and reached for his spoon.

She caught his hand in hers, bowed her head, and said, "Dear Creator, thank you for the food you've provided us and for each other. We trust in you—always." She squeezed his hand before letting go and picking up her spoon.

He dug into his stew.

When they finished, instead of moving in their normal routine, his mother pushed her bowl to the center of the table. "*Tollarb* Ke'ev stopped by today."

His mouth felt full of sand as he forced a nod. He should have known the *tollarb* wouldn't forget to drop off his mending despite his busy schedule.

"He commented on seeing you near the bakery, that you seemed distracted." Her lips tugged upward.

"I'm sorry I forgot to tell you he was coming by." Vivian flooded his mind, her cream-colored outfit this afternoon the same as the one the woman at the bakery wore. They had to be one and the same, but he should have asked to be sure.

"You were pretty distracted by your mystery woman from the bakery." Her eyes twinkled. "Ever learn who she was?"

"Um ..." He dropped his gaze from hers.

"Never mind." She chuckled and clasped her hands in front of her. "I need to talk to you about something."

His muscles tensed and his hands fisted.

"Many moons ago you traveled to the north to meet your father." She caught his chin and tugged his face toward hers. "From your abrupt return, I knew what you found was not to your liking. And ever since, you've run off with Astra at every turn and not taken your apprenticeship with David seriously."

"Mother ..." His heart raced faster than a train on open track.

"You always avoid this conversation, Hamal." She released him and clasped her hands again. "I can't force you to stay or to listen."

He looked at the scratched surface of the table instead of at her.

"I'm not mad at you for leaving, and I'm not upset you are angry with your father. I don't care if you never tell me why you went or what you found. All I ask is that someday you forgive him." She sighed. "It saddens me, this yoke I've seen you bear because you won't let go of what you found. Left too long, your yoke will choke you, choke your relations with others. Please, Son, give your burdens, your yoke, to the Creator to bear. Forgive your father not for himself, but for you so you may move on."

"I'll consider it." He snatched up the bowls and dropped them on the counter by the bigger bowl used for washing. "I'm going out."

"When will you be back?" She sat there, still as a chair, with her shoulders slouched and hands still clasped—all of it emphasizing her smallness.

His hand hovered over the doorknob. "I'll return after dark." He grabbed the doorknob, yanked the door open, and left.

A small *thunk* against the door caused him to cringe. He'd forgotten his gizmo, but he wasn't going back for it now. He needed to get away.

CHAPTER 20

Hamal trembled. His hands clenched and unclenched, and he yearned to punch something, anything. How could his mother ask him to forgive his father? How could he give his burden over to the Creator? His troubles weren't anything large.

Soft, feminine singing intruded on his turmoil, and he paused. The words were too quiet to be discerned, but the melody touched his soul. His churning emotions quieted like a sandstorm dying out.

He turned, trying to discover the direction and maybe the source of the singing. But he saw no one. He followed the sound, weaving between the buildings of Nahrot in a familiar direction.

The song changed to humming in front of Astra's home, the sound younger, but still feminine. He slipped through the gate, approached the door, and watched the curtains covering the window part.

Ehsan grinned. "Hamal. Come in." She lifted the window and used a board to hold it up. "Astra mentioned you'd be coming by."

He smiled and tried to hide his upset as he groaned inwardly. He'd promised Astra he would tell her about his connection to Vivian. How could he have forgotten?

The door opened. "My sister just took Sonji for some training exercises." Ehsan ushered him inside, the room smelling of sweet, dried apricots and vanilla-flavored bread. "I'm making dinner. Are you hungry?"

"No. My mother and I just shared some dinner." He stayed close to the door, something feeling off.

She spoke a mile a minute. "Astra and Sonji are signed up for the race now. You should have seen how the *jundiin* looked Sonji over."

Ehsan paused and craned her head, like she was looking to see behind him or above. "Where's Mo?"

Guilt gnawed at his stomach. "I left it at home."

"Oh." She turned from him, pulled a loaf from the oven, and stirred something in her stewpot. A bubble popped and the stench of rotten vegetables overtook the sweeter scents. Ehsan pinched her nose. "I think I used the cabbage meant for the chickens in my stew."

He tried not to gag and took a half-step closer to the door. "Where are your parents?"

"I don't know." Ehsan broke a piece off the steaming loaf of bread and nibbled. "I've not seen them since Papa sent Astra and me to the market."

Being alone with a girl under age for courtship tended to be frowned upon—but she seemed so alone. "You mentioned a visitor when you came by the blacksmith shop."

She nibbled some more. "He left a note for Mama, and I'd hoped when we came back she'd be home and tell us why she was upset."

A note. He still needed to return his mother's note to her.

The door creaked open. "Hello, my darling."

Ehsan dropped her bread and leaped into her father's arms. "Papa, where have you been, and where's Mama?"

"I was with your mother. We've been discussing some ... things." Jabir Paksim set down his daughter, pulled his turban off, and scratched the bald spot on his head.

Ehsan led her father to the table. "I made bread, but I think I ruined dinner." She broke off a piece for him and darted to the door, craning her head one way and then another. "Where's Mama?"

"Not here." Jabir eased into a seat, set his turban in his lap, and grabbed himself a chunk of bread. "Hamal, lad, Astra is in the yard unsaddling Sonji."

"Thank you, sir." He backed toward the exit, his hand reaching for the knob.

"Where's Mama?"

The door shut and muffled the answer.

"I feared I'd missed you." Astra stopped beside him, her sinar crooked and stray strands of hair framing her face.

"A promise is a promise." His heart twisted as he glimpsed Jabir and Ehsan through the open curtains.

"We can take a walk in the dunes." Astra rubbed her mare's forehead.

"A walk sounds good." Too many memories and regrets over his own father burdened his heart—he couldn't watch Ehsan and Jabir a moment longer.

"Good." Astra led the way out of the yard, leaving the back gate partially ajar.

Hamal patted the white mare's neck. "The life of a horse is surely easier than mine."

Sonji snorted. There was something in the brown eyes peering back at him, something ancient and far wiser than any animal.

Astra called for him, waiting on the other side.

Sweat slicked his palms as he closed the gate and broke the connection. "This way." He led Astra into the dunes, away from her father and sister and the strange horse.

CHAPTER 21

Astra could tell by the stiffness in Hamal's shoulders and the way he wouldn't meet her gaze that he dreaded sharing with her how he knew Vivian Rose. She wondered if she should drop the topic. But the stranger filled her with too much curiosity ... and the way the two interacted ... She shoved her ideas aside.

Once the village was tucked behind a dune, Hamal stopped.

Astra waited, straightening her sinar and tucking her loose hair in its folds before she twisted the end of her falling apart braid around one of her fingers.

He congratulated her on signing up for the race and selling her needlework to Mrs. Zilfel before he sat in the sand and leaned his back against a dune. His hand slid into his pocket.

She nodded a "thank you," released the end of her braid, and said, "Ham, if you don't want to talk about Vivian, I understand." Then she sat next to him.

"I do ... I just ..." He sighed, long and agitated.

She drew her knees up and wrapped her arms around them. "Ehsan mentioned your mother waved a paper at Mama, one that looked a lot like what the messenger brought us, and that our mothers discussed something after the Shabbos gathering. Has Omaira mentioned anything about yesterday?"

"No. But …" He reached in his pocket and removed a rumpled paper which he smoothed on his lap.

Silver words glittered in the evening light. *You are summoned.* And above those, in the same ink, was the symbol of the Creator.

"Mother dropped this yesterday on her way to bed, and I keep meaning to return it to her." Hamal handed Astra the paper.

The paper was indeed the same size and pale white as the one Mama received. "How did Omaira get this?"

Hamal shrugged, sand dripping off his shoulders. "I don't know."

Chills spread up her spine and along her arms, her hands trembling. "Ham, this is a summons to the Palace of the Creator." She dropped the note in his lap and paced. "And I'm pretty sure the messenger brought Mama the same kind of summons this morning."

His brow furrowed. "Our mothers have been summoned by the Creator? Why?"

"I don't know." Stories of legendary figures summoned to the palace swirled in her head. Most never returned home. She sat beside Hamal again. "Why were the men and women in the legends summoned?"

Hamal folded and returned the note to his pocket. "For Princess Gefen, there aren't any details about her visit—all we know is that afterward she set about gathering the people to rise against her father."

Astra nodded, the old tale replaying in her head better than a memory. "A man who'd become possessed by a Destroyer because he enjoyed darkness."

"According to legend, yes." Hamal stood, brushed the sand from his lap and the worst of the wrinkles from his shirt.

SONJI

Astra shoved aside her trepidations. "I'm sorry to worry you, Ham. You came ready to tell me about Vivian."

The sharp ring of a bell echoed across the desert.

Both turned toward Nahrot, where a slender trail of black smoke lifted into the darkening sky.

Her heart constricted before beating at triple the normal speed. Were the thieves back to take her mare again? Or was something else wrong?

She and Hamal ran toward the village, bypassing her home.

Around a dune, shouting men and women raced along the edges of Nahrot. Several held buckets, probably the beginning of a waterline from the village well to the source of the fire.

Astra flashed to two days ago when Papa's furniture shop burned, and the family well ran dry—and the bandits stole Sonji.

"I'm going to help with the fire." Hamal slowed to a halt. "You should check on your family and your horse."

"You think—" Her heart about stopped with his insinuation that matched her thoughts.

"Yes. But I'm hoping the bandits aren't back—and they haven't tried their fire trick again." He bounced on the balls of his feet. "Stay safe." Then, he took off.

She watched him blend into the chaos before running home to find the front gate open and Ehsan clinging to Papa.

"Stay here while I see what's going on." Papa pushed Ehsan inside. "Check on Sonji, and wait for your sister. I'm certain she will be home soon."

"But Papa—" She stayed, her hands clasping and unclasping and her eyes full of worry.

"Stay, my darling, please." He ran toward the village.

Astra, breathing heavily, stopped beside the gate for a moment to give herself a chance to slow her breaths and ease the ache in her side. She entered the yard. "Ehsan."

"Astra." Her sister gripped her in a fierce hug. "Do you know what's happening?"

"No. I'm guessing a fire since I saw smoke." Astra patted Ehsan's head and held her close. "Hamal went to see what's wrong, and I saw Papa leaving as I came home."

"He went to see why the bell rang." Ehsan eased back a step, but did not let go.

"I'm sure he did." Her sister was safe, her father and friend were investigating the trouble, but what about her horse? She pulled out of her sister's grip. "Have you seen Sonji?"

"Yes, by the barn." Ehsan led the way around the house.

The back gate stood ajar.

CHAPTER 22

A stranger stood in the backyard with Astra's mare. He wore a faded brown turban, a draping cloak, and baggy clothes. He petted Sonji and smiled, barely lifting the sides of his drooping mustache. "There, there, beautiful girl. You're where you belong."

Astra felt drawn to the man, despite his appearance. "Sir, why are you here?"

"Hmm?" He patted Sonji's shoulder before holding out his hand. "Hello."

Ehsan glanced at Astra, her hands still and an eyebrow raised.

Astra shook the stranger's hand, a warm hand covered in callouses. "Hello. Who are you?"

"I'm Zeb." His chestnut-brown eyes were kind, and a few gray hairs disturbed the pure blackness of his mustache.

"Nice to meet you." She shifted, unsure where the stranger came from and how to treat him without Papa around. "Why are you here?"

"I found the gate open and your horse slipping out. Thought I should encourage her back where she belongs."

Deep in her bones, she sensed Zeb was a friend and there was more to his story, but she doubted she would ever hear the rest. "I see. Thank you for bringing her back."

"I must be going." He bowed to them, his turban nearly falling off because of the grand gesture. "An honor to meet you and your steed." He backed a few steps, swirled around, and left.

Astra locked the back gate, too stunned for words.

"He bowed to you," said Ehsan. "I thought outcasts like us were unworthy of special treatment."

"Me too." Astra touched her mare's shoulder, ensuring she was real and ensuring the moment with the stranger was real.

"Astra, do you suppose what he said was true? Sonji really was trying to sneak off?" Ehsan pulled a dried apricot from her pocket and held her hand out to the mare.

Sonji slurped up the treat, and then pushed at the small hand as if asking for a bite more.

"Maybe." Astra rubbed her mare's scooped face. She'd never seen another horse with the decisive curve until she met Vivian and her dark horse yesterday.

Ehsan knotted and unknotted the end of her cloth belt. "I hope he was telling the truth. He seemed like a nice man."

"Me too." *Even if he is, who or what opened the gate?* "Is there any dinner?"

Sonji nuzzled Astra's pockets and blinked her big brown eyes.

Astra chuckled. She could almost hear her horse asking for more goodies. "I'm sorry, my girl. You've been given dinner and now a treat. No more for you." She ran her fingers along the mare's soft side, and silently thanked the Creator for her and the kindness of the stranger.

The sisters headed inside, and Ehsan lit an oil lamp to push back the night that stole the last of the sun.

"What died?" Astra wrinkled her nose, her stomach roiling in protest to a sour-cabbage stench.

"My stew. Papa tried to help me scrub the stewpot of the rotted vegetables, but the bell rang ... and ... you returned." Ehsan washed their father's plate.

Astra nibbled on the loaf of bread on the table. "Did Papa say anything about Mama while I was out with Ham?"

"He did." Her sister set the plate on the drying rack before wiping spilled stew off the counter.

Astra sipped from a cup of water. "What did he say?"

"Mama went to stay with our great-uncle." Ehsan rinsed her rag out in a bowl of soapy water.

"Why?" Astra took the rag from her sister and wiped off the kitchen table before sliding the cooled loaf into the bread box on the counter.

Ehsan shrugged. "The siren sounded and interrupted him." She headed for the door with the stewpot. "Maybe if I scrub the inside with sand, the rest of the dead cabbage will let go."

The siren. The smoke. She'd forgotten. Now she prayed Hamal, her father, and her fellow villagers were safe as she followed Ehsan outside to help her clean the stewpot.

CHAPTER 23

Hamal wiped ash from his face and gave the dirty, wet rag to a woman. He wanted to know her name, thank her. In the back of his mind, he felt he knew her from somewhere—he'd just forgotten where.

She tended to the other men passing buckets, offering drinks of water and cool rags. Who was she?

Where did he know her from? She had simple features, dark brown eyes, dark brown hair, and no scars or discerning features. Her tan clothes—a dress and a shawl—were covered in soot like everyone else's. She never complained, always offering a kind word.

The man next to him, a visitor from what little Hamal had already gotten out of him, elbowed him. "Awful shame about the Zilfels' trading post."

"You're familiar with the Zilfels?" Hamal passed a water bucket closer to the fire.

"Trade with them any time I have anything interesting turn up." The man wiped his face with his sleeve. "I remember Mrs. Zilfel's son, Isaac, was training a young lad to help him a few years back. The lad was good. Could take one look at an animal—any animal—and know right off if it was good or not. Did the same with merchandise. What an eye. And honest. Wonder whatever happened to him."

The man stole a drink before passing on a bucket. "Isaac's tried teaching several young'uns into the trade business, but none have worked out. He's got a young girl who's good at restocking and cleaning. Too bad trade requires more."

Hamal clenched his teeth. More than likely the man had a point for all his talk.

"Guess young Mr. Zilfel won't have to worry too much about leaving the shop so he can tend to his pregnant wife. He'll be busy salvaging instead of selling. Sad shame. I bet if he still had the lad, the shop wouldn't have caught fire, and he'd never had to worry about taking time off."

"Last pass," someone shouted in the dark.

Hamal tried to stop the woman so he could thank her, but she continued on her way, dabbing faces and offering drinks too fast for him to offer his kindness. Maybe he'd catch her another time.

The last bucket went up the line, and the mayor designated men to watch the ashes at the back of the trading post. Then he dispersed the citizens.

Hamal paused outside his home, staring at a pale light flickering below the front door. After a long moment, he braced his nerves and entered. "Hello, Mother. I'm sorry I'm late."

She slept with her head on a pair of torn trousers and her bottom on a hard chair.

His gizmo darted from under the pile of mending to hover in front of his face, wings softly beating and giving off a faint *click-click* noise.

"You are not normal." He sighed and held out his hand. "And I'm sorry I left you behind, but I needed some space."

Mo settled in his palm, and Hamal twisted, deactivating the wings before dropping it in his pocket.

He touched his mother on her shoulder, and she moaned but didn't stir further. He carried her to her room where he laid her on her pristinely made bed. "I really am sorry I'm late, Mother." He kissed her forehead and unfolded the spare blanket over her.

When he returned to the main room, he blew out the oil lamp and headed for his room.

The woman tending the bucket line still lingered in his mind. Who was she?

CHAPTER 24

Hamal woke to the sound of conversation. His bedroom door limited him to phrases—but because of those, he was certain who waited for him. His mother and Wisewoman Yasif. He groaned and buried his head in his pillow.

After a long minute passed, he crawled out of bed and cleaned up for the day by the little bit of sunshine filtering through the cracks of his shutters. If only he could avoid the inquiries of the women.

He entered the main room and spied a honey bun on the far side of the table. His mouth watered.

Mother laid out a pair of trousers, her sewing needle stuck in the top of a tear. "Good morning, my son. Sleep well?" She smiled.

"Yes." *Sort of.* His muscles were a little stiff and his mind a bit groggy.

The wisewoman sipped on a steaming cup of something, probably tea. "What do you think your friend Astra's odds of finishing the race are?"

"Excuse me." He swallowed.

"You heard me." Wisewoman Yasif finished her drink and set her cup on the table.

Pins in her mouth, Mother raised and lowered her eyebrows, her signal that he should behave and answer his elders.

"Astra always finishes what she starts," he said.

"This race is no ordinary challenge." The wisewoman stood and collected her walking stick from where it leaned against the table. "Your confidence in the Paksim girl is noted. I'll spread your opinion, and hopefully it pays."

"People are betting on the race results?" Hamal shook his head. "She hasn't even boarded the train in Urugha for Latif City yet."

Wisewoman Yasif shrugged. "She's registered, and you've given your vote of confidence, so I think we're operating under fair conditions." She moved away from the table. "I'll see you all tomorrow."

The door thumped.

Mother placed the last pin in the torn seam of the trousers. "She's been a busybody since I first met her, and I doubt she'll ever change."

"Why did she come?" Hamal slid into the seat the wisewoman vacated, the honey bun tantalizingly close.

"Curiosity." Mother pushed aside the trousers and slid the plated honey bun between them. "What happened last night?"

"The back of Isaac Zilfel's trading post burned." His hands fisted.

"Hmmm." She pushed a thread through the eye of her needle. "Purposeful or accidental, you think?"

"Purposeful. The fire played out like the burning of the furniture shop." His fingers tightened further. Would he find another woodchip with the engraved image of a horse?

"But?" She knotted the end of her thread and stuck the needle in the pants.

"Astra hasn't come over again saying her mare is gone." He relaxed a little.

"True." She cut into the honey bun with the knife setting on the edge of the plate. "Perhaps, if this fire was purposeful too, it was aimed at the Zilfels, but I'm hoping for no foul play. Maybe the young girl Isaac's had cleaning and restocking for him bumped into a lamp and didn't realize the harm she'd caused, or there was a dog or some other animal where it didn't belong."

"Maybe." His thoughts stirred like cross breezes creating a dust devil.

"I can see in your eyes another thought bothering you." Mother nibbled on a slender slice of the honey bun. "Your presence is no guarantee the fire wouldn't have started."

Hamal grabbed a larger piece, the honey sticking to his fingers and nuts dropping onto the tabletop.

She covered his free hand with hers. "Your choosing to learn under David instead of Isaac is not wrong. Don't feel guilty over an accident you couldn't have prevented." She squeezed. "I mean it, my son."

"You're right." He picked up the nuts that had fallen from the top of his slice and ate them, ignoring the tiger-sized guilt gnawing on his stomach and unsettling his breakfast.

She wiped her sticky fingers on a wet rag, then reached in her pocket and set the cog on the table. "I found this in your room. Where did it come from?"

"Wisewoman Yasif's garden." He licked his fingers, and removed the note from his pocket but kept his hand on it.

Sadness filled her brown eyes.

"Why were you in my room?"

The door banged open, and Ehsan stood, panting in the opening. "Astra's laid out her racing map and since Mama is, uh, occupied, we wondered if you and your mother might act as, um, I forget the term."

Mother rose gracefully from her chair and slipped the cog back into her pocket. "Hamal and I would be honored to help Astra."

"Astra will love hearing you're in." Ehsan stepped back from the door. "Now, come on." She darted out of sight.

He stuck the note back in his pocket—he'd get his answers later.

His mother walked into the sunny street. "This will be interesting."

CHAPTER 25

Astra saddled Sonji, checked the fit of her tack, and walked her mare in a figure eight. Her mind reviewed yesterday and the plans she had shared with Hamal, Omaira, Papa, and Ehsan. *Please, Creator, don't let my preparations for the race go to waste.*

Ehsan jogged out of the house. "Going for a ride?"

"Yes, this is my last chance to." Astra tugged her horse away from several squawking chickens and their feed.

"What's the challenge for today—climbing, travel?" Ehsan slipped the mare a carrot. "And, if you're doing either, will pushing Sonji be wise since she was stolen, and you don't have any idea what the thieves forced her to do?"

Astra rubbed her chin. "I need to make sure she'll fare well for the race, so we'll do a little of both. Nothing extreme—only enough to make sure she's feeling all right."

"Good." Ehsan fussed with her belt until the mare pushed at her hand, clearly after another treat. She giggled and patted Sonji's shoulder. "Sorry, pretty girl, I don't have any more for you."

Astra tied her day pack to the saddle and checked her cinches. Finding everything in perfect order, she headed for the back gate.

"Any idea why the bandits stole her?" Ehsan hurried ahead and unlatched the gate before pushing it open.

Astra led Sonji out and mounted. "No. I wish I knew."

"Do you think they'll try again?" Ehsan stood by the gate, her freehand again fussing with the end of her belt while she used her foot to push a chicken back inside the yard.

Astra shook her head, the end of her braid waving about. "I hope not."

"Ride safe, and I'll let Papa know you left." Ehsan picked up the sneaky bird and shut the gate.

Astra glanced at the ruins of her father's furniture making shop; the blackened projects, the caved-in roof, and all the walls, except the one acting as part of the fence, falling apart. A breeze whipped up the stink of ash.

She turned Sonji toward the desert, and they trotted three miles before stopping. Astra pressed her fingers to Sonji's neck, then smiled as the pulse count recovered to sixty in seven minutes. They trotted further, and she verified her results.

One more challenge. She surveyed the dunes and picked a promising, sandy slope, which Sonji climbed with ease. They paused at the top for another count. Astra grinned and whispered, "Thank the Creator." They descended the dune and worked a couple more sandy slopes.

Astra mentally reviewed her list of supplies—her cloak, a rolled cot, extra clothes, medical supplies, dried fruits, mixed nuts, some salted meat, her map, a compass, mint soap, a small bag of salt in case she ran low on winklls, two canteens, two bowls, a tent, and feed for Sonji.

A shadow passed over them, and Astra looked up. A bird flew too high up for her to identify the kind.

She checked the western horizon, found the sun glowed two hand widths above it, and decided to return home. She recalled the snake slithering in front of her after sign-up, and watched her surroundings more closely than before.

The thieves could return. She prayed they didn't because the day after tomorrow, she, Papa, Ehsan, and Sonji would travel half a day from Nahrot to Urugha to ride the train for seven-and-a-half hours to Latif City. And the next day, the race started.

CHAPTER 26

Astra stowed Sonji's tack and slipped her mare half an apple.

"Hamal's here." Ehsan sprinted around the house and snatched Mo from the air. "You're coming with me."

An odd humming sound echoed from Mo, like a purr but not quite.

"Sorry, not today." Hamal took Mo, twisted the wings in, and tucked it in his pocket.

"Hey," Ehsan shouted.

"You can play with it another time." He patted her on the head like a dog and turned to Astra. "Enjoy your ride?"

"Definitely." Astra tried not to laugh at her glaring sister, even biting her lip to hold in the giggles. "The fire at Isaac's ...?"

"No one was hurt. Just a lot of inventory ruined." He gestured toward the back gate. "Do you have time to talk?"

"Sure, and sorry if I smell like a horse." She followed him out, heat filling her cheeks. Why had she said that?

"I can't smell much after working in David's shop all day." He raised and lowered a shoulder.

They sat in the stretching shadow of a dune and watched the sun vanish below the horizon, the sky fading from blue to gray and pink before darkening to black. Stars sparkled to life and a small, almost crescent moon peeked over the eastern horizon.

"Astra, I'm pretty sure I know why Sonji was stolen."

"Oh?" She turned toward him, but there wasn't enough light to see his face.

"By the gate to Isaac's corral was a woodchip with a running horse engraved on one side." He put something in her hand. "My father used a woodchip like that as his calling card."

"Calling card ...?" She rubbed the carving, feeling the incredible detail.

Hamal stood, brushed sand from his clothes. "My father is Kaseem Nuru, the greatest thief in Dryzza, and last I checked, the bounty on his head—dead or alive—is five hundred gold winklls. Other countries have a higher or lower price depending on how often he's stolen from them."

She dropped the chip. "Nuru is such a common last name that I never would have ..." She searched in the dark until the moon rose high enough to cast pale light on their dune and reveal the carving.

Hamal cleared his throat. "I prefer to keep my distance from him. Mama loves him, talks about the good man he is, but I noticed she never mentions him in front of Wisewoman Yasif."

Astra shook her head. "Why are you so sure he stole Sonji? I mean, beyond finding his calling card?"

He invaded her space. "Three years ago, I left to meet my father. He'd run off when I was little, leaving me few memories of him, and Mother spoke only about his goodness. So, I tracked him down. But what I found was a world-renowned thief, a man obsessed with greed. He and his partners wove tales over their campfire about the legendary Sonji, the white horse ridden by Princess Gefen, and the key to the Creator's treasury—home of the ultimate bounty."

Her heart hammered, her hands sweated, and she tried to look anywhere but at him. "Ehsan named my mare 'Sonji' because she's white and reminds her of a princess's steed. She's not the horse from legend."

"Stories circulate of a horse that never dies. A white horse who's carried men to battle, freed countries from tyrants, saved outcasts, fought Destroyers. On her shoulder she bears the mark of the Creator, and when I've seen your horse standing in the sunshine, that old mark you call a scar looks like a flower made of three petals." His breath warmed her face.

Astra gulped and tried to keep the sound quiet. "I found her tied to an abandoned wagon, Ham. If Sonji is so special, why would she have been left like that?"

He backed away, pulled off his turban, and messed his hair with a hurried ruffling. "I don't know. All I do know is ... your horse isn't exactly normal. Sort of like Mo. But I can't figure out why."

She gave him back the woodchip. Held onto his calloused hand a moment longer than necessary. "Thank you for sharing this with me." She tucked her hands in her pockets.

"I'm not done sharing." He pocketed the woodchip and returned his turban to his head. "I ran north with my father and his band to escape the *jundiin* hot on his trail.

"We snuck aboard a ship, and I was seasick the whole voyage. Once we docked, the only thing that drew me out of my misery was hearing some horses whinnying. I followed the sound on wobbly legs, and found people from every walk of life gathered for an auction. I inspected the horses and kept out of sight.

"I spotted this colt, hardly more than a yearling, but solid and spirited. And then I heard this girl and her father talking about her getting a horse, her first horse.

They seemed smart and better-off than most, money-wise. Anyway, I caught her eye and led her to the colt just before the auction started.

"Willard, my father's right hand man, spoiled the moment by dragging me off.

"A few days later, my father's men forced me to pickpocket from people in the local market. A young horse spooked. The owner—I'm not sure he'd ever worked with a horse before—tried to quiet her and keep anyone from getting hurt, but he worked with her all wrong. I slipped through the crowd and sweet talked her, eased my way to her head and calmed her.

"Vivian's father was in the crowd, and he saw me. He offered me a job, so I snuck off to work for him. But my father found me and tried to get me to help him steal from Vivian's family. I refused. The Roses were broke after Vivian's mother's illness and death. My father's greed blinded him. So, I ran home and hoped he'd never come for me."

Astra touched his arm, her heart aching.

"When we stole back Sonji, a man wearing an eyepatch chased her. That man was Willard, and wherever he is— my father is sure to be close." His face shone serious and worried in the moonlight.

She tucked her hand back in her pocket. "I'll be careful." She didn't know what else to say.

CHAPTER 27

Why did she persist on racing? It wasn't a life-changing event, was it? Hamal grumbled and shoved open the front door.

Mother sat at the table, the cog in front of her, glittering in the glow of the oil lamp. "We need to talk." She didn't sound angry, more tired and nervous.

His gizmo wiggled in his pocket.

He dropped Mo in a pile of mending and put the summons on the table. "I agree." He sat in the other chair.

She pulled the paper in front of her, unfolded it, and smoothed the wrinkles. The silver writing sparkled.

"Fourteen years ago, Fatima and I each received a summons. At the time, we both lived elsewhere. We came to Nahrot, families trailing behind, to find the trail to the palace and cross the desert. What we discovered was not what we expected." She sighed. Picked up the cog. "Fatima and I received orders to find a machine, an ancient machine, lost in the desert for some time, and to bring it to the palace."

She turned the cog, the light catching on an engraving of a flower with three petals. "On our way out, we saw a tapestry. Angels fought with Destroyers. The Great War. Hidden in the shadows were little angels busy working on machine-looking-things. Fatima and I presumed we were looking for one of those things."

She sighed again before setting aside the cog. "What we found in the desert was a demolished machine. We collected cogs and gears as far as five hundred yards from the main, ruined mass of metal and loaded them in our wagon. But as we left, a Destroyer attacked us." She shivered. "We managed to ditch it for a while. But when we were half a day from Nahrot, the Destroyer found us again. Fatima and I grabbed what we could and ran for the trail. Before we got there, the Destroyer bit me. Fatima fought it away and dragged me back to the village, but I was in no shape to travel further. She bagged every piece we'd managed to get away from the Destroyer and went to the palace. She told me she made the delivery, but she has never told me anything more." Mother covered her face with her hands a moment.

Eventually, she looked up. "The wagon where Astra found Sonji, I'm positive it's the one Fatima and I used to haul the pieces of the machine." She tapped the cog. "Fatima and I saw that mare resting at the palace between tasks. And now you've found this cog bearing the Creator's flower. Fatima and I didn't get all the pieces to the palace. Our summons is not finished. We have to get the rest of the machine and deliver it. We have to. Or I fear more of the Destroyers will find the weakened point, break through the Veil, and start the war all over again. But this time, we humans will be underfoot."

Hamal blinked. "Destroyers? Summons? Machines? The Veil? Isn't all of that part of children's stories?"

She frowned. "You don't believe me."

With its little claws, Mo climbed the leg of the table, grabbed the cog, and waved it around.

"There's something strange about my invention." Hamal, glad for a topic change, picked up Mo and looked at it from one way and then another.

The cog dropped to the table and the claws clicked inside.

"You've scared it." Mother pocketed the cog and the note before pushing her chair away from the table and placing the kettle over the fire in the stove. She leaned against the counter, her arms shaking slightly. "Did you remember to get my medicine from Wisewoman Yasif the other day?"

"I did." He slipped his gizmo in his pocket, went to his room, and brought back the medicine. The fragile vial was something he dared not keep in his pocket for longer than necessary.

She held the fragile vial in thin fingers. "I need this because of the venom from the Destroyer's bite." She poured two generous drops of medicine in her cup, added a heaping spoonful of honey, and, when the kettle whistled, added steaming water.

"But Astra's grandmother diagnosed you with a degenerative disease."

"I wish that were the simple answer." She stored the vial in a little basket on the counter. "Good night, my son. I love you." And she gimped to her room, closing the door.

CHAPTER 28

The sky shifted from black with stars to a pale gray as Hamal snuck from the house. He'd made sure his mother slept soundly before leaving because he didn't want her catching him near Vivian.

And as the sky shifted again, a soft pink hovering over the horizon, he wished he could find Vivian and make up for how he'd acted. He'd already checked the bakery and the inn near the House of Citizens for her and her horse, but found no sign of them.

Where else to look? He didn't have time to search every building in Nahrot. He'd need to report to work soon.

A whinny and the hoarse grunts of camels drew him to Isaac's. He walked around the trading post and found a woman helping a trader load his animals.

Beside the barn, Isaac shook hands with Vivian, her horse standing beside her.

Hamal eased closer to her until a breeze stirred the ash at the back of the trading post, revealing a woodchip with a running horse engraved in its center. He grabbed the chip and stuck it in his pocket with Mo. The second fire had been his father's fault, but why did Astra still have Sonji?

Isaac moved to the couple with the camels. They conversed, the trader mentioning he would return from Urugha and the train station late that night.

Vivian crossed her arms and faced Hamal. "You've never been able to sneak up on me, so why are you trying now?"

He shrugged, his words vanishing, and held out the chip.

She turned it over. "I found one of these the morning we discovered you'd left … and we'd lost several of our promising stock." She gave back the chip and patted her horse's neck. "Lucky for me the thieves seemed not to know Midnight's worth."

He pocketed the woodchip. "I'm sorry for the trouble I caused, for the property you lost."

She caught his shoulder and squeezed. "There's no reason for you to seek forgiveness for something you probably couldn't have prevented, and you couldn't have known he'd still follow through on his plans without you. Besides, what we lost we didn't need. My father's other ventures covered what we lost and then some." She chuckled. "The Creator, or the 'Light,' where I come from, is very good at meeting needs, surprising us when we trust him."

She released Hamal's shoulder and mounted. "My guide is ready."

He stepped in front of her horse. "Wait, Vivian, why did you come here?"

"I've been laying out my supply stops for the Great Desert Race, making sure the change in elevation wasn't hard on Midnight. Why?"

"Just curious." He moved out of the way.

She smiled. "May the Light bless our paths to cross again." She waved and trotted after the line of camels.

Hamal glanced at the sun, figured by the angle of it he should grab a bite to eat and hurry to work, but he needed to speak with Astra first. A second of his father's calling cards should have meant another try at Sonji … unless there was something valuable in the trading post he hadn't known about.

He learned from Jabir Paksim that Astra had gone out with Sonji and her throwing knives, but he didn't know where.

Hamal had an idea of where she'd wondered off to—her thinking spot on the outskirts of town—and that's where he found her, her knives *thunk*ing into the side of a broken-down wagon until she ran out of blades to throw and had to retrieve them.

"Aren't you supposed to be working?" Astra sheathed her weapons, her cheeks reddening.

Sonji lifted her head and nickered, her relaxed ears flicking toward him. She seemed to be in agreement with Astra.

"Yup. But I wanted to see you first." He gestured to the wagon. "Nice throws."

"Thank you." Her hazel eyes sparkled. "Now, why are you here? I'm sure you have something more important to say than a compliment on my aim."

Mo clawed its way out of his pocket, dropped to the sand, and then clicked in its claws and rolled away.

Hamal chased his gizmo. "Wait. Stop. Mo!"

Astra joined him, even leaping and sliding after Mo.

But the crazy thing avoided them and kept on rolling, only pausing a moment by the wheel to click out its claws. Mo climbed the wheel and disappeared under the wagon. Clunking noises resonated from within.

His mother's story from the night before filled him. Could this ancient wagon really be the one his mother and Fatima had driven, trying to escape a Destroyer bent on preventing them from delivering an old machine to the Creator? He remembered Astra showing it to him after she found Sonji two years ago, but it still looked as unimportant and dilapidated as it did then, maybe worse. How could this wagon and the one his mother used be the same? He didn't recall seeing it before Sonji appeared. He and Astra had explored the desert near the village a million times over the years.

Clunk-cuthunk. Plop. From beneath the wagon, Mo pushed a dirty gear, and both landed in the sand.

Hamal picked up the find. "What is this?"

The sunlight caught on a clean spot, revealing an imprint of a flower bearing three petals.

CHAPTER 29

Astra rechecked her tack and supplies for the twelfth time and tried not to let yesterday's events clutter her mind. She needed to get to the town of Urugha, find the station, ride the train to Latif City, and hope come morning she could follow her directions to the starting line correctly. She still had a race to run.

Astra helped Ehsan into the saddle before slipping half of an apple to her mare and whispering in a slender ear, "Keep track of Ehsan for me, all right?"

Sonji bobbed her head as she ate the treat.

"Are you sure about this?" Ehsan knotted the reins, unknotted them, and then knotted them again. "She is your horse."

"You're lighter." True. "And you won't get to play with her for a while." Also, true. But her heart warred with her decision.

Zeb, a trader of Isaac's, asked a camel to kneel and offered to help Astra aboard. "You're very kind to let your sister ride your mount."

She smiled a little, unsure what to say and not quite ready to get on the camel.

"Astra, wait." Hamal sprinted around the side of the burnt trading post with his gizmo flying close behind, sliding to a stop a short way from her.

Zeb tied the camel for Astra before he helped his wife Ruth mount one. Then, he checked on Papa and a third camel.

Astra approached her friend. "Ham, aren't you going to be late for work again?" Why couldn't she talk about something other than responsibilities—like how handsome he looked today? No. Compliments might come across wrong.

"Yes. But I wanted to wish you well on your trip." His hands slipped into his pockets.

She pressed on the pendant hidden beneath her shirt. Mrs. Zilfel had brought the flower pendant to her yesterday afternoon and mentioned Mama had ordered it months ago as a token of good luck for the race and an early birthday present. Why had Mama left? Had she been summoned by the Creator and failed to bring him an ancient machine because of a Destroyer? Was the Veil compromised?

She pushed her crazy thoughts away. "Thank you ... for coming and for your help with race preparations and everything."

"You're welcome." Hands behind his back, he pushed sand around with the toe of his shoe.

She brushed her lips against his freshly shaved cheek and backed toward her camel. "I need to go, but I'll see you soon."

Hamal seemed to be blushing. *Impossible.*

Zeb handed her the reins and helped her mount.

Hamal waved as Mo flew around his head, and she returned the wave before Zeb led the way into the desert.

After a while, Astra pulled her necklace from under her shirt and recalled Mrs. Zilfel's parting words: "You are not an outcast, Astra."

Not an outcast.

So why, when she looked in the mirror and saw her green-flecked brown eyes staring back, did she feel like one? Why did the scruffy old vendors in the market harass her? Why had she been called one in school?

Papa turned toward her. "You've been very quiet this morning. If you're having second thoughts about the race, perhaps want to back out, we'll understand."

"I want to race, Papa." Probably said that too fast and forcefully. "I do." Astra rubbed her finger over the pendant.

"Then, why so quiet?" He met her gaze with his warm brown eyes.

She forced herself not to bite her lip. "I'm sorry your shop and projects burned."

"You are not responsible for their ruin, my darling. Please, don't blame yourself for what you cannot control." He reached across and squeezed her knee. "And remember, you, your sister, and your mother mean more to me than my work does."

"Yes, Papa." Her fingers curled tighter around her pendant. "But what about rebuilding? I know my gold winkll could have helped."

"No." He released her knee and slashed with his hand. "No more worrying. A regular client of mine has promised to help me rebuild in return for a few pieces of furniture. Your gold winkll is yours—to enter the race, to buy thread, to do whatever you desire."

A weight lifted from Astra's shoulders, and her guilt over using the gold winkll to enter the race dissipated.

Papa pointed ahead of them. "Zeb and Ruth seem to be handling Ehsan's enthusiasm quite well."

Astra watched. Sonji kept pace with the camels, the reins resting on her neck. Ehsan's hands flew every which way, and her voice carried across the warming desert. Ruth and Zeb nodded their heads or contributed simple questions to the conversation.

"Papa, how do you know Zeb and Ruth?" She tucked her pendant back inside her shirt.

"I can't remember anymore." He scratched his whiskered face. "They worked for Isaac's mother before working for him ... might have even worked for the lad's father. Why?"

She shrugged. "I don't remember seeing them around Nahrot before."

"They're nomads—they prefer the wide open spaces to crowds."

Her forehead wrinkled. "Don't most nomads travel in family groups? And why are they taking trade goods to Urugha?"

Papa sipped from his water skin. "They are a family group, even though there are only two of them, and even nomads need to make a living."

"I didn't think about that." Her hand touched her chest, right where the pendant rested under her shirt. The word "family" had her thinking about Mama and that she wasn't there to see her off for the race.

Papa chuckled. "Your mama convinced me to let you race because there was no stopping you. Better for us to wave you off than have you sneak away in the dead of night."

"I wouldn't have snuck away." Her hand dropped from her chest, and she faced him.

He raised a dark eyebrow.

She ducked her head. "Well, maybe not."

He chuckled again. "I love you, Astra, and I love your mother. The Creator has big plans for the both of you. Please know I will always be here, and you never need be afraid to talk to me."

"Papa, why did Mama run away?" The question burst forth before she could think it over.

His mouth thinned and sadness filled his dark eyes. "I cannot answer for her." He pointed to the pendant. "Know that she loves you and your sister always, and she prays for you both."

They rounded a large dune, and Urugha spread before them. To the left waited the train station, and to the right, people and animals packed the streets. Dryzzian flags flapped from rooftops. The stench of humans and animals sweating in the hot sun mixed with the aromas of cooking meats and cinnamon-sweet bakery goods. And the sound of too many creatures and people occupying the same space scratched her ears.

Maybe, on second thought, she did want to back out of the race.

CHAPTER 30

The acrid smell of coal smoke cut through the tangy scent of body odor, animals, and ripening foods. More people crisscrossed the Urugha train station than Astra had ever seen in one place before. The wooden boards of the platform groaned under the weight of the foot traffic.

Astra waited with Sonji on the platform.

The crowd swallowed Papa and Ehsan as they headed for the seats listed on their tickets.

The constant activity unnerved Astra. She reached deep in her pocket for her special bell, the last item she'd packed for the race. Train stations and towns were bigger than what she'd read about in books and a perfect place for pickpockets.

Ten minutes later, her father appeared at her side. "Ready?" He pointed to the stock cars at the end of the train.

She forced a nod and hoped her face didn't reveal the fear swirling in her stomach. She removed her hand from her pocket and gripped Sonji's lead rope with white knuckles.

On their way to the first stock car, they passed a post with a wanted poster. The name listed was Kaseem Nuru, and the man pictured reminded her of an older, harder version of Hamal.

Part of Hamal's confession circled her mind: "*A man obsessed with greed. He and his partners wove tales over their campfire about a white horse … the key to the Creator's treasury.*"

Boys about Ehsan's age rushed up and down the planks loading the big, wood-sided cars. One lad led a familiar dark bay horse into a car.

A boy wearing an eyepatch darted over to Astra and stopped in front of her. "Hello, Miss. Are you picking up or loading?"

The thief who'd chased Sonji wore an eyepatch, too. Ham said he was his father's right hand man, and he went by the name Willard. Her friend's voice filled her head again: "*… and wherever he is—my father is sure to be close.*"

Papa stepped in front of Astra and held out a yellow slip. "We're loading."

Eyepatch looked at the paper. "Do you want to lead your horse in, or would you like me to care for him?"

"Sonji's a girl." Astra's grip on the rope tightened further, and her knuckles popped. Her senses were overloaded by colors, smells, and movement. Where should she look? What was worth her attention and what wasn't?

"Pardon me," said Eyepatch.

"You're pardoned." Papa gestured to the first car. "We'd like you to show us her stall."

"This way." The boy waved, spun around, and led them up the plank and into the car.

Astra paused inside the doorway to the car and tried not to gag on the stink of manure. The floorboards were worn smooth and nailed together tight while slits of light wiggled between gaps in the warped wooden slats of the walls. A patch of light from the ceiling illuminated a two-foot-by-two-foot square on the right side of the entrance. A narrow hall led to mooing cows, squealing pigs, and squawking caged chickens who roomed in all but one stall.

Sonji touched Astra's shoulder with her muzzle, and Astra rubbed her mare's forehead. "Thanks for steadying me, girl." They followed the boy.

Eyepatch opened the gate to the empty stall. Over the noise of the animals, he said, "There's a chest to store your saddle and things. Cover her in the blanket and leg wraps so if the train jolts, she doesn't get cut on anything."

"Where should we tie her lead rope when we're done?" Papa stepped into the stall and to the side.

"Don't tie her. She could get tangled in the line during the trip." Eyepatch patted the wooden gate. "I'll make sure the door is secured before the train departs."

Astra led Sonji to the back of the small stall and tied her. Methodically, she worked her way through the cinches and buckles of her saddle.

Papa took the tack and set it in the chest before bringing her an oversized blanket and bands of fabric. Then, he stepped back and spoke with the boy by the gate.

Astra showed the items to Sonji, who sniffed them and then chewed on some hay in a feeder, before setting to work wrapping her horse. When finished, Astra disconnected the lead rope from the halter.

Eyepatch held out his hand. "There's a hook here I can hang that on. Keeps ya from rummaging through the chest for it later."

She gave him the rope and moved close to her father. "Thank you."

"You're welcome." Eyepatch dropped the rope on the hook by the gate and fastened the lock. "Hope ya have safe travels." He sprinted out of the car.

"Nice boy." Papa led the way back to the platform.

Astra watched someone else hand an animal off to a lad and give him a coin. "Papa, should we have given the boy a coin?"

"Yes, we should have."

Astra searched the crowd but couldn't spot Eyepatch. She did see another lad, this one bigger than him, fighting with a gray horse. She shuddered. The animal had to be unnerved by all the movement and noise and smells. While those things intimidated her, at least she had Papa and Sonji and even Eyepatch to help her. She prayed for the gray horse and the boy.

Papa escorted her up several steps and into a passenger car.

Ehsan waved from a seat a few rows back. "How'd loading go?"

"Good. Sonji never batted an eye." Papa pushed Astra onto the bench beside her sister before plopping into one across the aisle.

"She's special." Ehsan grinned, her brown eyes glowing.

Astra agreed. Then, she pulled her pack off her seat and onto her lap and hugged it, hoping her heavy load would help ground her. So much had occurred. So much more would happen. Was she ready—really ready—to run in the Great Desert Race?

Someone hollered, "Last chance. All aboard for Latif City," a moment before the train whistle blew, and with a screech of iron on iron, the giant, smoke-breathing contraption jerked forward.

She hugged her pack harder now, because it was too late to back out.

Creator, please lend me your courage, your strength. And keep the bad men away.

CHAPTER 31

Astra's kiss this morning sent a ripple of electricity through every nerve. Of course, she'd given the standard goodbye kiss and nothing more. Her father and Ehsan were there. But even with company, this kiss touched Hamal more deeply than any other. He wondered why, and touched his cheek for the umpteenth time as Mo flew around his head.

"Hamal." Dirty and sweaty, Isaac Zilfel walked away from the ruins of his shop and shook hands with Hamal.

"Isaac." Hamal pushed his thoughts of Astra to the back of his mind and removed the woodchip from his pocket. "I've been meaning to talk with you."

"Oh?" Isaac wiped his face with the tail of his turban, rearranging more soot than he removed. His wiry beard stuck out in every direction.

"Yes." Everything in Hamal screamed to leave and admit to nothing. "I'm certain I know who burnt your shop, maybe even why."

His former mentor led the way to the sturdy front of the trading post and sat on the shaded front steps. "Who?" Not a hint of accusation or upset on his face.

Hamal handed Isaac the woodchip. "Kaseem Nuru. I found his calling card in the ash."

Isaac turned the chip over in his hands and returned it. "How do you know?" Again, no accusation. More curiosity.

"Three years ago, when I left for a while ... I saw one of these at a, um, mansion that had been recently robbed by him ... according to the local *jundiin*." Hamal winced inwardly at having not told everything to his friend, but admitting his ties to his father could cause trouble.

Isaac's forehead wrinkled. "The detailed inventory of the post that my wife and I did revealed nothing missing, and when we asked everyone in Nahrot if they were missing anything, we learned no one was. She'd thought our fire might have been set like Jabir's, to cover a theft, but I've not found any sign of it."

"Strange." Hamal caught Mo, deactivated its wings, and slid it in his pocket.

"Indeed." Isaac stood and stretched his back. "At least my dear Peridot convinced me to build an extra storage shed before this happened. Never have figured out how she knows we need something before we do."

He patted Hamal on the shoulder. "If you ever want your apprenticeship back, or some extra work, let me know. You're the best I've ever had."

A girl of about fourteen sprinted up the street, one hand keeping her sinar on her head and the other lifting her skirt. She skidded to a stop in front of the post. "Good morning, Mr. Zilfel." Her face was a little small for her camel-brown eyes, and her dark brown hair escaped her braid. "Sorry I'm late, sir."

The stinging comments Hamal had heard about the young girl rang in his ears. She was good enough to restock the shelves and sweep, but she had no mind for trade.

She tipped her head to him. "Good morning, Mr. Nuru."

"You can call me Hamal." Being called 'mister' made him feel older than his seventeen years. "I'd best be going. David's expecting me today." He tipped his head to Isaac. "But I may drop by this evening to give you an extra hand cleaning up." He slipped his hand into his pocket and rubbed Mo and the two woodchips.

Nerves zinged and desert flies buzzed in his stomach. His father was behind the fire. He knew it. But since Sonji hadn't been stolen again, why was Kaseem here?

CHAPTER 32

After he and his mother packed his bag for the train ride and ate dinner, Hamal slipped into the night. His head pounded with a million thoughts, most of them centered on his father.

He rounded the corner of a darkened alleyway and saw a familiar figure—the woman who helped with the bucket-line—walking ahead of him. Why was she wandering Nahrot in the dark?

He kept back and followed her as she wove through one alleyway and then another before crossing a street and entering the *mople*, the building reserved for worship and Shabbos gatherings.

He paused in the shadows, his heart thundering in his ears and sweat slicking his palms. A million questions buzzed in his head before he steeled his nerves.

And entered the *mople*.

Rows of empty benches lined either side of the dark aisle Hamal walked. Moonlight illuminated the *Creato*, the book containing the stories of the Creator, sitting on the pulpit at the front.

He stopped in front of the pulpit. "Hello? Is anyone here?" His voice echoed in the large space.

No one answered. No human shape emerged from the shadows. Where had the woman gone?

Hamal backed several steps, spun around, and hurried back into the night. His chance for answers had disappeared like a figment of his imagination. How could she not be real? She had given him a wet cloth the night of the trading post fire.

He pulled his restless gizmo from his pocket, unleashed the wings, and tossed it in the air. He watched Mo zoom ahead and hover as if checking on him. He smiled at his special invention. Blacksmith work suited him better than trading.

Nabila knew how to trade. When he helped clean up the burnt mess of the post for an hour before dinner, he'd heard her whisper the appropriate pricings and quality of items to herself. Her lack of confidence when put on the spot was what kept her from shining. Maybe a few more years under Isaac would curb her nervousness, grow a bit more confidence. He hoped.

He wandered his way out of the village and paused at Astra's house. The windows were dark, the chickens quiet, and the sharp scent of smoke hung in the air.

She was off on an adventure.

Strange not being beside her for the Great Desert Race, but he'd meet her at the halfway point to refill her supplies.

Her train had probably steamed into Latif City by now. She'd be tired. She, Jabir, and Ehsan had left Nahrot for Urugha before the sun fully rose.

His heart ached.

"You miss her already." Wisewoman Yasif walked up the trail and stopped next to him.

"Huh?" He turned from the Paksims' to her.

"You've never done well at hiding your feelings, boy." Her cat, proudly carrying a dead mouse, trotted over and sat beside her feet. Then, she leaned and patted her pet on the head. "Good job."

A cross between a purr and muffled meow emanated from the cat before he trotted up the trail, his tail up with a proud tweak at the end.

"I'll see you at home shortly." She chuckled and turned to Hamal. "Trust the Creator. Your Astra will stay safe."

"She's not mine." The words slid out faster than he expected, and an uncomfortable heat filled him.

Wisewoman Yasif cocked a graying black eyebrow. "All right. But I still say trust the Creator, because his ways are beyond ours—and Astra has caught his attention."

Hamal struggled to say something in return, but failed.

"Will you be able to care for my garden tomorrow?" Her teeth flashed in the light of the waning moon.

"No, I'm supposed to be on the train." He knew he should have told her about his travel plans on his way home from the post … but the thought of dinner had been more alluring than talk.

She stepped closer to him. "Did you ever hear anything about the messenger?"

"Nothing more than he visited. Why?" His senses tingled.

"There's a shift in the wind, a tug in my gut." She inhaled deeply and tipped her head back. "I can almost taste what's coming."

A cold breeze rustled their clothes and rattled a loose board in the gate.

She shivered and gripped Hamal's shoulder. "Take care, boy." She walked back to the village.

He stared at the dark house again and, for the first time in years, prayed. *I know I don't deserve to be heard, but please watch over my friend.*

He returned to Nahrot, climbed a fence, and snuck along roofs toward home, his heart slightly lighter than before.

CHAPTER 33

Morning in Latif City was noisier than the afternoon at the train station in Urugha. Astra listened to tens of thousands of people waking and starting their day beyond the walls of the stable attached to the inn.

"Today's the day." She forced her quivering hands to still before she slipped the halter on Sonji and tied the lead rope to a ring by the stall door.

Ehsan, standing on a stool, held out a comb. "Being nervous is all right."

Astra shook her head. "I'm not nervous, and I'll take the hoof-pick. You can comb her today."

Ehsan dropped the pick in Astra's hand and set to work combing the cream-white mane. "She'll be the most beautiful racer." Her nose wiggled and her forehead wrinkled. "Are horses considered racers?"

"They're usually considered mounts, and, yes, Sonji will be the most beautiful." Papa entered the stable through the door from the inn.

Ehsan beamed, her smile wider than her face and her eyes bright as amber stone.

In minutes, Sonji stood groomed and tacked, Astra's bedroll, tent, and saddlebags full of supplies strapped onto the saddle.

Astra, her family, and Sonji exited the stable and stepped into a street filled with people and animals. Bright-hued streamers stretched between buildings and danced in the cool early morning breeze. Fresh-baked bread, roasting meats, and sugar desserts flavored the air and almost squashed the smell of uncleaned people and animals. Children squealed, adults shouted, dogs barked, and goats bleated.

Astra stopped not far from the stable door as the same unease from the train station engulfed her.

Ehsan gripped her free hand, Papa stepped to the front, and together they squeezed through the chaos.

Nearly to the starting line and the open sands, Astra spotted a wanted poster for Kaseem Nuru tacked to the side of a building. Was the Creator trying to warn her about something?

Her hand holding Sonji's reins strayed into her pocket and found her brass bell. She pushed aside her unease.

Thirty minutes later, Astra waited in the check-in line.

A tall, buck-toothed woman with dark brown eyes leading a big red horse stopped beside Astra. "Are you even old enough to race, half-jug?" she sneered.

Astra met the stranger's gaze even though her legs shook. "I am."

The woman's sneer deepened. "And you're a half-breed to boot, might as well give in now. You've not got enough desert blood in ya to last a day in the race." Her horse snorted as if he agreed.

Astra stepped back and wished she were brave enough to stand up for herself.

A gimping man wearing rags bumped into the woman. She cussed at him but finally left when another person called out to her.

Men and women of every age imaginable roamed the area with their horses, steeds of every color and size, following along. Astra hadn't realized the size and diversity of her country until now. Rumors claimed some of the riders came from other countries, but she couldn't imagine crossing borders to participate.

Weaving through the participants, her dark horse trailing her, was Vivian Rose. They paused by the water trough.

Astra contemplated leaving the line to speak with Vivian. She glanced ahead and behind, and found the line stretched twenty-five people in front and more than fifty behind. Better to wait and check in rather than leave and wait longer later.

Vivian and her mount disappeared in the sea of people and horses.

Astra eventually reached the check-in table, where a young man efficiently checked names and paperwork. As she signed in, she wondered why one person manned the station when there were a lot of people to care for. Finished, she searched the shady areas near the starting line for Sonji and her family.

Ehsan, wearing her blue, flower-patterned sinar, waved beside Papa.

Astra joined them, her stomach grumbling and her hands stuffed in her pockets. "I'm glad I listened to the commander back home and arrived early."

Papa nodded and handed her a honey-and-raisin roll. "You've studied for this, my darling. Asked every former racer in Nahrot and then some about first day expectations and travel conditions for every inch of the two hundred miles of desert you'll be riding. There's no need for you to be nervous."

"True." Astra nibbled her roll and licked the honey from her fingers.

Ehsan pointed across the way. "Isn't that dark horse over there handsome?"

A man about Papa's age, instead of Vivian, led the beautiful mount.

"He is." Papa handed Sonji's reins to Astra. "I need a minute, my girls. Excuse me."

The sisters allowed their father to pass. He approached a man of the same light skin tone as Vivian and with hair lighter in color than anything Astra was used to. The man carried a satchel and wore a hat with a wide brim. And he seemed to know Papa, the way they shook hands and traded smiles.

"What do you suppose they're saying?" Ehsan shaded her eyes.

"I'm not sure." Astra wished they were closer, and startled when Sonji nuzzled her pocket. She pushed her mare's muzzle away. "I don't have anything for you right now."

Ehsan pulled a dried fruit from her pocket. "Here's an apricot."

Astra straightened the stirrup of her saddle. "How about you take a short ride on her and then give her the treat?"

"Deal." Ehsan stuffed the treat back in her pocket and climbed aboard.

Astra led Sonji through the crowd and spied open sand in the distance. She paused, forced herself to inhale deeply and exhale slowly. Her nerves steadied, mostly.

"Hello."

Astra stopped, turned. "Vivian Rose."

Vivian smiled, her blue eyes twinkling. "You know my name, but I seem to be at a disadvantage." She rubbed the nails of her fingers with her right thumb.

"I'm Ehsan Paksim"—Ehsan tapped her chest before pointing—"and this is my sister Astra." Then she patted the white mare's shoulder. "And this is Sonji."

"Pleasure to meet you." Vivian dropped into a curtsy in a skirt split like pants.

Ehsan attempted to return the gesture even though she was still atop Sonji. "You, too. Are you here to race?"

"Yes. You?" Vivian still rubbed her nails, and never looked at them.

Ehsan shook her head, her sinar falling and her ebony hair flying. "No. My sister is."

A sharp whistle cut through the conversation, and Vivian's cheeks turned pink. "Excuse me. My father needs me." She ran to the man speaking with Papa.

How did Papa and Vivian's father know each other?

CHAPTER 34

Astra, her hands trembling, triple-checked the buckles and cinches of her saddle before she tested the ties for her equipment. She ensured Sonji's hooves were clean and her shoes firmly in place. Everything checked out.

Sonji touched her arm with her muzzle.

Astra rubbed the familiar face and looked deep into the warm, brown eyes. "Maybe I should have checked in later."

Hundreds of spectators watched behind ropes lining the starting area as more than a hundred racers eased into position.

Her white mare tugged the reins she held and led the way to their starting position. Astra, her stomach flip-flopping, followed and mounted her horse in a sea of riders and people. A flash of blue drew her attention.

Ehsan, atop Papa's shoulders, waved her sinar like a little flag.

Astra smiled and waved back, her constricting fear easing.

In the distance, bright colored flags flapped from the top of the creamy white and gold palace walls. A teardrop shape topped each of the four yard towers and the fifth taller tower in the center. The city spread from the palace center in a patchwork of tan, white, and brown. Beautiful. But uncomfortably huge.

A booming voice cut through the chatter of the crowd and the whinnies of the horses. "Welcome to the annual Great Desert Race of Dryzza."

She strained to see who called from the starting line, but too many riders and people blocked her view. She sighed and sat back in her saddle.

Movement to her right drew her attention. She scanned the spectators.

A tall, mustached man wearing a brown turban hurried through the crowd. Zeb? Why was he here? She remembered him and Ruth saying they were returning to Nahrot after making their delivery in Urugha.

"On the sound of the shot," said the booming voice, "the race will begin. One ... Two ... Three."

A sharp pop rang out.

A few of the horses startled while Sonji and the rest trotted with the flow.

Astra, her heart pounding in her ears, held tight to her reins and passed under the banner stretched over the starting line. If only Mama were here to watch her.

She glanced over her shoulder to catch one more look at her sister and father, but dust and the crowd hid them.

Please, dear Creator, watch over my family—Mama, Papa, and Ehsan. And watch over me, too, as I race.

Soon the banner disappeared, the city shrank, and the crowd blended into the sands.

For over a mile, the racers stayed in a bunch and then spread out. A few seemed to know each other and hung in clusters while others kept to themselves.

Hours passed. Surrounded by open desert, Astra breathed easier and sipped from her canteen as her mount kept to an easy, ground-devouring trot. She recalled from her time on the train her papa reminding her to stay hydrated and ration her supplies because getting lost was easy and surviving could be tricky.

In the distance, the check-in point appeared like a wavering mirage. Tents, palm trees, and people pulsed in the late afternoon heat until Astra drew close enough for them to solidify. She guided her horse toward the tent marked for checking in.

A plump woman stirring a large pot of stew stood by the entrance. She pointed to the paper held down by rocks.

Astra dismounted, dipped a sharpened stick in a pot of ink, and scribbled her name below dozens of others.

"You can eat in a few," said the woman. "Outhouses are that way, and over there you can send messages." She waved at a row of narrow tents before pointing to a tent similar to her own and closer to the pond in the center of the oasis.

"Thank you." Astra led her horse to the pond, passing many of her fellow racers and their already-pitched tents.

Several yards away, Vivian Rose watered her horse. She tipped her head.

Astra returned the gesture while Sonji, ears flicking and tail swishing against flies, sucked several large gulps from the pond.

Vivian's horse lifted his head, and the two walked into the field of tents.

Astra stared at where Vivian and her horse had disappeared. *If she traveled to Dryzza for the race, why visit Nahrot? Hamal? And why did Hamal and I cross paths with her at the abandoned homestead?*

CHAPTER 35

Breakfast dishes cleared away, Hamal set the woodchip with the engraving of the horse on the table. "I've found two of these—one by Isaac's corral and the other in the ashes at the back of the trading post. I think they mean my father is nearby. Any idea why?"

His mother stopped wiping clean the tabletop and sat heavily in a chair. "How did he find her?" Her voice was softer than a breeze.

Hamal wrinkled his forehead. "Sonji?"

"Yes." She picked up the chip and patted the extra chair.

"But she wasn't taken after the second fire." He pulled his gizmo from his pocket, set it on the table, and sat beside her. His gizmo rolled onto the cleaning rag.

"She wasn't taken again because someone interfered." Mother set the chip on the table and pushed it away. "Years before Princess Gefen was born and found her beloved mare Sonji, a young man wandered lost in the wilderness. The sand dunes he climbed sometimes flattened and hardened to dried dirt, allowing rocks and scraggly brush to grab his feet. The smallest amount of food or water was a blessing. But he yearned to find civilization because the loneliness of the wild ate at his soul.

"One day, hot and sweaty, the man saw a fine palace and garden in the middle of the desert. He rubbed his eyes, certain heat and exhaustion were trying to make a fool of him for the thousandth time, but the palace did not vanish. Intrigued, he crossed the sands.

"Before evening, he reached a tall stone fence surrounding the palace and interrupted by a pair of wooden doors. He touched the doors, and they opened. Startled, he fell back … yet no one appeared, so he entered.

"A forest rose around him, full of trees, grass, and exotic flowers. A trail cut through the thick vegetation. Brightly colored birds danced above him while other creatures—a white horse, a black panther, a parade of elephants, and more—filled the grounds.

"He followed the trail to the beautiful palace he'd seen from afar. Carvings of stories from the *Creato* lined the walls and seven tall spires reached for the sky—the center one nearly touching the clouds. Tending several small plants beside the palace was a small, older man with twinkling eyes.

"The young man asked the older one who owned this place, and the older man said, 'I do.' The younger pretended to believe as his stomach growled and greed grew.

"The older took the younger in and offered him food, clothes, a room, free roam of the palace and the grounds, but there was one request—leave the small, white horse alone.

"The young man agreed and thought nothing of the request because there were many horses—all of them finer than the small horse.

"With his needs met and his time free, he roamed the palace looking for a sultan, for someone to trick riches from. The old gardener couldn't be the owner, but if he was, well, there had to be a treasury somewhere, because this palace was too fine to exist without riches. The young man knew these things from past experience—experience that had brought about his exile in the wilderness.

"Yet he never met anyone other than the gardener.

"The young man passed the time by following the engravings in the walls depicting the story of the Creator's love. The day he finished and turned to find a new way to entertain himself, a tree branch shivered in a breeze. Tucked in a dark corner were several small carvings mentioning the small horse … and the hidden entrance to the palace treasury.

"The man broke his promise and caught the small, white horse. He took her to the treasury and followed every step he'd seen outlined in the carvings until the door opened.

"He glimpsed the most wondrous treasure he could ever imagine, only to be forced to flee when the animals—birds, horses, lions, and more—attacked.

"When he fled, he took the small horse with him because she never attacked him as the other animals did. They crossed miles of desert and stumbled into civilization. The young man told anyone who would listen about what he'd seen.

"No one believed him.

"He worked until he had enough money to gamble. But he cheated at his gambling and got caught. To keep from losing a hand for his crime, he disappeared back into the desert … and left behind the small horse. Rumors from his stories about her lingered, but nothing could be confirmed, so she passed from one man to the next before crossing paths with Princess Gefen."

Hamal glanced at the clock and brought his mother a cup of water. "Quite the tale for one horse."

"Yes, my son." She accepted the drink.

He knew in his gut she'd shared the truth, but he wished she'd told him fibs. "How could you have seen Sonji at the Palace of the Creator if she was stolen?" He stuffed his gizmo in his bag. He needed to leave.

"I'm not sure. Perhaps after you find out, you can tell me." She shakily stood and forced him to meet her gaze. "May the Creator bless your trip, my son." She rubbed her thumb along the side of his cheek.

He stepped out of her grasp. "I have a train to catch."

CHAPTER 36

Hamal walked the long route to the trading post to catch the caravan headed to Urugha and hoped the extra steps would help him relax—until *Tollarb* Ke'ev opened his front door and waved.

Hamal bit his tongue to keep from asking *Tollarb* Ke'ev a million questions brought on by his mother's story of the man stealing the white horse. Why would the Creator allow someone like him through the front gates? How could a horse unlock the Creator's treasury? And what was in there?

"I'm glad to see you." Two long strides brought the slender man alongside him. "There's something I feel I need to share with you: Never be afraid to place what you do not understand, like the fires, in the hands of the Creator."

"Uh-huh." *Please, go away before I say something crazy.* Hamal's original questions burned on the tip of his tongue along with a new one about why the *tollarb* said what he did.

Wisewoman Yasif stepped from her house. "Hamal."

Tollarb Ke'ev stopped. "Thank you for listening, Hamal, and, if you could, please let your mother know her mending work is appreciated. I need to be going now."

"Uh-huh." Hamal adjusted his grip on his pack and watched *Tollarb* Ke'ev stride away before forcing himself to slow and face the old woman. "Good morning."

"Yes, yes." She batted his words away like they were flies. "I forgot to tell you something the other night."

"You did?" His stomach twisted and he tried to recall their conversation at the Paksims'. What would be so important she needed to stop him on his way out of town?

"Yes." She picked up her cat. "The change in the wind, perhaps it means a miracle is in the making?"

He struggled with a response, but her door slammed shut before he could think of one, and so he continued to the trading post. His conversation with his mother caught in a whirlwind of thoughts brought about by *Tollarb* Ke'ev and Wisewoman Yasif.

David crossed his path. "I know we spoke yesterday before you left work, but I forgot to tell you not to worry while you're gone. I'll keep an eye on your mother and help her care for the Paksims' chickens."

Hamal stopped, faced his mentor. "Thank you, sir." A weight lifted from his shoulders, but a new one settled because he wished he'd not been grumpy with Mother.

"You're welcome, and may the Creator bless your travels." David walked away.

At the trading post barn, Hamal found a woman tending to several camels. Her hair was the color of unsweetened chocolate, her eyes a common brown, and she wore a brown sinar, a tan blouse, and a brown skirt. Her skin was the same tanned tone as the locals. Nothing about her seemed unique. And then she smiled, and he remembered where he knew her from—the bucket-line.

"You," he managed to say before Isaac walked around the post, patted him on the shoulder, and greeted him.

Isaac's wife Peridot followed him, her belly the size of a camel hump, and said something about how she doubted they would ever find what ignited the fire. She stopped and smiled. "Good morning, Hamal."

Hamal tipped his head to the Zilfels. "Same to you."

Peridot rested her hands on her belly. "Are you excited to be traveling to Gefen?"

Before he could answer a little boy raced from behind the trading post, wrapped his arms around Isaac's leg, and peered at Hamal with large eyes.

Peridot giggled and ruffled the child's hair. "My boy, Hamal won't hurt you."

"He look like man with match." The child hid behind Isaac.

Isaac picked the boy up. "What man?"

"The one who burn post." The boy stuck his thumb in his mouth and peeked at Hamal before burying his face in his father's shoulder.

The color in Peridot's face drained. "Isaac, we need to speak with the commander—immediately." She hustled away, and her husband tried to keep up. A minute later, they disappeared around the corner.

Nabila, still as awkward as Hamal had seen her last, raced up the street and stumbled to a halt in front of him. "Ready for work, sir." She pushed her drooping sinar and loose strands of hair from her face. "Mr. Nuru ... Hamal?" She looked around. "Where is Mr. Zilfel?"

Hamal shifted from one foot to the other. "Isaac and his wife went to speak with the commander."

"Oh." She stopped looking and fussed with her sinar, tucking her stray hairs underneath.

"You're good at trade, Nabila." He forced the words out, nervous because she was nervous. "I think with a bit more time and practice people will be just as interested to work with you as with Isaac."

She faced him, hope shining in her camel-brown eyes and her voice soft as a whisper. "You think so?"

"I do." He smiled.

She beamed, standing straighter than normal and her lips tipped up in a smile. "Thank you, Mr. Hamal, and please tell Miss Paksim my grandma and I are praying for her." She scurried off faster than a desert mouse to the trading post.

"I will," he said to her disappearing backside.

"What you told that girl was very kind."

"Huh?" Hamal turned, found the woman from the bucket-line.

"You heard me." She smiled and lifted her dark brown eyebrows. "Now, why are you traveling to Urugha?"

"To catch a train." He could hardly breathe—the woman he'd sought to speak with over the last few days stood before him as not a ghost but a living, breathing human.

She tipped her head, her eyes narrowing. "I'm guessing you're riding the train because you are helping one of the racers, possibly resupplying him somewhere along his route."

"Good guess." He wanted to pinch himself to make sure that he wasn't dreaming.

"Several locals mentioned one of their own is partaking in the Great Desert Race this year." She removed a tattered paper and a pencil from her skirt pocket. "Racing isn't an easy challenge. I'll pray for your friend. What's his name?"

His conscience gnawed at him. "*Her* name is Astra."

"Astra. Pretty name." She set the paper against her open hand and scribbled before putting her writing tools away.

Hamal liked the name, but mostly he liked the girl, his best friend … or maybe something more? He'd never even sat close to her without a good reason, so dreaming of holding her and kissing her were too farfetched and presumptuous, right? And … what if she didn't see him as more than a friend?

"Daydreaming?" She chuckled and headed for the camels. "I still feel the same for my Zeb."

"Huh?" Hamal snapped out of his thoughts and followed her. "I saw you last night going to the *mople*."

She shook her head and faced him. "I didn't go to the *mople*. I stopped by the *tollarb*'s."

"Why?" He doubted *Tollarb* Ke'ev was even awake when she had dropped by late last night.

Her face paled, and she backed up a step toward the shifting, grunting camels. Hamal turned to see what was behind him.

Thunk.

And everything went black.

CHAPTER 37

After dinner, Astra pitched her tent on the outskirts of the check-in point. Papa had warned her against secluding herself and becoming easy prey for bad men, but pitching closer to the pond meant people surrounding her. She hoped by leaving Sonji loose to watch over her that the men would keep their distance.

She inhaled the clean, cool, night air and marveled at the black dunes butting against a dark blue sky full of stars that sparkled like polished diamonds.

Sonji nibbled on a pile of hay as Astra ran her fingers over her mare, the familiar muscles, limbs, and scars comforting. Her hands hovered over the faded scar on Sonji's shoulder, the barest hint of a shape lingering there. When she'd found her mare two years ago she thought the mark a brand, but when the commander and his *jundiin* inspected the mare, no one commented on it.

Now, she touched her finger tips to Sonji's warm shoulder and followed the outline she saw by firelight. One ... two ... three ... petals. She tugged her pendant free from beneath her shirt and held it next to the mark. They were the same design.

She dropped the pendant and backed away from her horse.

Was her Sonji the same steed the princess had ridden … the key to a treasure in the Palace of the Creator? Was a renowned thief after her? Was Hamal right?

She sat in the sand in front of her tent and ran her fingers through her tangled hair, her sinar sliding to her shoulders. She bit her lower lip and listened to people laughing and jabbering until the noise faded and the fires mellowed to embers. Then Astra crawled into bed, the racing questions in her head dulling to a thrum.

A feminine voice sang into the night, the tune and the voice tugging at a buried memory. But even as the sound aroused her curiosity, her eyelids drooped and sleep drew her in.

Her dreamworld unraveled on a dark canvas. Light splayed over the horizon, glinting off Papa's shovel leaned against the barn. The chickens scratched and pecked the sandy yard. The water bucket hung over the well near the barn.

Around the side of the house, she found Mama and Papa whispering. Astra ducked behind a grouping of old crates and a barrel.

Tears dripped off Mama's dust-covered face, and Astra snuck closer, wondering why she cried.

Mama wiped at her tears with the back of her hand. "Everything went wrong, Jabir. Everything."

"Tell me." Papa led her to the bench he'd finished building and they sat.

Mama sniffled. "Omaira and I found the device by Angel's Wings, but it was in a million pieces—like it had exploded. We scoured the area for hours and, when we thought we'd found everything, we turned our wagon toward home. And then things started going wrong." She strangled her handkerchief.

"What went wrong?" Papa caught her hands and stilled them before wiping a fresh tear from her cheek.

"Something huge behind the Veil chased us. One of our horses broke the rigging and plummeted to the bottom of the canyon. Then, night fell on us. The ... something ... kept coming. We managed to take refuge in a *mople* in a village somewhere, got a new pair of horses for the wagon ... but the thing found us again. Chased us. Kept chasing us all the way here." Her whole body shook.

Papa pulled her against himself. "Shh, shh, Fay, you're safe now."

"How do you know?" She hiccupped and buried her face in his chest.

He held her, kissed the top of her head. "Because a new day is here. Because you are here. Because the Creator has answered my prayers." A tear trickled down his face, passed his beard, and into her hair.

Mama pushed herself off Papa's chest. "The thing—the Destroyer—chasing us managed to poke through the Veil. Omaira's been bitten."

His face paled. "Has she seen ...?"

"My mother, yes, and been given a special medicine, but there's no telling if it'll be enough. The fangs sank deep." She blew her nose in her handkerchief. "And we still haven't finished answering our summons—we haven't taken the machine to the Palace of the Creator."

"How can I help?" He caught more of her tears on his thumb.

Astra shifted and bumped the barrel over, her legs going numb from crouching behind the crates.

Her parents stiffened, and heat flooded Astra's face.

Papa left the bench and picked her up. "Astra, my little darling, what are you doing out here?"

She felt small and loved, her voice coming out young. "I heard Mama."

Something warm pushed on her arm, ending her dream. She stared into the familiar brown eyes of her horse.

She gently pushed her mare from the entrance of the tent and looked out. The sun rose half over the horizon, revealing most of the tents and racers were gone. A *jundiin* and a woman disassembled the check-in tent and loaded it onto a pair of camels while a boy tied caged pigeons onto another camel.

"Oh, no. We're behind." She scrambled free of her tent.

Her note for her mother crinkled under her feet. She'd written about entering the race and asked Mama if she would meet her for supplies, but after dinner she'd become too concerned with her need for space to remember to stop by the tent with pigeons.

She grabbed the paper and ran to the boy. "Wait, please. I have a note for my mother I need to send."

"Where to?" He paused and set down the covered cage in his hand.

"Sultan's Elbow."

He lifted several cages already hung on the camel, mouthed like he was reading silently, and nodded. "Here we go."

She handed him the paper, reached in her coin purse, and tipped him a copper winkll. "Thank you."

"There's no need to pay me, your entry fee covers this." He shook his head, dropped the coin in his pocket, and attached her note to a bird. "You'd better be off."

"I am." She ran back to her campsite.

CHAPTER 38

Astra stopped at a small oasis and ate dried dates, a hard biscuit, and a salted piece of meat while Sonji slurped from a small pond, more like an overgrown puddle, and lipped her rock to ensure she'd gotten every crumb of her handful of grain. The angle of the sun indicated the time at around midday. Astra guessed she should have packed a pocket watch, but why time how long she slept or ate or rode? Keeping track of the days and the miles was most important.

She checked her map after she finished her lunch and traced her path from the palace to the first check-in point to where she figured she was along the race route. According to her figures, she'd reach the second check-in point before dark.

A few riders she recognized from the day before rode by. She waved, but none waved back. Astra rolled up her map and remounted her horse. Sonji walked a few steps before transitioning to her ground-covering trot, easily passing the racers who didn't wave back and following the hoofprints of the leaders.

Mile after mile passed to the steady beat of Sonji's hooves. With Sonji, Astra traveled over the sands better than birds ... yet today and yesterday felt slow.

Astra's thoughts strayed to her dream. Had Mama run to Great-Uncle Trev's because of the note brought by the man in purple ... or was there another reason? When trying to complete her summons, had she and Omaira been chased by a Destroyer, and had the creature bitten her friend? Was Omaira dying from Destroyer poison instead of a degenerative disease? And, if so, had Grandma known?

The harder she thought, the fewer answers Astra found. Frustration tightened her hold on the reins, so she shoved aside her questions and loosened her grip. Sonji needed her head—she knew best where to step and the pace to keep.

Astra counted her blessings—the Creator had gifted her a loving and supportive family, her horse was sturdy and smart, most of her neighbors were kind, and she was racing. Every hoofbeat, another blessing counted, and so the sands slid by like the blue sky overhead. Peace wrapped around her.

Soon, evening shadows stretched over the dunes, and the town of Sultan's Elbow spread before her. Would she find Mama at Great-Uncle Trev's? She hoped so and that her note had arrived ahead of her because any hiccups could cost her the win and her chance to rid her family of the title of outcast.

Astra eased her mare to a walk and approached the check-in tent sitting at the edge of town and glowing in the fading light. A *jundiin*, his eyes closed, waited with his boots propped on the table, so she cleared her throat.

He dropped his feet, his eyes opening wide. "Hello. Wasn't expecting anyone."

"Why?"

He offered her a wetted quill. "This is the third check-in point. Hardly anyone gets here so soon."

She thanked him and accepted the quill, scratching her name at the top of the paper, but she struggled to believe him—the third check-in? "Where was the second check-in?" And how had she missed it? She'd read her map, plotted her course, and followed the hoofprints of the lead racers, so where was it?

He shrugged and settled back in his chair. "Doesn't matter as long you visit the rest of the check-in points."

A pigeon landed on the table, and the man fished a note off its leg before sticking the bird in a cage. "The second point was lost in a sandstorm. Several racers are suspected to be lost." He shook his head. "I'd hoped this year would have fewer calamities than previous races. You're lucky you started out early this morning."

Heat flashed up her neck to her cheeks and she forced a noncommittal sound from her mouth before hurrying away.

She'd risen late, so how could she have escaped the sandstorm and arrived in Sultan's Elbow early? She glanced at Sonji. Her horse was special, but literally as fast as the wind? Impossible.

CHAPTER 39

Based on the angle of the sun through the open tent flap, Hamal figured he'd been knocked out for most of the day. He tugged against his restraints. No-go. He tried to spit out his moldy, sweet-tasting gag. Again, no-go. So, he tried not to puke.

The stiff legs and seat of a chair dug into his back, and he wondered why they'd tied him and leaned him against it instead of tying him in it. Maybe if one of his captors removed his gag, he'd ask.

Sitting in view of the open flap were three fair-skinned men roasting a scaly creature over a fire and speaking in a tongue native to the north.

One bearded man, his blonde mustache trimmed short, laughed loudly at something one of the others said.

Hamal wished he'd practiced his knowledge of other languages after he returned home because all he could decipher were snippets about money and how easy this job was.

The tent wiggled in an evening breeze, and the warm air stirred up the scent of the rag, nauseating him further. He jerked harder on the knots digging into his wrists, but nothing loosened.

A form lay to his right, revealed by the moving of the tent. Dark hair escaped a brown sinar. Astra?

Please, Creator, let her be free!

None of the goons faced him, so he struggled once more against his bonds, but still nothing loosened. How to escape? His tied-together legs were numb—he couldn't crawl out like a worm.

A familiar stirring and rolling motion in his pocket lifted his spirits. His gizmo.

Willard stepped into the tent, lit the lantern tied to the support post, and sat across from him. "Been a while, Hamal."

Chills spread across his body. Hamal wished he were anywhere other than here, wished he'd never searched for his father.

The light caught on Willard's ruined eye and the scar stretching across his face. "You stole my good looks from me. Lucky for you, women are enchanted by scars and their stories. Otherwise I'd return the favor." He knelt, removed a knife from his boot.

Hamal read the menace in Willard's intense gaze and tried to lean away—but there was nowhere to go, and the chair dug deeper into his back.

"Your friend here may not be so lucky." Willard stood.

Astra! Hamal squirmed against his bonds.

Willard grabbed the feminine form and lifted her to a sitting position. He yanked her sinar away, and thick, dark hair fell around a simple face.

She blinked and winced, revealing brown eyes.

Hamal stilled—not Astra, but the woman from the bucket-line.

Willard leaned close to her. "Your husband and I have some business to attend to." He tossed her back on the sand and faced Hamal. "And when you're not so tied up, we'll have a proper conversation." He smirked, extinguished the lantern, and left quieter than a spotted sand snake.

How could they escape? There wasn't a knife lying about, no sharp edges on the gas lantern, no hook on the main support pole of the tent—no sharp edge anywhere.

Again his gizmo stirred, and he held his breath as a crazy idea filled his head. What if Mo acted without orders to free him? The little invention had cut Sonji's rope of its own accord over a week ago.

Mo rolled from his pocket onto the sand.

Maybe the sand tiger won't bite. His slow, nervous heartbeats echoed in his ears. *Please, prove you're more than metal and my creativity, and free me.*

Feminine singing drifted on a breeze, and the gizmo rolled behind him. *Click.* A tug, the sound of sawing, and finally the ropes binding his hands loosened.

He pulled his hands free and checked the three men around the fire—they laughed and passed burnt-smelling meat between each other, but none of them watched the tent.

The sun dipped below the horizon, painting the sky pink, orange, and yellow, and showing Hamal that if the thieves did look back they'd be able to see what he was doing inside the tent.

He worked on the knotted rope around his legs while Mo rolled from behind him to his tied-up feet and sawed on those ropes with a sharp little knife.

The feminine singing stopped, and the blade retracted inside the gizmo with a *click.*

"I don't remember designing you with weapons," Hamal whispered and rubbed his numb leg muscles, spreading a tingling sensation that faded to an ache.

Mo rolled toward his pocket and stopped. Hamal crawled passed Mo to the woman.

Something bumped his shoe as he reached for her ropes. Then, a blade met his throat but didn't break the skin. He lifted his gaze.

Willard smirked. "Did you really think you could escape so easily?"

CHAPTER 40

Two drooling men lay beside a pile of embers, at least from what Hamal could see—and neither of them was Willard. He recalled during his time working under his father, his uncle never drank or seemed to tire.

Hamal tested his new bonds, found the knots tight, and closed his eyes, grateful he was alive, but wishing he were free. He leaned his head back until he touched the main support pole of the tent, the taste of the gag—mold and maybe honey, definitely something sweet—turning his stomach.

Willard hadn't skinned him alive because his father Kaseem had walked into the tent and, in the sharpest, no-argument tone Hamal had ever heard, said, "Release him."

Willard didn't let go. "He was trying to escape."

"And you look ready to kill him." Kaseem was still—too still.

"We should. He's never been good for more than causing trouble." But Willard's knife dropped away.

"Leave," said Kaseem, and Willard did. Kaseem grabbed Hamal, tied him to the chair, secured the chair to the support post of the tent, and left.

Hamal wiggled his foot, and Mo rolled around inside his boot. The crazy invention had crawled in there after Kaseem departed.

A warm breeze brushed his wrists, and when he looked over his shoulder, he saw no one. So where did the breeze come from?

Mo crawled from his boot to the sand and exchanged its claws for wings before flying away.

Hamal hollered a muffled, "Mo," and struggled against his bonds. Why did the gizmo leave without him? Why not cut his bindings again so they could they leave together?

Kaseem entered, two plates in hand, and set both on a table near the chair before lighting the lantern. "I'm sure you're hungry."

Hunger was the least of Hamal's problems.

Kaseem went to the woman. "Don't scream. My men will gut you. And we're too far from civilization for anyone to hear you and come to your rescue."

She groaned as he righted her against the table and pulled the gag. Then she spit in the sand. "I guessed as much."

"You're smarter than most." Kaseem wiped the spit dripping from her mouth, ripped a loaf of bread and some greasy meat into small chunks, and fed her.

When the plate was almost empty, she said she was full, and he wiped her mouth and helped her drink from a canteen he'd brought. She thanked him before he stuffed the gag back in her mouth and tied it.

"I'm sorry about kidnapping you." Kaseem tore up more bread and meat.

The woman's eyes were kind and she seemed to be communicating that she was not upset with him. How could she not be mad or scared?

Hamal wanted to shout, *So there's no connection to Mother's crazy theory about my friend's horse because you've kidnapped us? You've asked someone to pay a ransom for us to go free?*

His father removed his gag. "The same warning goes to
you too, son—no shouting."

Hamal's teeth ground. "Son? I'm not your son."

Kaseem winced, the action showing for only a moment,
and then, a hardness covered his face. "Suit yourself." He
hand-fed him pieces of meat and bread and offered Hamal
a drink.

Hamal accepted the food and water because he knew
he'd need his strength to escape. "Why the change? Why
the kindness?" The questions slipped out before he could
think them through.

His father stuffed the gag back in his mouth and
tightened it. "Better I care for you than my men do." He
collected the plates, tied the canteen back on his belt, and
turned off the lantern, filling the tent with darkness.

CHAPTER 41

An empty alley stretched along one side and a narrow space along the other of Great-Uncle Trev's two-story home. Humming drifted from inside as Astra knocked on the thick front door, but no one came to greet her. She knocked again, louder this time.

The humming stopped. "Hello?"

A moment later the door opened, and her great-uncle appeared. He smiled and pushed his full-moon spectacles up his nose, magnifying his eyes to the size of chicken eggs. "Astra, my dear, we've been expecting you and your horse."

"My note reached you." The tension in her hands eased.

"Indeed." Great-Uncle Trev stepped aside, revealing a tidy interior filled with sturdy furniture. "Please, come in."

"Can I enter through the backyard? I need to stable Sonji." She patted her mare's shoulder.

"Oh, of course. I'll go unlock the gate." Whatever else he said was muffled by the door he closed as he spoke.

Astra led Sonji along the alley and through a gate held open by Great-Uncle Trev. The scent of fresh blossoms and the sound of trickling water welcomed her. A fountain of layered stone bowls sat in the middle and stone paths crisscrossed an immaculate garden created by the hard work of multiple generations. "Even more beautiful than my last visit, Uncle."

"Indeed, my dear, thanks to your mother's diligent pruning." He disappeared amongst the plants, calling back, "I'll see you at the house."

Astra kept the reins short as she led Sonji to the two-horse stable at the back of the yard. In the first stall, feed overflowed one bucket and water filled a second—a good reward for Sonji not stealing any blooms. Astra stored her tack in the second stall and rubbed down her horse, sand leaving pale brown spots across Sonji's white body. "You know," she said with a chuckle, "Ehsan will want to give you a bath when she sees you."

The horse snorted and ate her supper.

"I'll see you tomorrow, Sonji-girl." Astra wove her way through the bushes and flowers of Great-Uncle Trev's backyard and entered the back of the house to the scent of honey and fresh-baked bread. "Mama?"

"Astra."

She crossed the kitchen and fell into her mother's bread-dough covered arms. "I've missed you. Papa and Ehsan miss you, too." Tears wetted her face and her mother's blouse.

"I've missed my blessings and your papa." Mama kissed the top of her head before stepping back and wiping away the tears. "I'm sorry for causing everyone grief."

"Why did you run to Great-Uncle's? Was there something on the note the man in purple gave you?" Astra waited, standing on tired legs.

Mama sat by a blob of dough on the kitchen table. "How has your ride been?"

"Why did you leave?" Astra needed a bath to sooth the exhaustion gnawing at her legs and arms, and rid her of the scent of days of hard riding.

Mama turned, worked the dough. "Dinner will be ready late—I wasn't expecting you so soon. How hungry are you?"

"Mama? Mama, why won't you answer me?" Her throat tightened with her upset.

Mama moved her dough to a stone bread plate and tucked it in the oven before stirring the contents of a pot on the stove. The scent of stewing goat meat and garlic joined the baking bread.

Astra left, her stomach growling and her eyes watery. Her riding boots thudded against the well-worn wood as she headed for her usual room on the second floor.

Great-Uncle Trev waved to her on her way through the main room and she limply raised her hand in return. She climbed the stairs, holed up in the guest room, and slid into a tub of warm water. She scrubbed herself clean using a bar of mint soap, the bits of mint leaves floating in the water reminding her of working in Grandma's garden and learning how to make medicines and salves from plants. What would Grandma do with Mama?

A tapping on the door drew her from the bath.

"One moment, please." She wrapped her hair in a towel, dried off, dressed quickly, and then opened the door. "Great-Uncle."

He lifted his lips in a sort of smile. "I have something to show you." With an old book in hand, he brushed by her and sat on the bed.

"All right." She left the door ajar and perched next to him like when she was little and listened to him read bedtime stories.

He pointed to the image embedded on the cover—the same image as on the pendant, on Sonji's shoulder, etched in the wall above the doors to the *mople* ... and inked in silver on Omaira's summons.

Goosebumps lifted along her arms.

He raised a bushy, white eyebrow and smiled, deepening his wrinkles. "Astra, my dear, you've been called."

CHAPTER 42

Her great-uncle rubbed his chin. "Your horse—she's not the average mount, is she?"

Astra bit her lip, her mind full of thoughts—the message the *jundiin* read about the sandstorm, Ehsan's comment about Sonji running as fast as the wind, and Hamal saying his father might be after her. Yes, her mare seemed to be far more than a mount.

Great-Uncle Trev plowed ahead. "I saw the mark on your horse's shoulder, the call for you to visit the Creator, but I wonder why he wants you to come?"

He smiled, his dark eyes sparkling. "I know he never sends for his best without a reason. He must be calling you for a visit to prepare you for a possible summons someday ... and the chance to receive a gift. Oh, I wonder what you might receive, what might be added to the garden."

"Me, receive a gift?" Her thoughts spun, but she'd managed to say something.

"Maybe someday." He pointed out the window to the garden. "Each and every plant there came as a reward for a summons answered by our family." He lowered his hand, and his expression grew distant. "They're the best flowers and shrubs I've ever raised—masterpieces with their fragrant blossoms and thick, healthy vegetation that defy the boiling hot sun and bone-dry sand, as well as the overbearing rains."

A cool breeze flicked through her room and extinguished the candle on her nightstand. She shivered, the memory she'd visited in her dream returning to her, filling her head with the conversation between her mother and father about the chase by a Destroyer and Omaira getting bitten ... and the broken machine at Angel Wings ... and Mama's fear.

A loud clatter, like pottery crashing against the floor, resounded through the night.

Astra jumped from her bed and poked her head into the hallway. "Mama? Mama, are you all right?"

More clattering.

She tiptoed from her room, down the stairs, and into the kitchen to find her mother muttering and sweeping broken pottery into a pile. "Mama?" She touched Mama's shoulder.

Her mother stilled, and Astra wrapped her arms around her. "I'm here, Mama."

For the longest moment nothing happened. Then, she dropped the broom and returned the hug, her shoulders shaking and her crying, soft and wet, echoing in the kitchen.

Astra wished she could steal away her mother's fear and return her to the strong, courageous woman she was. "I'm here, Mama."

They stayed standing until Astra's legs ached, and they moved to the kitchen table.

Mama wiped her face with the edge of her apron. "I'm sorry, my blessing. I know you're hungry and tired."

"Don't worry, Mama." She squeezed her mother's hand.

From her skirt pocket, Mama removed a crumpled piece of paper and slid it across the table with a candle. The words *You are summoned* were written in silver ink, and glittering beneath them was the seal of the Creator, a flower with three wide petals.

SONJI

Astra's heart nearly froze before beating at triple time. Most summoned individuals never returned home—and this was her mother's second. If she answered a second time, would she return again?

CHAPTER 43

With his father standing a few steps away, Hamal took care of his business in the dark. He knew after working for the man that if he ran he would get a knife in the back, so he didn't run, didn't even try.

"Finished?" Kaseem said.

"Yes." A wet, soapy cloth dropped in Hamal's hands, and he washed.

Afterward, the cloth was jerked away and a *plop* was followed by droplets of water wetting his hand. His father caught his elbow, led him around the dune and back to the tent.

A dark figure—Willard—sat near the other thieves and sharpened a dagger in the low glow of the fire.

Kaseem fastened Hamal to the chair, stepped away, and stopped. He removed the gag he'd just tied. "How is your mother?"

"Fine."

His father retied the gag and raked his fingers through his hair. "I never wanted to leave you and your mother."

You have a lousy way of showing that. Hamal's eyes narrowed.

Kaseem left.

Hamal recalled three years ago when he had hid with his father and the other bandits in a cave in the mountains.

They'd lit a fire, roasted a deer, and kept their horses in a makeshift corral at the back, certain their pursuers had given up the chase thanks to the clouds further darkening the night and the rain turning the rocky trail slick. Lightning split the sky like skeletal hands reaching for them and the treasure they stole.

That night, Kaseem had told a story.

A young couple survived a particularly bad sandstorm that wiped their village off the map. Instead of staying, they became nomads. They visited every inch of the desert and tried a few places beyond. During their travels, they stopped in Sh'va Nahrot. They'd worked there many times before, but this time was special.

This time a man in purple gave them a special paper. A summons from the Creator.

They answered.

Hamal heard a rustling in the sand and guessed the woman was changing position in her sleep.

Outside the tent, Kaseem stiffened and unsheathed one of his knives, and Willard stopped sharpening his blade. Both men disappeared from view.

Chills raced along Hamal's spine. Trouble had kept his father from finishing the story on that stormy night in the mountains—but what drew him away from the campfire tonight?

Shouts and the roar of a tiger shook the dark.

The two men by the fire jumped to their feet, and Hamal struggled against his bonds. Sand tiger teeth were sharp, their claws sharper, and their strength unmatched.

"Guard the tent." Kaseem's shout cut through a second roar, the tiger sounding mad and large.

The men surrounded the tent.

"Kaseem!" Willard. Had to be Willard yelling.

Someone screamed in pain.

CHAPTER 44

Hamal's heart about stopped in his chest. He hated his father, but he didn't wish the man dead. He fought against his bonds, fought harder than he ever had, yet they refused to give.

A shout and a blood-curdling scream echoed across the desert.

Hamal yelled but all that came through his gag was a garbled moan. He yanked against his bonds again, wishing Mo hadn't left and was cutting him free.

One of the thieves charged into the dark, toward the sounds of battle, while the other stayed near the tent flaps with his sword drawn. He prayed under his breath in his native tongue, the words rushed, almost tripping over each other, something like, "Protect us, Light, from the night monster."

A second blood-curdling scream, this one more animal than human.

The thief shivered, his sword wiggling in his hand.

Kaseem called. "I need a cot. Find the medical supplies."

The thief ran off, and a moment later raced by the campfire with a rolled cot and a saddlebag.

The commotion promised a perfect time to escape ... if he could figure out how to free himself from his bonds. Hamal stopped fighting, forced himself to think.

Someone shouted and cursed. Sounded a lot like Willard.

Hamal held his breath and tried to think harder, faster, but no plan formed. He jerked against his bonds—this was a horrible time to be tied up.

A few more curses were followed by silence.

He stopped, strained to hear anything, but the woman rolled over and mumbled something. He looked at her. She faced him, hair in her face, and again mumbled something.

"What?" His word came through the gag no better than hers.

The tent flaps rustled, and his father and one of the other thieves hauled Willard inside, lowering him to Hamal's left. Kaseem lit the lantern and brought it close to Willard's bleeding thigh. "Looks like the bite isn't too deep, and you're already showing signs of clotting." He turned to the thieves, speaking to them in their northern tongue.

One ran out and returned with a bulky bag while the other disappeared from view.

"Hold him," said Kaseem, then he repeated in the other language, and the thief held Willard by the shoulders.

Willard glared. "You're not planning to play medicine man, are you?"

"Until we can get you to a real one, yes." Kaseem passed his belt to his fellow thief and gestured to Willard's mouth before saying something in the northern tongue.

"I can put the bloody thing in my mouth without his help." Willard grabbed the belt and groaned.

"I told you to be careful moving." Kaseem yanked several items from his bag. "The way that tiger fell on you I'm sure your ribs are cracked—and I don't want them breaking."

Willard bit down on the belt and turned his face away, the woman rolled her back to the scene, and Hamal tried not to stare—but there was so much blood—and yet the others didn't seem bothered by it.

Kaseem cut Willard's pants and tugged the fabric away from the bite. Willard groaned.

Hamal tried to avert his gaze and not lose what little food he'd had to the iron scent of blood mixing with the moldy, sweet scent of the gag. He never could understand Astra studying to be a wisewoman, her wanting to deal with blood and broken bones and illness.

Kaseem hollered for the man standing by Willard's head to make sure the other one was boiling water like he'd been told to.

The thief left and hurried back in with a bucket of hot water he set near Kaseem, who said, "What about my clean rag?" He repeated himself in the other language.

Kaseem hardly ever traveled with men who knew only a single language—at least Hamal couldn't remember any from before, so why were these two part of this job?

The second thief entered with shredded bedsheets.

Kaseem crushed Dryzzian mint into the boiled water, stirred with the blade of a clean knife, and then wetted a large rag. He wiped around the wounds and wrung out hot liquid on Willard's leg.

Willard's fisted hands were white and his jaw muscles looked ready to pop.

Kaseem cleaned, salved, and pressed several layers of ripped bed sheet over the wound before wrapping it. He gently felt along Willard's sides.

Willard grabbed Kaseem and spit out the belt. "Enough is enough, brother."

"Definitely cracked." Kaseem pulled away and gathered his supplies. "Try to keep your movement to a minimum and don't try to get up." He washed his hands in the bucket. Then, he crushed more mint and left it on the table. "I mean it, Willard. Don't move."

He exited the tent and returned a minute later with a steaming cup. He stirred the crushed mint into the contents of the cup, blew on the steam, and then helped Willard drink. A moment later, the lantern was extinguished, and Hamal's father left.

Hamal glanced at Willard. Even wounded, the man could be dangerous—usually more dangerous. Fear tingled all over ... even his numb legs and arms.

He'd have been better off with the sand tiger.

CHAPTER 45

Pale streaks of light broke through the night and hid the stars as Astra stood with Sonji by the gate to the backyard. "Thank you, Great-Uncle."

"You're welcome." He kissed her on the cheek. "I'll be praying for your safe travels."

She returned the gesture, briefly scratching her lips on his rough cheek. "How can I ever thank you?"

He grinned. "By finishing the race."

Mama waved from the kitchen window, and Astra waved back, the summons from the Creator's messenger floating to the forefront of her thoughts. Why did the Creator want to meet with Mama? Was her previous summons unfinished or was there something else?

Astra mounted Sonji, and they trotted to the edge of Sultan's Elbow. She reined in her horse, watching from the shadows as a fellow racer and her mount visited a well. "Looks like Vivian survived the sandstorm."

Sonji snorted and pawed the ground.

"You're right. We need to move on." She patted Sonji's shoulder, and they resumed their trot.

Dunes surrounded them. They stayed low, hiding in the shadows to stay cool. Occasionally, when Astra needed to consult her map, they climbed to the top of a dune and searched for landmarks, but often there were none, and she had to use the sun to gauge their direction.

"I think we're headed the right way," she said when they stopped for lunch and a chance to stretch her legs and rub her sore back muscles. "The next check-in point should be a bit ahead of us." She turned in a full circle, sand and more sand surrounding them. "It has to be."

Sonji emptied her bowl of water and nuzzled the bag of sweet feed.

"No." Astra ensured the clasp on the bag was firmly tied before taking a sip from her canteen. "You've had more than your share already." She dropped the bowl in a saddlebag and swung onto Sonji. "Time for us to go."

Nothing changed for miles, and soon the sun sank low on the horizon. Astra guided her mare to the top of a dune, searching for a sign of the check-in point. Instead, she spied someone on a dark horse, maybe Vivian—but there'd been a number of dark horses entered in the race, following her trail. Perhaps her headings weren't off ... and that someone was a racer and not one of the thieves Hamal had mentioned ...?

She squeezed Sonji's sides with her heels, and the mare eased back to the valley, trotting in a southerly direction.

Somewhere out there waited the next check-in and Sh'va Nahrot, a resupply stop for racers. Would they rest there this evening? Doubtful. Yet the thought of home lifted and constricted her heart. Ehsan and Papa would probably be there, waiting for her. But Mama would not.

Tears pressed the backs of her eyes. "Sonji, I'm pretty sure this is the second time Mama has been summoned. What will happen if she answers him again?" A teardrop escaped and slid off her cheek.

Sonji tipped her head like she was trying to see Astra better, to reassure her there was nothing to worry about.

Astra sniffled. "Mama came home once. She can come home again—she has to, because I'm not sure I'm strong enough to lose her." Another tear slid off her cheek.

Her mare faced forward, her ears flickering.

"And if Mama can answer a summons and come home, I can answer the call of the Creator and return ... right?" Astra wished her Sonji could talk—flickering ears weren't much of a reply.

CHAPTER 46

Astra never found the fourth check-in point and the oasis with the crooked palm tree. Her map and the commander of the *jundiin* stationed in Nahrot had promised they existed, but her pursuit left her pitching her camp in the dark.

With Sonji standing by the entrance to the tent, Astra slid her bell under the saddle-blanket she used for a pillow—the bell was better there than in her pocket because otherwise it would dig into her leg as she slept. She tugged her cloak tightly around herself and laid out on her bedroll. Tonight, the desert felt cooler than normal. She wished for the campfires of her fellow racers.

Her horse whinnied, and she poked her head beyond the flaps of her tent.

A person and a dark horse with a crescent-shaped forehead marking stood a few feet away.

Astra kept her cloak around herself as she exited her tent, her pulse pounding in her ears. "Vivian Rose?"

"Yes." Vivian stepped into the starlight which barely revealed her face. "I thought my Midnight to be a sturdy mount, but yours is incredible."

"Thank you." Astra sighed, her pulse slowing to normal. *And I thank the Creator you aren't thieves.*

Sonji and the dark horse sniffed each other. Her ears flicking back, she squealed and stomped her foot before smacking him in the face with her tail on her way back to Astra's tent. There, she pushed at the sweet feed bag.

The dark horse snorted and stepped closer to Vivian.

"I guess your Midnight passed my Sonji's test." Astra chuckled and rolled her eyes. "Would you like to join our camp?"

Vivian's teeth flashed white in the night. "I'd be honored." She unrolled her bed by Astra's tent, removed her tack from Midnight, and clipped a long rope tied to a spike to the halter he still wore before hammering the spike deep into the sands. "Sleep well, my friend." Then, with her cloak wrapped around her, she plopped on her bed.

"Good night." Astra returned to her tent and slipped back inside. She patted down her bedding—no scorpions or snakes—but as she adjusted her makeshift pillow she heard something *plunk* on the ground. Between the dark and her growing exhaustion, she decided to search for the source of the sound in the morning.

CHAPTER 47

Something blacker than the night sky drifted above the dunes in his sleep and frightened Hamal awake as the barest of sunrays illuminated the desert. He watched the sky shift from dark gray to blue. The creature in his dream still felt chillingly real, shouts and screams rang in his ears, and each time he closed his eyes, tongues of red, orange, and yellow flashed across an ebony background.

Two men slept by the fire embers and to his left slept Willard, drool dripping from his mouth. This was the first time Hamal had ever seen Willard asleep.

The tent flap rustled, and Kaseem entered with the woman. He helped her sit, then tied her hands and feet. He glanced across the tent, turned back to her, and said in a whisper, "We will release you in a couple more days."

"Thank you." She smiled.

Kaseem grunted and gagged her before passing Hamal and touching Willard's forehead. "Good, no fever."

He towered over Hamal. "I will untie you so can take care of your business—but no games, Son." His hand rested on the pommel of his knife, through the holes in his worn sheath sunlight glinted off his sharp, clean blade—a blade he must have stayed up late to shine. Blood stained his clothes. Was all of it Willard's or was some of it the tiger's?

Hamal nodded, and his father freed him. He stretched and rubbed his joints, everything creaking and tingling. He stood and wobbled.

Kaseem grabbed his shoulder, steadied him. "Your eyes are an awful sight. Did you get any rest last night?"

"Some. You?"

"Enough." Kaseem released him and pointed out.

Hamal hurried from the tent and around the dune, nearly wetting himself on the other side.

A sand tiger, a gold bodied cat with dark orange stripes and a white belly, lay in the sand like it was out early to sun itself.

"He's dead."

Despite the statement, Hamal kept clear of the giant predator while taking care of his needs.

In camp, Kaseem had him wash his hands in a bucket of mint water. Hamal wanted to comment on the irony of washing his hands when his father had not changed his blood-soaked clothes, but he knew pushing his luck wouldn't end well.

Kaseem tied him to the chair. "I'll bring you something to eat later," he said and left.

Hamal watched his father kick the two thieves from their slumber, reprimanding them in their language for not cleaning and skinning the tiger before daylight, for risking the meat spoiling.

Willard chuckled.

The hairs on Hamal's arms lifted.

"Idiots." Willard winced. "They'll wind up whipped the way they keep slacking."

He breathed shallowly. "Today's the third day of the race. Your friend and her little horse should be drawing close soon." He grinned. "The Creator's treasure will be ours any day now."

A deep chill reached from Hamal's toes to the top of his head. His father was smart to have him gagged because he might have said something stupid to Willard like "Leave Astra and her mare alone."

"I wonder how Kaseem plans to steal her this time?" Willard's brown eyes gleamed.

Hamal prayed. *Please, Creator, keep Astra and her horse safe.*

CHAPTER 48

Hamal watched Kaseem and his men prep the sand tiger's hide for tanning, smoke the meat, and treat the bones. His father never wasted anything from a successful hunt ... or protecting his camp.

But none of what Hamal saw revealed how his father planned to steal Sonji again.

Willard drooled and muttered during his afternoon nap, ruining any chance Hamal had of catching part of his father's conversation with the other thieves, so he prayed again that Astra and Sonji would escape Kaseem's plans. They had to.

The woman rolled in the sand, shifting from facing the side of the tent to him and Willard. She wiggled over to the table and used the edge to push down her gag. "Better," she whispered while breathing heavily.

Hamal tugged on his bindings ... and nothing gave.

She shook her head. "I know you're thinking you need to escape, to signal your friend about Kaseem's plans, but that's not what the Creator wants us to do. We wouldn't have been kidnapped otherwise."

"What?" he tried to say around his horrible tasting gag. Was she crazy? The Creator wanted them tied up and wherever they were in the desert with his thieving father?

"I'm not crazy." She narrowed her eyes.

Willard's string of drool dripped onto his makeshift pillow, and he made a gargling sound.

"Out of the three of us, he's the one that should be wearing a gag." The woman winced, and Hamal agreed with a bob of his head.

Her forehead wrinkled. "You look a lot like Kaseem. Are you his son?"

He paused. The resemblance was uncanny. Finally, he nodded.

"I didn't realize when Isaac mentioned my passenger would be Hamal Nuru that I'd be traveling with someone related to Kaseem. After all, Nuru is pretty a common last name."

He'd enjoyed being anonymous, but he doubted he'd ever live without association to his father now.

"My name is Ruth—"

Kaseem entered the tent and fixed her gag. "You're lucky I'm the one who came to check on you, and Willard didn't wake. My men don't get much womanly company ... and when they do, they prefer the women not to talk."

He moved her away from the table and shook Willard's shoulder. "Tonight we're heading out. There's a wisewoman nearby willing to see you."

Willard groaned. "Nice of you to arrange a proper nursemaid for me."

"I'll be back in a little while to rewrap your tiger bite." Hamal's father left.

A bit before dusk, Kaseem returned and cared for Willard. As soon as he finished, the tent came down, Willard was strapped onto a stretcher pulled by a camel, and Ruth and Hamal were tossed on the back of another camel.

Night wrapped around them. While cooler than the day, it presented a heap of problems—sand tigers, scorpions, snakes ... maybe even Destroyers. The desert was not blessed like people's homes to ward away the dark things.

Kaseem mounted a horse that Hamal didn't remember seeing, but then he'd been kept in a tent and not brought out much during the day.

Whinnies interrupted the quiet night.

Hamal tried to yell, struggling against his bonds.

Kaseem called his men to a halt. "I'll scout ahead."

A long while passed before the sound of hoof beats on sand cut through the quiet. His father said, "She's here. And I have the girl's bell."

Hamal's heart constricted. *Astra. Sonji.*

CHAPTER 49

The sun barely broke the night as Astra crawled off her bedroll and wiped sleep sand from her eyes. Outside her tent, she yawned and greeted her fellow racer who'd already braided her hair and saddled her horse.

Vivian fussed with the end of her braid, wrinkles marring her forehead. "I've not seen your horse this morning … and I found hoofprints leaving camp."

"What?" Astra reached in her pocket—no bell. Then she remembered hiding it under her makeshift pillow and dove back into her tent, yanking aside the saddle blanket, but there wasn't a bell. Her stomach soured, the plunk from the night before returning to haunt her. She reached for the tent flaps by the head of her bed.

Vivian peered around a flap and held out a woodchip. "Is this what you're looking for?"

"Do you see a bell?" Astra tried to speak clearly, her throat constricting. Dear Creator, where was her bell? Where was her Sonji? The thieves couldn't have stolen her horse while she slept in the middle of the desert.

Vivian shook her head. "No."

Astra crawled out. "I'm going to call for Sonji, but if she doesn't come … will you please show me the tracks you found?"

"Sure." Vivian slid the woodchip in her pocket.

Astra nodded, her heart hammering and her hands quivering. "Sonji, Sonji-girl, time for breakfast." She clicked her tongue as loud as she could.

No whinny.

No running mare.

She called three more times.

Still nothing. So the thieves had come, and the woodchip couldn't be random.

"What if I followed the tracks and you stayed here?" Vivian looped her reins over Midnight's head. "Maybe your horse will come back while I'm gone."

"Yes, please." Panic thickened Astra's throat and tears threatened to fall. *Creator, where is Sonji? Why would you allow her to be taken now?*

Vivian mounted Midnight and trotted away.

"Sonji, Sonji, where are you?" Astra whispered and fell to her knees, the night cooled sand chilling her as the sun warmed her back.

Half an hour later, Vivian and Midnight rounded a dune coming back.

Astra stood. Please, let them have good news.

Vivian reined Midnight to a halt and shook her head. "I have bad news. The hoofprints and some footprints intersect with other prints—I think someone took her. I'm so sorry, Astra."

"Show me." Astra stepped in the direction she'd seen them ride from.

Vivian held up her hand. "Let's pack up camp before we try following."

"Really?" Astra stared for a moment before rolling up her cloak and bedroll. "You'll be losing your lead in the race by helping me."

"I know, and I don't mind." Vivian dismounted and helped take down the tent. "I didn't come to win, only to challenge myself and my Midnight." She shared jerky and a canteen with Astra.

Even if you don't need the win, I do. Astra thanked her, ate the over-salted jerky, and returned the canteen. Soon the camp was packed, and she hefted her heavy saddle in front of her. "Let's go."

Vivian grabbed the saddle from her and tossed it on her horse. "We'll both walk. My Midnight can handle double saddles."

"Thank you." The kindness of this foreign girl befuddled Astra.

"You are most welcome." Vivian pointed. "The prints go that way." She led.

CHAPTER 50

The day before Astra had traveled too far north. She knew because an hour following the tracks in a southerly direction brought her and Vivian by the fourth check-in point and the oasis with the crooked palm tree.

Vivian checked in and forged Astra's name, later whispering she believed Astra would rejoin the ranks on her horse.

Astra hoped Vivian was right.

They traveled all day and into the night. Vivian carried a torch to help them see. The prints they followed skirted the racing trail and delivered them in Nahrot, far from the check-in booth.

Vivian yawned, lifting her hand to cover her mouth. "I need to check-in."

Astra tried to stifle the groan climbing up her chest. "You're not planning to write my name again, are you?"

Vivian shrugged. "You and your horse are traveling the right way—even if you're not traveling together at the moment."

Astra chuckled, her lips tilting up. "I'm not sure the *jundiin* or the sultan are inclined to follow your thinking."

"You never know." Her new friend smiled broadly.

Astra yawned. The hour was late and most of the houses were dark. "Do you have a place to stay tonight?"

"My *vater* is a merchant. He sells wood to a man here and buys furniture from him. If I can find his home or remember where Mrs. Zilfel lives I'll have a place to stay. You?"

"This is my home village." Astra tried to hold back a second yawn. "Your father sells wood to someone in Nahrot who makes furniture?"

"That is what I've been told, yes." Her blue eyes glowed in the fading light of her torch.

"Is his name Jabir Paksim by chance?" Astra paused by the village well.

"Yes, I think so." Vivian kept walking.

"He's my papa." Astra hurried to catch back up. "You're more than welcome to stay the night. I'm sure my parents and sister won't mind, especially after hearing about all your help."

"Thank you."

The check-in tent, lit by a pair of torches, appeared beyond the trading post and a familiar *jundiin* waited with his feet on the table.

Vivian stopped by the barn for the trading post. "I'll go sign us in and come back. You can show me the way to your home, yes?"

Astra shook her head. "No. I'll go with you."

"All right." Vivian raised a blonde eyebrow.

"If he asks about Sonji, I'll tell him I dropped her at home." Astra tugged her saddle off of Midnight and dropped it on the corral. "He did the inspection of my horse when I entered, so he knows I live here."

Vivian bobbed her head. "Oh, all right."

"Right." Heat filled her cheeks. Lying. Her mother spoke against the habit.

They approached the booth and found the *jundiin* asleep, his hat pushed over his eyes.

"I usually ask for messages at each check-in ..." Vivian wrote her name. "I'll wait until tomorrow."

Astra added hers and they left, grabbing her saddle on their way toward her home. At the gate, they paused—there was no sign of anyone there.

Vivian caught Astra's shoulder. "I did not want to say earlier, but I feel you should know, now that the tracks of the horse thieves have connected with your village, they will be harder to follow."

"I know." Astra opened the gate. "Maybe we'll get lucky, though. Maybe someone will have seen her and can help."

"Maybe." Vivian entered.

Astra closed the gate before leading Vivian to the barn. The chickens squawked a bit as they cared for Midnight and closed him in Sonji's stall. Astra shut the door, her heart aching.

A candle flame glowed by the window and Ehsan appeared at the side door. "Astra. Vivian Rose. Come in, come in." She grinned and stepped out of the way. "Papa told me about how he and your father work together."

Vivian and Astra slipped by Ehsan.

"How's the race going? Tell me everything."

Astra dropped the woodchip on the table. "The thieves struck."

"How do you know?" Ehsan set her candle on the kitchen table.

Astra told Ehsan about what she and Vivian discovered that morning. Then, she added everything she'd learned from Hamal about the woodchip with the carving of the running horse. Tears spilled over. "They took my bell, too."

"How?" Her sister raised her eyebrows.

"I'd tucked the bell under my saddle blanket, but I think I knocked it off my bedroll and out of the tent while I was sleeping. All the thief had to do was pick it up off the ground." Astra began to sob.

Ehsan hugged her. "You'll get Sonji back. You did once—you can again." She rubbed Astra's back. "Everything will be all right."

"How do you know?" Astra's voice cracked. She hated falling apart in front of her sister and her new friend.

"Because everything else has. So this has to, too."

She kept crying. Sonji was gone. Hamal's gift gone. Why?

CHAPTER 51

Early the same day and after an all- night trip across the desert to Nahrot, Hamal hated his father more than ever—Kaseem acted like a starved sand tiger after a fresh steak in his quest for the treasure.

Mother's kind voice filled his head, encouraging him to forgive the man, but Kaseem didn't deserve forgiveness. He'd left Astra in the middle of the desert without her horse and didn't even care about what he'd done.

Hamal's fingers curled, his nails biting into his callused palms.

Desert heat permeated the shack he and Ruth had been dumped in. And the one to help his father? Wisewoman Yasif! She tended to the wounded Willard and offered this shed to keep Ruth and Hamal.

Hamal had watched her wince as she closed the door.

He glared. *I've never liked her, and now I know why. Being the town gossip is one thing, but helping my father kidnap two people and leave another unhorsed in the middle of the desert? Criminal.* He hated her about as much as he hated his father. He'd only worked for her to procure the medicine his mother needed. Now, he'd tell the commander about her and gladly find another source for the medicine.

A bee buzzed in through a hole by the roof of the shed, then overhead, and out the gap between the top of the door and its frame.

Hamal's chair was nailed into the floor and his gag on too tight for him to make much noise. Ruth had fallen asleep stuck in a similar setup. But the heat kept him awake.

A shovel, a hoe, a bucket of dirt, and other garden supplies littered the shed—the perfect place to cut the ropes if his father's work wasn't so thorough.

His mind strayed to stealing back Sonji. What had happened to the camels, horses, dogs, women, and men traveling with Kaseem and Willard? How did they factor into everything?

The door creaked open, and he blinked against the bright sunshine.

"I know you've never liked me." The voice feminine and older, the figure hard to discern because of the sunlight. "But I'm not a bad person."

The ropes loosened and the gag dropped.

Ruth mumbled, stirring awake. "Ah, rescue."

Hamal rubbed his wrists, trying to draw circulation back into his hands and to keep from saying something he might regret.

"Thank you." Ruth hugged Wisewoman Yasif.

The old woman stepped away. "I'm righting a wrong I committed. Nothing more, ma'am."

"Admitting to a mistake takes courage. Fixing the mistake requires real bravery." Ruth ran her fingers through her hair and adjusted her sinar.

Wisewoman Yasif backed out of the shed. "Kaseem has left with the white horse. I gave his men some sleeping herbs in their tea, but I wouldn't bet on that holding long if I were you."

"Thank you." Ruth hugged the wisewoman again and hurried into the sunshine.

Hamal followed until Wisewoman Yasif caught him by the shoulder. "Your mother's not doing well. I upped her medicine, but she's weak and in a lot of pain." She released him and fussed with her apron.

"Thank you for telling me." His stomach clenched.

"Ehsan is sitting with her now. I'll go back later when your father's men are awake and can keep an eye on their own. Thankfully they can't roam the village with their wanted posters hanging in the House of Citizens." She waved toward the yard gate. "You'd best hurry out of here."

"What will happen if one of them comes to check?" Why the sudden worry for her? He couldn't explain it.

Her cat walked over, sat by her feet, and she picked him up. "I can take care of myself. Go on."

"Thank you." He awkwardly patted her shoulder before heading for the gate.

Ruth led the way into the village, pausing by the well, where she inhaled deeply and closed her eyes. "Dear Creator, you are ever wonderful."

Hamal rolled his eyes.

She pointed in the direction of the trading post. "I need to speak with Isaac, see if Zeb has sent me any messages."

"All right. I'm going to see my mother." He shoved his hands in his pockets, his fingers brushing one wooden chip. Why had Mo left?

"Let's meet at the *mople* later. Maybe we can figure out a way to check on your friend, the owner of the white horse, and make sure she's all right."

"Yes." He watched her stride away, amazed the stranger he'd been kidnapped with was offering help.

CHAPTER 52

Hamal entered his home as Ehsan, carrying a cup and bowl, stepped from his mother's room. She dropped the dishes and ran to him, her arms wrapping tight around his middle. "Hamal, thank the Creator you've come."

"Thank you for being with my mother." He patted the girl's back. "How is she?"

Ehsan released him and gathered the cup and bowl. "You should see for yourself." She washed the dishes.

He found Mother sitting on the edge of her bed.

She smiled. "I thought I heard you out there."

"Hello, Mother." His heart wrenched at seeing her as fragile as a dying flower, skinny as a flower stem, her hair brittle and arms shivering. He should have been here for her, not causing her to worry.

"Astra hasn't been this way yet." Mother grabbed a cane beside her bed.

"Kaseem kidnapped me and Ruth, the woman who was going to take me to the train station in Urugha. Then he stole Astra's horse." He bit the inside of his cheek, released it. "Ruth said she'd help me look for Astra. I'm to meet her at the *mople* in a while."

She shakily crossed the room to him, slid an arm around his middle, and leaned her head on his chest. "I never received a note requesting money for you to be returned to me—you were not kidnapped, but stolen." She looked up, her brown eyes glistening, full of sadness and love. "I had hoped when Kaseem left that his father would not ruin him again ... and he would not try to take you from me." She pushed out of his embrace and edged out of the room.

He followed her, every muscle in his body tense watching her move slower, more unsteady than ever before. He wanted to pick her up and carry her wherever she wanted to go, but he knew if he did, she'd smack him with her cane. She'd done it on her other not-so-good days.

"Your father was a good man once." Mother sat at the table. "And he was a bad man before he was good. I'm sorry, sorry my influence on him has been lost, and you and your friend have suffered." A tear slipped down her face, and she wiped her cheek with the back of her hand.

Ehsan, pins sticking from her mouth and pincushion, attempted to sew a patch on the elbow of a shirt. Her stitches weren't as even as his mother's or Astra's, and he doubted the conversation around her helped her focus.

Hamal's heart ached for his mother. "You have nothing to be sorry for, Mother. Kaseem is a grown man. He will face the consequences of his actions, actions you didn't make him commit."

"Your father visited me after he came into town." She rested her cane in her lap. "He told me he wanted to see you, but he knew his men would not treat you well if you were welcomed back into their company. I had no clue he'd seen you, taken you. I'd apologized he'd missed you by a few days and guessed about when you'd be back from helping Astra."

Hamal struggled to form a response.

She gestured to the bench by the front door. "Set the basket and clothes aside and bring the bench over to the table. There's no need for you to keep standing."

He did as his mother said. "Kaseem came to see you."

"Yes. Despite what you may think, he still loves me and honors his vows to me." She cupped his chin, and he leaned into her touch.

Ehsan glanced at them, poked her finger with her needle, winced, and returned to sewing.

"Your father did not leave us because he wanted to hunt for treasure. He left to protect us. His father is not a man to be trifled with, and no matter how hard your father was on you in the five months you spent with him, that was nothing compared to what your grandfather put him through in his childhood." She pulled her hand away.

Ehsan scooted a cup closer to Mother, a few drops of water spilling over the top.

"You need to forgive him, Hamal. Not for him, but for yourself." Mother used both hands to lift the cup to her cracked lips, sip, and set the cup down. "And a small part of me does still believe his misguided actions are from a place of love."

Hamal abandoned the bench and paced. Kaseem had kidnapped him. Kept the other men from caring for him. Fed him. Stayed away from the family, from his mother, for years. Never let him meet his grandfather. Because Kaseem loved them? Doubtful.

Hamal spun around. "He stole Sonji and left Astra in the desert."

Mother tapped the table, and a little metal ball rolled from beneath the shirt Ehsan had patched. "A friend of ours claims she was not left alone in the desert, but with a fellow racer, and she's all right and headed for the village."

Wings clicked free and Mo flew around his head.

"I say you and this Ruth lady stake out the check-in booth and see if my report is correct."

"How'd Mo tell you?" He stared at his gizmo, then his mother.

Mother's eyes twinkled. "That's a secret."

Ehsan grinned and stuck her last pin in her cushion.

CHAPTER 53

Papa wasn't home. According to her sister, he'd gone into town to speak with Isaac Zilfel and Bartholomew Rose at dusk. What was taking him so long?

Astra unrolled her bedroll on top of two benches she'd pushed together in the main room. She'd needed space, so when Vivian and Ehsan fell asleep in the room she shared with her sister, she snuck out. Now, she wrapped up in her cloak, ready for some sleep of her own.

Tap. Tap.

She leaped from her makeshift bed and opened the front door.

Hamal, not Papa, stood in the dark. "I guess I don't need to save you."

"Ham." Astra launched into his arms, inhaling the scent of mint on his clothes. "I've missed you." She pulled out of his arms and led the way around the house to her favorite bench. "What did you mean by 'need to save' me?"

His brow furrowed, barely visible because of the lack of a moon. "Isn't Ehsan here? Didn't she tell you about this afternoon?"

"Yes, my sister is home." She shook her head. "And, no, she didn't tell me about this afternoon ... although, she did mention Omaira isn't doing well." She pushed her tangled hair away from her face. She'd left her sinar and hair tie inside. Not proper. But she was tired and she was with Hamal, not *Tollarb* Ke'ev.

"Kaseem stole me and a woman named Ruth. He didn't kidnap us because, well, I never heard of anyone receiving a ransom note."

Astra gasped and covered her mouth with her hand. "Poor Zeb, he must have been out of his mind with worry over his wife."

"Zeb?"

"Ruth's husband. They let Papa, Ehsan, and me travel with them to Urugha when I needed to catch the train."

Hamal sat on the bench and ran his fingers through his hair.

"Your turban." Astra sat beside him.

"I lost it days ago. Must have fallen off when he grabbed me." He dropped his hands in his lap. "Astra, when was I supposed to catch the train to meet you in Gefen?"

She counted the days since the race started. Four, almost five. She'd left on Shishi, traveled on Shabbos and Rishon, and walked today—Ahad. Tomorrow was Ethnyen. So ... she rubbed her chin. "You'd need to be catching the train tomorrow. I figured I'd need to ride two more days to get from Nahrot to Gefen. And I didn't want you waiting there long. Why?"

"The tickets I had when I went to travel with a caravan for the train station had me leaving a day after you did." He smacked his hand against his leg. "I should have listened better when you explained your plans."

"What matters is you're free. We'll find Sonji."

"I'm sorry about Sonji, and I don't know how easy that'll be. I told Ruth about my father and why he stole your horse. She says the gateway to the Palace of the Creator isn't here in Sh'va Nahrot like legend claims, but to the south of us, near the haunted shack."

"No wonder we could never find it here." Astra shuddered. "But why there?"

"I don't know." He sighed. "Ruth said there used to be a village by the abandoned shack. A couple decades ago, the place was covered up by a serious sandstorm. She said the couple who lived at the shack moved away, and there never was a double murder or a murder and a suicide. The story may have been passed around to keep people like my dad from figuring out where the gateway was. And because a couple moving from their sand-buried town wasn't an interesting story for an abandoned shack."

"Hmmm." Her eyelids drooping, she leaned her head against his warm arm.

He picked her up, took her inside, and set her on her cot. "I'll come by tomorrow morning. Ruth said she'd guide us to the gateway."

"Uh-huh."

Her eyes closed, and she thought she heard Hamal and Papa greet each other. Then, a kiss on her forehead, followed by "Good night, my darling," before sleep claimed her.

CHAPTER 54

"What you seek is beyond ..." A kind, grandfatherly voice whispered in Astra's ear, interrupting her deep slumber.

Feminine singing swirled around the words, taking shape in a plum-purple sash floating on a breeze. Soon the sash blotted out the darkness of her dreamworld and its movement formed shapes.

First, Mrs. Zilfel giving her the pendant. "You are not an outcast, Astra."

Then, the day at the market, picking up her mother's mended basket. The scrawny old man yelling, "Now get out of here, you worthless freak."

Zeb bowing, and Ehsan commenting on his action, his acknowledgment of them.

Astra lining up to sign in for the race. A tall, buck-toothed woman with brown eyes calling her a half-breed, laughing, and taunting her for even trying.

Her mother appearing over the image of the stranger, smiling and catching Astra's chin. "My blessing."

A customer entering her father's furniture shop when she was twelve. His roving eyes making her uncomfortable as he said, "No wonder Jabir's been banned from the village."

Again, the dream drifted. But this time was different. Hamal sat beside her on a sand dune, and they watched the sunset. She commented, *how pretty*. He agreed, but she could tell by a glance out the side of her eye that he was looking at her and not the sky.

She rode Sonji, and they neared the finish line, but someone on a red horse beat her. Cheers filled her ears while her heart crumpled in her chest. She'd lost her chance to rescue her family from their lot.

Her sister approached her, smiling. "You finished. You were amazing."

Papa lifted Ehsan on his shoulders. "You were, my darling. Be proud of your accomplishment. I am proud to call you my daughter."

Mama stepped from behind Papa and gripped Astra's hand. "I also am proud of you, my blessing." She smiled a real smile and her eyes glistened with happy tears.

The singing and the sash faded, returning her dreamworld to an endless blackness. Softer than at the beginning, the words said by an older male repeated. "*What you seek is beyond ...*"

What did that mean?

CHAPTER 55

Hamal left his mother in Ehsan's and Wisewoman Yasif's care. Leaving her tore at his heart. Her fragile state—why, Creator? She was the sweetest, kindest person he knew. He prayed she'd do all right while he was away, but praying she'd be healed felt too far a stretch to make.

Astra waved and stood by the front gate of her home. Early morning sunlight highlighted the jewel tones in her eyes, and the tail of her braided ebony hair hung over her shoulder.

He waved back, wishing his prayer that Sonji was not stolen again had worked. But at least Astra appeared unharmed and ready to retrieve her horse.

She jogged over to him. "I sent Vivian and her horse on since one of us should have a chance to win. She said if she won she'd split the winnings with me and claimed the night I let her camp with me saved her or something." The right side of her mouth pulled up and she giggled. "I doubt that."

Ruth called to them while she led three camels up the trail to Astra's home. "I thought meeting here best because, well, the shack and the lost village are this direction."

Hamal and Astra agreed and thanked her for the camels before they mounted and followed her into the desert.

Hamal's pocket wiggled. He removed Mo, twisted, and tossed it in the air, wings clicking into place and flapping.

"Think your gizmo will help save her again?" Astra stared at the gizmo, her smile wide as the desert.

"Maybe." Hamal smiled, unable to turn away from her.

Astra, her gaze lowered to his, leaned toward him. "I wish you'd been kidding about us going to the shack, though."

"I know, but Ruth assured me no one was ever killed there."

She bit her lip, released. "The place is still creepy."

He agreed.

For the rest of the ride, Ruth filled the silence—first with stories about her and Zeb's adventures and then about their destination. "The lost village had a name, not much of one, but a name nonetheless—Desert City. Never had enough residents to be considered a city, barely had enough to be a village. A trader had started the village to care for caravans traveling to the rich southern countries—he'd hoped to create a cultural center beyond Latif City. Unrealistic hopes for a sand pit, in my opinion."

She shifted in her saddle. "The real treasure he'd stumbled upon was the beginning of a trail to the Palace of the Creator. Desert City never boasted much in the way of residents because not many of the visitors ever came back. Most people were unsettled by the disappearances. Family members of the lost sent many messages which were never answered.

"Although, I've always wondered if the visitors traveled a different path home. That would be a better reason for why the messages weren't answered."

Astra sipped from her canteen. "How do you know so much about Desert City?"

Ruth glanced over her shoulder. "Zeb and I lived there for a while."

"Why is the trail in Desert City?" Astra capped her canteen. "Legends have always claimed Nahrot."

Mo zipped ahead, casting a little shadow across the sands.

Ruth turned in her seat. "I've always wondered if the names for the two villages were swapped. What if the crossing of the seven rivers is beneath Desert City and not Nahrot? What if the trader started both towns—one to cover the truth of the other and help keep the greedy from easily finding the palace?" She faced forward again. "But there's no way to prove my theories. The trader is long gone, and now Desert City is buried."

The winds kicked up, and the camels startled.

Again Ruth turned. She squinted and then her eyes widened. "Sandstorm dead on our heels. Head for the shack."

The camels ran, and Hamal held on for all he was worth. Camels did not run like horses—they swayed like ships.

The wind screamed in his ears and sand bit at his backside.

His camel ran harder.

A shriek.

He tried to glance back, sand scratching his face. He faced forward. And hoped nothing more than the wind made the sound. Hoped Astra was safe.

The shack appeared around a dune.

Ruth jumped from her camel, covered its face with her sinar, and brought it inside the one-room building.

Hamal followed her and yanked his cloak from his pack to cover his upset camel's face.

A third camel crammed itself inside the shack, and Ruth wrapped its face in her cloak.

Astra didn't follow.

Hamal ran for the door.

The sand was thick, and the wind howled. The camels grunted, but didn't react further.

Ruth grabbed him and shoved him low in a corner. She covered him with her body. "Too late. Pray she is somewhere safe," she shouted.

He tried to fight her, but she was stronger than she looked. "Astra ..." His voice cracked on her name.

CHAPTER 56

Something hard struck his boot, and Hamal struggled to move under Ruth.

She tightened her grip. "I won't let you go unless you promise you're not running into the storm." Sand and wind howled beyond the shaking shack.

Again something struck his boot.

He prayed Astra was somewhere safe. "I promise." Running out wouldn't do anyone any good. He'd seen the shredded mess a storm left of flesh—both human and animal.

"I hope you mean that because I don't want to find you buried under sand." She released him and pulled back.

He grabbed the round, metal object next to his boot. "Mo?" His gizmo had zipped ahead. Had it known a sandstorm was coming? Impossible ... right?

A purring-whirring noise reverberated from Mo as he rubbed it with his thumb before tucking it in his pocket. "Glad you're here."

"That the flying thing you keep playing with?"

"Yup."

"Lucky thing, whatever it is." She stayed protectively over him, reminding Hamal of his mother ... before her disease.

The sandstorm stayed for hours and, when it cleared, stars sparkled in a dark sky and a foot of sand reached up the wall.

Hamal ducked beneath the doorless-frame.

Ruth followed him with the camels, pausing by the well to stake them. "The stillness after a storm always takes my breath away. How can chaos rule one moment and peace rule the next?"

"I don't know." He strode for the old shed and found it empty. His heart tightened in his chest. "No ..."

Ruth came up behind him. "Perhaps she found another place to hide out the storm."

"Maybe." What if she didn't?

"We can look for her at first light." Ruth squeezed his shoulder. "Trying in the dark could get us lost, and she knew we were coming here." She walked back to the shack.

Did she? Hamal tried to recall how well he could hear when the storm caught them. Not well. And Astra had fallen off, so she probably heard less.

He slammed his fist against the sand-smoothed wood of the shed. The building shook, but didn't collapse. Where was she? "Creator, I'll make a deal. If Astra is alive, if I find her, I'll ..." The promise he was about to make hurt him, hurt him in his core. "I'll forgive my father for his sins against me and my mother, and I won't ask why he committed them."

The faint echo of feminine singing tugged at him, and he scanned the desert, making a complete circle and squinting into the night to find the source until the sound vanished.

Strange. He and Ruth were too far from Nahrot for him to hear Peridot comforting her boy. And the sound hadn't come from the shack.

Who was out there? How did she survive the storm? Did she save Astra?

"Please, Creator, let Astra be alive and safe."

CHAPTER 57

The wind had picked up, and she remembered watching Ruth glance back, say something about a sandstorm.

Astra looked around. She had to be sure of what she was hearing. Miles to the left, miles to the right stretched a sandstorm. Fear locked her joints. Her throat dried.

Her camel tripped.

She tumbled off, smashing into the ground.

A man rode a camel out of the storm. His beast's hooves smacked the ground fast.

"Run. Run." The shouts barely cut above the roar of the wind.

Astra struggled to her feet before an arm cinched around her waist and she screamed, her bottom landing hard on a stiff camel saddle.

"Hold tight," said whoever held her.

She gripped the saddle so tight her fingers turned white. She refused to look back.

Out of the desert rose an abandoned village, doors and shutters hanging crooked in frames and holes filling several walls.

They ducked inside a building with a tall entrance, perhaps a House of Citizens.

The rider pulled Astra from the camel's back. "Cover your face and hide in a corner." He wrapped his camel's face with his cloak, led them to the soundest-looking corner in the place, and closed every window and door near them.

Terror ran rampant through Astra's body, blurring her vision and fogging her mind.

"Cover your face." He pulled his turban over his eyes.

Her heart thundering in her ears, Astra covered her face with her sinar and snuggled deep into the corner and the man's side. Something bit her hands, and she yanked her sleeves past her wrists.

Her sinar barely muffled the sound of whooshing sand and screaming winds. The sound overwhelmed the thundering beat of her heart. *Creator, please stop this storm.*

Despite the storm's fury, she fell asleep.

Later, she awoke to a deafening silence. She shook her sleeves before sliding her hands free and pulling her sinar from her face.

Sunlight streamed through the cracks in the shutters and walls, revealing the man and his camel were gone and a layer of sand covered the floor.

She stood and stretched her stiff muscles before she took a step, tripping on her pack and Sonji's bridle. She'd tied those things to the saddle of her camel. How could they be here?

She untied her canteen from her pack and sipped. Her stomach gurgled and her throat sighed with relief. She closed the canteen, dug out a few dried dates, sent a quick prayer of thanks, and ate. Next, she gathered her gear and followed the mix of hoofprints and footprints from her corner to the partially open front doors.

Bright morning sunshine revealed knee-high sand filling the streets.

She lifted her shirt, checked her middle, and found a bruise from being grabbed and swung onto the camel's saddle. Her bottom hurt a bit from the bumpy ride, but then the floor beneath the sand was hard and could have caused her tenderness.

"Creator," she whispered into the unnatural quietness of the abandoned place, "thank you for more than my food. Thank you for the stranger who saved me from the storm. Watch over him. Watch over me. Thank you. I trust in you."

She climbed over the sand and out the door and slogged to the center of the street to try to get her bearings off the angle of the sun. Then she trudged in what she hoped was the direction of the shack—of Hamal. Deep in her heart, she hoped finding him and Ruth would yield some answers.

Creak. Creak.

A sign swung above her—Desert City Inn.

Or she'd found Desert City and was supposed to visit the Palace of the Creator to answer her call.

Maybe she'd find Sonji at the palace. After all, Kaseem seemed to believe the mare was the key to the treasury.

"Please, Creator, help me. Guide me." She hooked her arms in the straps of her pack. "And watch over my friends. I trust in you."

CHAPTER 58

Traveling the desert alone felt scary at first. Her fear mellowed to loneliness. She longed for company, for someone to talk to.

Miles and miles of sand stretched in every direction since the abandoned village had slipped into the heat and beyond the horizon. She considered returning. Ruth knew of the place. If she and Hamal hid out the storm in the shack, they might check the village for her.

But Astra needed to get Sonji back—the sooner the better, because the race was on. So she kept going.

Under her breath, she recited familiar prayers until her throat burned. Her sips from her canteen barely cut the dry scratch.

Sand in her riding boots aggravated her feet, so she stopped, removed her boots, and poured out the grains. She massaged her tender feet before switching her destroyed socks for fresh ones. Finished, she gathered her supplies and walked on.

A feminine voice sang, the music floating over the desert.

Astra stopped, turned a full circle, and saw nothing. She ignored the sound because too much time alone caused hallucinations—both visual and inside her head.

The singing grew louder, easier to hear, and the voice was soulful, almost hypnotic.

She again searched, but saw no one—not even an odd shape wavering in the distance because of the heat. "Creator, please clear my mind. Fend away Destroyers, demons, and tormented spirits. Wrap me in your loving arms for protection." Her throat ached with each word and her heart nervously pattered in her chest. "I trust in you."

"Do not be afraid, child," said a feminine voice.

"Who's there?" Her heart about jumped out of her chest.

"A friend."

"How do I know?" Her dry lower lip cracked and bled. She wiped at the wetness.

Mama and Papa spoke of the love of the Creator. And they'd warned of the trickiness of the Destroyers.

Once again, she wondered if she experienced something or hallucinated.

"The Creator loves his creation."

No Destroyer could say love, or claim the Creator loved his creation.

She fussed with her lip, aggravating her fresh sore. Then, she decided. The tension in her muscles eased, and the constricting of her chest relaxed. "I believe you. Why are you speaking with me?"

"I wish to help."

"Help me. Why?"

"You are a creation of the Creator."

The riddle-like answers reminded her of stories in the *Creato*. "How are you going to help me?"

"Leave your burdens behind and follow my voice."

"I'll follow." Astra stepped toward where she thought the feminine voice came from.

"Leave your burdens behind."

"You want me to leave my pack? But the camel man brought me everything in spite of the sandstorm." She clung to her items. "How will I survive without water or food? And ... what if I find Sonji?"

"The Creator provides for your every need. Trust him."

"But you asked me to follow you."

"I did."

She tugged the pendant, her mother's gift, from beneath her shirt, wrapping her fingers around the solid reminder.

"The Creator is more than that—like a flower is more than its center and petals."

Astra set down her pack and let the pendant rest on top of her shirt. Doubts circled her.

"Trust, child."

She stepped away from everything.

"Good. Now follow my voice."

She followed.

CHAPTER 59

Hamal and Ruth awoke early, mounted the camels, and rode back toward Sh'va Nahrot, but found no sign of Astra.

Ruth stopped them a few miles from the shack. "I don't think we're looking in the right place."

"Why?" Hamal freed Mo from his pocket and watched his gizmo fly to the top of a dune just to drop to the sand and roll to the bottom.

Ruth closed her eyes and rubbed her forehead. "When Zeb and I escorted your friend and her family to Urugha, her sister rode the white horse and talked to us. I remember a mark on the horse's shoulder."

Mo flew back to the top of the dune and rolled down again.

Ruth lowered her hands and opened her eyes. "There are stories of animals with certain marks, marks different from brands, that mean their person has been called to the palace."

The muscles in Hamal's jaw tightened. "My mother has received a summons. So has Astra's."

"A call is not the same as a summons. It's more a request to visit." Ruth turned her camel around. "I think we need to go back. We need to check Desert City."

"But it's buried in sand." He scrunched his forehead.

"We need to go back." She led the way.

Mo zipped ahead, came back, circled Hamal's head, and zipped forward again.

"You annoying hunk of scrap, you." Hamal glared at his gizmo before hurrying after Ruth.

Half a mile south from the shack, hidden by several large dunes, spread a village. A well sat in the center surrounded by a House of Citizens, an inn, and some businesses. The place was empty. No bodies. No living people. No furniture. Just empty buildings.

"Strange," whispered Hamal. The silence unnerved him.

Mo darted in and out of open windows and doors.

Ruth pointed to a trail of footprints leading away from the village, but instead of following them she reined her mount to a halt. "My camels and I go no further. We've not been called."

"That makes no sense." Hamal slid from his mount, tossing her the reins. "Keep your camel. I have to find Astra." He whistled, caught Mo, and stuck the gizmo in his pocket. He'd not leave it behind if he could help it. Then, he untied his pack from the camel's saddle.

"Be careful. There is more out there than desert." She turned the camels. "We will wait for you by the well."

"Sure."

Hours passed, shadows lengthened, and dunes flattened. Vultures flew overhead.

Hamal's stomach growled. He didn't remember eating any breakfast, so he paused, dug around in his pack, and removed some nuts. But his mouth felt like sand, so he untied a water skin from his pack and drank. Then he ate.

An hour later, pink, orange, and purple painted the western horizon. The sun vanished, replaced by a dark blue sky full of twinkling stars.

Hamal stopped long enough to make a torch. Then, back on the trail.

An image of Astra floated in his mind and blurred to his father. Hamal didn't deserve her friendship, her kindness, her smile. He was the angry son of a notorious thief. His mother's voice drifted to the front of his thoughts: *"Forgive your father—not for him, but for yourself so you may move on."* How could forgiving Kaseem help him more than his father?

A low, throaty growl reverberated in the dark.

CHAPTER 60

Hamal turned, drew his dagger. He remembered the sand tiger his father and Willard faced the other night. The bite in Willard's leg.

His heart hammered in his chest.

"I smell fear." The voice was growly, like a big, mean dog.

"Who's there?" Hamal raised his torch higher.

A pair of red eyes glowed. They were farther apart than a man's and higher than Hamal was tall.

"You're the son of that woman, the one my brother bit." The same growly voice spoke.

The eyes circled him.

"A Destroyer?" Chills raced along Hamal's cold limbs. He wished for the sun, for warmth and light.

A deep growl. "That is your name for us."

His mother's stories weren't fiction.

The eyes circled him again. "Have you come to finish your mother's work?"

"No." His hand shook.

"Interesting." Another circle. "Why are you here?"

"None of your business."

"Must be something important." A row of sharp teeth flashed, like a fanged smile. "Or someone."

His heart smashed against his ribs. Astra. Where was she? Why did she have to have found the white mare? Why not a normal horse no one cared about?

"Definitely someone." A growl. "You reek of fear now."

Hamal never should have doubted the *Creato*. It was full of the truth—not children's stories.

"Who are you chasing? Your mother?" A gravelly laugh. "I doubt that. The poison has to have wasted her by now. So, who?"

He gulped.

"Leave him alone."

The eyes stopped, lifted higher. "Kaseem, old friend. What brings you here?"

"I said, leave him alone." Kaseem stepped from the dark of night into the light cast by Hamal's torch. He drew his sword.

Another gravelly laugh. "I thought nothing would stop you from claiming your precious treasure."

Kaseem turned to Hamal. "Give me the torch and leave."

Hamal hesitated.

"The flame is how he found you. Give it to me."

Hamal surrendered his torch.

"Listen for a woman singing. She will guide you to safety."

Palace. Treasure. The words clunked in his head, reminding him what was missing. "Where's Sonji?"

"She escaped." His father waved with his sword toward the dark. "Go."

"Then where's—"

"Go, listen for the voice, you'll find what you're searching for."

"But—"

"Go." Kaseem sighed, the hardness in him softening. "Please, go."

Something had changed Kaseem in the last three years. Hamal wondered what. What had softened the hardness? Stolen the greed? What had brought him to defend Hamal from the Destroyer?

"I will be all right. Go." Another wave of the sword.

Hamal touched his father's shoulder. "Thank you." He snuck behind his father and into the dark.

CHAPTER 61

Astra followed the feminine voice to an oasis. The cool water soothed her sore throat and she plucked figs from a little tree before resting in the shade of a cluster of palms.

After a while, the voice encouraged her to rise.

And she did.

Later, she asked her burning questions. "Have you seen a white horse? Perhaps she was being led or ridden by a man?"

Silence.

"Voice?"

"What you seek is beyond."

Tingles spread along Astra's spine and her limbs. "I've heard that before. What does it mean?"

"You say you are seeking a horse. What you seek is not the horse, but what you think riding her will bring you—a better identity for yourself and your family."

A second round of tingles. "Um."

"You must know human approval is finicky."

She'd been told so by her father and heard such from the *tollarb* during Shabbos gathering ... but the thought never took root. Her dream the other night fluttered to the front of her mind: the disapproving comments, the endearments of love, and the bows from strangers. Bows—a show of respect usually reserved for high class citizens like *amir*s and the sultan—but she had received one, once.

"Your silence says I am right, yes?"

"Yes." Astra's heart ached.

They traveled in the heat until the sun hovered close to the horizon and her shadow stretched toward night.

In the distance, a stone wall interrupted the sand. A purple roof poked above the wall and seven weather vanes topped the roof. Tree boughs tickled the back of the place.

"Where are we?" Astra tried to find a latch or a handle of some sort on the wooden gate interrupting the stone wall, but located none.

"You'll find out soon."

CHAPTER 62

Astra knocked on the wooden gate, and torches blazed to life on either side. She stumbled back, tripped, and landed on her bottom.

The gate opened as the feminine voice said, "Are you all right?"

Astra stood and rubbed her behind. "I am."

"You may enter."

"Voice?" She bit her lip, staring at a garden far more magnificent than any she'd ever seen.

"Yes, child?"

She released her lip. "Is this the Palace of the Creator?"

A man wearing a purple turban and a dirtied purple vest stepped into view. His dark eyes sparkled, and he wiped his hands on a rag. He smiled, lifting his long gray mustache over his beard. "Welcome."

"Um, hello, sir." She tried to curtsy and nearly fell instead. She sensed the truth, her insides full of a special, tingling warmth.

He steadied her, a gentle touch on her shoulder. "I've been expecting you." He stuck his rag in a pocket and waved for her to enter.

She stepped inside, and the gate closed behind her without anyone touching it. The barefoot man leading her along a carpet of grass reminded her of an older version of

Papa. Thick vegetation lined the path and so did the most beautiful glow bugs. One glow bug landed on her nose for a moment. Such detail. Such pretty light.

A breeze wrapped her in the scent of fresh blossoms, reminding her of Great-Uncle Trev's garden and his claim that his plants were gifts for answered summons. Would her mother receive a blossom someday?

The path ended at a two-story, purple house. A lantern hung by the big front door and windows of various sizes and shapes lined the walls. Silver weather vanes sparkled on the roof.

"This isn't a palace." Astra covered her mouth.

"Oh?" The man turned, his hand on the doorknob.

She shook her head and lowered her hands. "No, it's better. Homier."

He smiled again. "Would you like to come inside?"

"Yes, please." Astra ran her fingers through her tangled hair, tried to straighten her sinar, and shook the worst of the sand from her clothes.

He opened the door and motioned for her to go first.

She hesitated, then entered. The house smelled of honey, baking bread with a hint of vanilla, and roasting goat. Her mouth watered. She removed her boots and set them by the wall.

A tapestry featuring a white horse drew her. "Sonji." How could she have forgotten? "Sir, have you seen a white horse?"

"Are you hungry?" He gestured toward the back of the house.

Her thoughts drifted to Hamal. Strange to think of him after searching so hard for Sonji. Heat traveled up her neck to her face as she recalled the night they'd returned home from rescuing her mare from the bandits. The formal goodbye kiss she'd placed on his cheek and the special glow in his dark eyes.

Did he feel the same for her as she felt for him?

Then she remembered meeting Vivian at the shack.

Hamal had stepped between her and Vivian. There was a bite in his words when Vivian asked for water. What kind of past did they share? Friends? Something more?

"Astra, my child, are you hungry?" The man held out a plate filled with slices of meat, a large hunk of bread, and fresh fruit and vegetables.

"Yes." She nodded and accepted the offering. "Thank you, sir."

"You don't have to call me sir." He led her to a table.

"What should I call you?" She set her plate down.

"I have many names. What would you like to call me?"

"Grandpa." The word slipped out without much thought. But his gray hair and wrinkles and kindness, well, it reminded her of how she always imagined her papa's father to be.

He chuckled warmly. "I'm honored."

Heat filled her cheeks and she smiled.

They shared dinner, and she helped wash dishes. Then, the man led her to the stairs. "You may pick any room you like."

"I'm not tired." She yawned.

He tipped his head, his smile never leaving him.

She yawned again, this time bigger and deeper. "Grandpa, why do the stories claim your home is like the sultan's palace?"

"What one man calls a palace is not another man's palace." The man leaned against the railing for the stairs. "And when one man repeats another man's story, he often embellishes the details to draw in a bigger crowd."

Astra sat on the bottom third step. "Grandpa, have you heard my every prayer like it says in your book?"

"I have." His eyes sparkled.

"If my mother answers her summons, will she come back to me and Ehsan and Papa?" She yawned again and her eyelids drooped.

He picked her up in his arms, as Hamal had done the other night. "You need rest, my child."

"Do you really watch over everyone all the time, even Hamal's father, Kaseem?"

"I do."

"So ... you love him like you love your better-behaved children?"

"I do." He set her on a bed and pulled a soft blanket over her. "Sleep well, my child."

CHAPTER 63

Hamal stumbled in the dark. Starlight illuminated little. His father facing the Destroyer for him—crazy. Sweat dripped from his brow, and he shivered. He'd run once he left the circle of light from the torch. Now, his side screamed in pain, and his legs were hardly able to support him. He stumbled again, but this time he didn't catch himself. Sand and little shards of rock bit into his palms.

He stayed on his hands and knees, gasping for air.

Destroyers were real.

His father cared about him—he'd had to in order to face that monster and send Hamal away.

Why had he left Kaseem to face the Destroyer alone?

"I should go back." The stitch in his side eased and, on quivering legs, he stood and wiped his hands on his pants.

Something moved in his pocket. Mo? It had to be.

Singing, soft and feminine, came from his left.

"Hello? Is anyone out there?" He stepped toward it.

The sound strengthened.

"Who's there?"

His father's words reverberated in his head: *Listen for a woman singing. She will guide you to safety.*

Mo crept from his pocket and launched into the air. Whirs and clicks mixed with the singing.

Hamal chased Mo. "Wait. Come back. Don't leave me again. Mo!"

A golden light appeared ahead. A dark figure stood beside the glow. Who was in the middle of nowhere? Had he circled back to his father? But there was no sign of the Destroyer. *Please, Creator, watch over Kaseem.* He couldn't believe what he'd just prayed, but he meant it.

The figure waved. "Welcome."

Hamal drew closer. A stony wall and a wooden gate took shape. The figure was a man wearing a purple turban and vest, and he held Mo.

The feminine voice singing in the night faded. Perhaps he hadn't heard Ruth or Peridot singing in Nahrot. If not, who possessed those pipes? He could almost swear the voice sounded the same as the one he followed to Astra's, and he'd heard it when he followed Ruth in the dark to the *mople*.

"Welcome, Hamal." The man smiled and stepped aside. "Please, come in."

"How do you know my name?" Hamal stood in front of the gate. "Who are you?"

"Let us escape the ears of the Destroyers and their brethren, share a bite, and discuss what troubles you." The man tipped his head toward the path illuminated by glow bugs. He still held Mo, the gizmo purr-whirring.

"I guess." Hamal glanced over his shoulder. Nothing there, at least that he could see.

The man led the way, and without help, the gate closed behind them.

Mo joined some glow bugs lazily floating up and down a grassy trail.

This place, the man, it all felt vaguely familiar. Why?

"Sir, my father is out there facing a Destroyer." Why did he blurt that out?

"Do not fear for him."

"What?" Hamal's step faltered, but he quickly regained his balance.

With Mo and the man, he entered a purple house. Small tapestries that looked like Astra's needlework lined the walls of the front room. One showed angels battling Destroyers. Smaller, angel-like beings worked around machines.

A chill slid up his spine.

The man sat in a chair with a purple cushion in the front room. "Come, sit. We have much to discuss." He smiled, and his brown eyes sparkled.

CHAPTER 64

"You're the Creator," Hamal whispered, his forehead furrowing. "But this isn't a palace." He'd dreaded ever coming near the Palace of the Creator, thanks to his father's greed, but this house wasn't it. Couldn't be.

"Are you certain of your claim?"

"No ..."

Mo again settled in the man's hand. The gizmo split, right down the middle, and out crawled a silver-colored-beetle the size of Hamal's pinky nail.

"What?" Hamal's jaw dropped.

The man smiled, his mustache lifting at the corners of his mouth. "Been a long time since our last meeting, my friend."

The beetle's antennas twitched and twitched and twitched some more. The action reminded Hamal of Ehsan waving her hands about as she told a story. No wonder the two got along so well.

The man bobbed his head now and again, sometimes adding, "Uh-huh."

Beetle. There was a beetle inside his invention. How? "What is that?" Hamal stepped closer and leaned toward his gizmo.

"A magic metal beetle," said the man. "He says you've been calling him Mo."

The antennas paused a moment. Then ... twitched again.

Hamal dropped into a chair.

The man continued to act as if he were having a conversation with the beetle.

Impossible.

Hamal tugged off his turban—his spare before he lost the other one during his sort-of-kidnapping adventure—and ran his fingers through his hair. He was a mess. He shook his head. Astra and her Sonji were lost somewhere in the desert. His father was facing a Destroyer. And now, the Creator of everything was having a conversation with a beetle—a magic metal beetle.

When will I wake up?

Something moved on the floor above him. The steps sounded lighter than a man, but bigger than a cat.

A short, slender figure crept barefoot down the steps behind the Creator. She rubbed her eyes. "Hamal?"

He stood, crossed the room in three strides, and stopped at the foot of the stairs. "Astra." Little flecks of sand clung to her wrinkled brown and tan clothes and drew out the gold in her eyes. She smelled like home, like hot dunes and baking vanilla bread. He ached to draw her into his arms.

She smiled and paused a couple of steps above him, putting them at eye level. "How'd you get here?"

His heart danced. "I'm not hallucinating ... am I?"

"No." She flung her arms around him, buried her head in his shoulder, and squeezed tight. "I was so afraid the storm swallowed you." She pulled back. "*Ruth.* Is she all right?"

Her hair smelled like sand and sweat and a hint of something fruity. "She's fine. She promised to meet us in Desert City."

"Ham ... how did you find me?"

"First, I followed your footsteps. Then, my father told me to follow a singing voice."

"Your father ...? Kaseem ...?" Her hands shifted to his chest. "Is Sonji here?" Her brown and green eyes glittered.

"He said she got away from him." Hamal backed away from her. "I left him in the dark to face a Destroyer ... the same creature that poisoned my mother."

"Oh, Ham." She descended the last two steps and pulled him into another hug, her head pressing against his chest.

"When I was a little kid, I thought him something from a legend. Stealing from the rich and giving to the poor. Keeping only what he and his men needed to survive." He sighed. "That dry season, when I was fourteen, I found him in Latif City. He and his men stole from everyone. They had no friends, no worthy goals. I ran home. He never seemed to want to come anywhere near Nahrot."

She looked up at him, her ebony hair a tangled mess around her face. "I'm listening."

"I told you he kidnapped me."

"Yes?" Her forehead furrowed, then relaxed.

"And when I was with him, the legend part of him I hadn't seen since I was a little kid peeked through—he kept his men from harming me, made sure Ruth and I were taken care of right, and left us in Wisewoman Yasif's shed so we could escape."

He chuckled, then sobered. "Kaseem ... my father ... found me in the dark, cornered by a Destroyer. He sent me off to follow a voice on the wind to safety while he challenged the creature. He gave me a chance to live." Hamal turned his face from Astra and tried to free himself from her grip. "Maybe he's always been the man I remember from when I was three. I just didn't see it until now."

The Creator cleared his throat. "Perhaps when you visited him you reminded him of that man."

CHAPTER 65

Sitting in the Creator's hand was a silver beetle and the shell of Hamal's gizmo. Astra stared. Where had the bug come from? And what had happened to Mo?

She released Hamal and leaned close to the silver beetle. "You're kinda cute, but what are you?" She held out her hand next to the Creator's, and the bug crawled across, touching her hand with his antennas.

"The beetle is Mo." Her friend laughed, deep and soulful.

She'd not heard such a sound from him in three years. She turned.

"How it—"

"He," said the Creator, his eyes twinkling.

Ham tipped his head to the Creator. "Excuse me. How he operates my invention—I don't know. My whole life anymore feels like a good Dryzzian legend told to thrill the children."

He turned from them, staring at something across the room. "There's a tapestry with angels fighting Destroyers, and below them I thought little angels worked on machines." He stared at Mo. "But maybe they weren't little angels ... maybe they were magic metal beetles like Mo."

The Creator smiled and nodded. "Mo's brethren have a special task in caring for the machines that keep the Veil operating."

An involuntary shiver skittered up Astra's spine. "Can a machine fail?"

His smile dimmed a little. "Yes, it can fail if tampered with, and when this happens a weak point is created, often allowing a Destroyer through to this side."

Hamal gawked. "You're the Creator. How could something you created fail? The machines are on the opposite side of the Veil from the Destroyers, and even if those things get to this side, wouldn't your magic keep them from breaking the machines?"

"Yes." The Creator sighed, his smile gone. "My magic protects the machines from the Destroyers and their kind, but it doesn't prevent one of *your* lost brethren from finding and tampering with it."

"Lost brethren," Astra whispered, the term reminding her of a part of the story about Princess Gefen and her brother saving Dryzza from their father, the part where he'd listened to the whispers of a Destroyer instead of the guidance of his advisors.

The Creator ushered them to the gathering of chairs in the front room. "We'll be more comfortable for the rest of our discussion if we are seated."

"Sure." Astra sat in a cushioned chair next to him and held her hand below the flame of an oil lamp. The light sparkled on Mo's silver shell. "I don't see a mark on Mo like there is on my mare's shoulder. My great-uncle said the mark meant I was called here."

Hamal looked as tired as she felt. His curly black hair stuck in a million crazy directions, and he sat across from her with his turban peeking from under his left leg.

The Creator held out his hand, and Mo lifted two hard back-plates, flying on little, almost transparent, wings to him. "Mo and the white mare are made of a magic I reserve for special messengers, but they are not supposed to be marked. The people are meant to listen."

The gizmo clicked back together like two magnets attracted. Wings flicked out and Mo flew about the room.

Astra faced the Creator. "What do you mean?"

The Creator leaned back in his chair. "Years ago, after my white mare was stolen from me, she landed in the hands of Princess Gefen. Gefen knew, one look at my mare, and she knew this wasn't a normal horse. So Gefen studied the *Creato* and learned where to find the beginning of the trail to my home. She brought my mare back to me, and she answered her call."

Astra pulled the blanket off the back of her chair and wrapped herself in it. "I don't remember hearing that in the legends."

"I'm not sure she told anyone about her visit. I thanked her for returning the mare, and she left. But my horse was not the same without Gefen, so I opened the gate and she returned to her princess. You know the rest because of the legends."

Mo returned and dropped in Hamal's lap.

He picked up the ball. "At least, I finally know what powers my gizmo. I can't really believe it, but at least I know."

A strange whirring purr echoed from the ball.

The Creator laughed. "Mo likes you."

"And I him," said Ham.

"Mo went with my mare when she returned to the princess. She and Mo were friends before she was stolen. He didn't want to be left behind again."

Astra grinned. "So that's why those two get along so well."

The Creator turned to her. "You asked me if I'd seen a white horse."

"Yes." She nodded, hope lifted in her chest. "Like I said, she has a mark on her shoulder. My sister named her Sonji after Princess Gefen's steed."

Sadness filled the Creator's brown eyes. "Your white horse is my horse. Gefen's father caught and branded her with my flower when she acted as lookout for Mo and Gefen. They were stealing the key to the palace from the sultan."

He continued. "Stories of a special white horse had been in circulation for over a hundred years. The sultan recognized the magic—*my* magic—in my horse and wanted her away from Gefen. He'd hoped greed-blinded men who saw the mark would help him. But Gefen had good friends, and her father's plan failed."

Astra's heart ached for Sonji. A thought stirred in her mind, the scene of her in-progress-needlework. "But can't Sonji shrink? Didn't Princess Gefen send her to get the key?"

The Creator shook his head. "No, my child. Legends may be based on truth, but not everything in a legend is truth. Sonji never could shrink. Mo collected the key, and Sonji kept guard."

Hamal chuckled. "If Sonji could shrink, she never would have been caught by my father and his bandits. She never would have been caught by the sultan and branded. And I doubt the man who stole her so Gefen had a chance to meet her could have ridden away with her."

"True." Astra rubbed her chin. "So the times in the legend where she shrank, that was Mo helping save the day."

"Indeed." The Creator smiled.

A shrill whinny echoed through the house.

Astra leaped from her chair and ran to the door. "Sonji!"

CHAPTER 66

At the gate, Astra found Sonji and Kaseem. Both were covered in blood.

Astra looped her arm under Kaseem's and Sonji held up his other side. Kaseem could hardly keep his feet under him, but he refused to ride the mare. The threesome walked through the gate and to the door of the house.

The Creator and Hamal waited there. Astra wondered why they had stayed back.

The Creator led them to a bedroom on the main floor near the dining table.

Kaseem sat on the bed, both hands pressed against a deep gash in his side.

The blood wasn't Sonji's. A part of Astra sighed with relief while another part struggled to remember everything Grandma taught her during her short apprenticeship.

Sonji nuzzled Astra's shoulder before she slipped outside, Mo flying after her.

Hamal, looking a bit green, sat in a chair in the corner.

The Creator stood beside her. "What can you do?"

"You're the Creator." She stepped back from her possible patient.

"And I gave you a gift." He gently pushed her toward Kaseem.

Hamal's father was pale, his black beard a sharp contrast to his whitened skin. "I understand if you don't want to help me. I don't deserve it."

"No, I want to help." She nibbled her lower lip a moment. "Grandpa, I need a pot of hot water, clean rags, Dryzzian mint, honey, and something for him to bite on. Something like a stick."

Hamal headed for the door. "I can get the stick."

"Thanks." She bobbed her head. "I need a sterilized needle and thread too. I'm hoping nothing important was punctured—wait. Mr. Nuru, were you slashed by a blade ... or bitten, or clawed?"

"Clawed."

Her heart fluttered and her hands slicked. "Clawed by what? A Destroyer? If so, I can't remember if their claws are poisonous like their fangs."

Kaseem Nuru gave a slight shake of his head. "Not bitten. Just clawed."

The Creator moved toward the door. "The claws are not poisonous, and Astra, I will bring you what you need."

Astra nodded to herself. "Good to know—and thank you."

Kaseem's breaths were shallow. "You've cared for the injured before?" He winced.

"My grandmother was the village wisewoman. She had started to teach me her work before she died." Astra moved closer to him. "Where were you clawed?"

"My worst one starts on my shoulder and ends at my gut. There are a few small ones on my back and arms."

The Creator returned and set a pot of boiling hot water on an extra chair he brought with him. He pushed Hamal's chair closer, left, and returned with the rest of the supplies. "Tell me what to do."

Green-faced Hamal entered with the stick, set it on his chair, and retreated.

Astra had forgotten about Hamal's discomfort with blood. She'd been away from caretaking for too long.

She turned to the Creator. "We need to remove his shirt and clean his gash. He said he has some smaller cuts on his back and arms. We can clean those after I look at the gash."

With help, Kaseem removed his shirt and bit down on the stick.

Astra smashed the mint leaves and mixed them in the hot water. She cleaned sand and long strands of black fur from the gash. Blood already tried to clot and create a scab. The gash did stretch from his shoulder to his gut—but by some miracle, it was not too deep, and his organs had not been punctured. Astra was sure some were bruised, though. He'd be sore a long time.

She sterilized the needle and the thread with hot water. "Kaseem, I need you to lie back and not move."

The Creator walked around the bed and held down Kaseem's shoulders.

Kaseem removed the stick from his mouth. "I'll do my best." He bit the stick and closed his eyes.

She set to work. The stitches were even, tight, but not too tight. She covered them in a special healing cream mixed with honey and Dryzzian mint leaves instead of straight honey to help keep the wound clean and sterilized. The cream was similar to what she'd used on Sonji's face, something she'd learned to make from her grandma.

When she finished tending to the gash, she and the Creator treated the smaller cuts, and then cleaned up the supplies.

She returned and double checked her work. "Try to be careful when you—"

Snores cut her off.

The Creator came in behind her. "I'll finish tending to him. Why don't you check on Hamal? He's in the backyard."

"Thank you." She hugged him.

"You're welcome." He hugged her back.

She paused in the doorway. "Grandpa, why didn't you heal Kaseem? Why did you have me tend to him?"

"Why do you think?" His dark eyes twinkled, and his mustache lifted in a slight smile.

She bit her lower lip, released it. "I'm not sure."

"What did I tell you earlier?"

"You gave me a gift."

"Mm-hmm."

She pondered the answer, rolling it over in her head. "I'll check on Hamal now."

CHAPTER 67

Hamal sat in the grass. The sky to the west shifted from midnight black to gray and added a tinge of green to the dark palm and pine trees spread across the back yard. The stars faded, and the glow bugs retreated. Mo danced among the flowers while Sonji, somehow clean of Kaseem's blood, grazed nearby.

The image of his injured father played over and over in his head. So much blood.

"Ham." Astra sat beside him, her hands washed and her clothes bloodstained. "Are you all right?"

"Sort of. How's my father?" His stomach roiled and he couldn't meet her gaze.

"He'll live. He's lost a lot of blood, and he'll hurt for a while. But he'll live." She sounded satisfied, hopeful.

"I'm glad." Hamal meant it.

"We found Sonji … maybe she found us. I don't know." She gestured to the white mare.

"Do you still want to race? I mean, are you going to finish the race?" He peeked at her, avoiding looking at the stains. "You'll be behind more than a day if you continue."

"Yes, I'm going to finish the race … even though I'm behind, but I don't have to win anymore." She smiled, took off her sinar, and finger-combed her tangled hair.

"I'm glad you're continuing the race, because Wisewoman Yasif said the whole town is betting on whether or not you're going to win, and I think somebody should be able to collect the prize." Ham faced her. "But I have to ask, what happened to having to win? Of taking home the prize and showing everyone you're not an outcast?"

"I'm not an outcast. I never was."

"And how did you come to that conclusion?" His eyebrows raised high on his forehead.

She pulled a pendant from beneath her shirt and tugged the necklace from under her hair. She handed it to him. "Mrs. Zilfel, Isaac's mother, brought this by. She said my mother ordered it for me. And she told me I'm not an outcast."

He turned over the flower pendant. Engraved on the smooth back was, *The Creator loves his children. All are special—none are forgotten.*

"I'm missing something." He handed the pendant back.

She slipped the necklace over her head. "I had a dream. I remembered times when I was treated like an outcast and times when I was treated special—or like a friend. Then I remembered what my mother calls me and my sister—her blessings. And the Creator having me care for your father—acting as a wisewoman—was the final clue." She pulled her knees up and wrapped her arms around them. "I am useful. I am worth something. I never should have let myself believe the lies—that I'm a worthless freak."

He gave her a crooked smile. "I could have told you that."

Astra laughed. "I guess." She released her legs and faced him. The happy light in her eyes shifting to one full of questions. "Ham, I know you said you and Vivian are friends. Are you sure?"

He gulped. Even a mess, Astra was more beautiful than any girl he'd ever met. "I'm sure, Astra. There's only one girl fo—"

The Creator stepped into view. "A new day has arisen. There are a few things we should discuss before your visit comes to an end."

Sonji looked up from her grazing and trotted over.

The Creator fed her a carrot and rubbed her forehead. "Welcome back."

She snorted and returned to grazing.

The Creator led the way back to the house. Hamal saw people and animals step from the trees and tend to the plants. Where had they all come from?

The back door closed, reminding Hamal of the closed door to his father's room.

The Creator sat at the kitchen table, and Astra joined him, patting the chair beside her.

CHAPTER 68

Hamal sat next to Astra. His stomach tightened as he watched the Creator rest his clasped hands on the tabletop and lean toward them.

His gaze met each of theirs. "Will the both of you encourage your mothers to answer their summons?"

"I'll try." Astra's confidence outside seemed to have melted. She braided her hair and tied her sinar.

So Wisewoman Yasif had guessed correctly that the messenger in purple was sent by the Creator. Hamal wondered if Ehsan knew the significance of the man.

"Good. Hamal?" The Creator's eyes were full of compassion and understanding.

Still, Hamal shook his head. "My mother is sick."

"I know. We have spoken in her dreams, but she is still unsure about answering."

"May I ask what my mother has been summoned to do?" Hamal knew if she could do something, she would.

"If she wishes to share, she may." The Creator stood.

"I'll talk with her." Maybe she would tell Hamal what she'd been summoned for.

"Thank you." The Creator headed for the backdoor. "Before this visit, Astra was in the midst of a race." He led Hamal and Astra from the house to a shed.

Sonji trotted over and nuzzled Astra's shoulder.

Astra traced the mark on her mare's shoulder. "You aren't mine." She wrapped her arms around her horse's neck. "But I wish you were."

The Creator brought out a bridle, a bucket of grooming tools, and a saddle with a blanket from the shed. "If she wants to go with you, she may leave."

Hamal held up a hand. "My mother said she saw Sonji here when she and Fatima answered their summons over a decade ago. How did she get from here to Nahrot?"

"Do you have to know?" The Creator handed Astra the tack and the bucket.

Hamal shrugged. "No, I don't have to know."

Astra slipped the bridle on her mare. "Sonji was here when Mama and Omaira came?"

The Creator nodded and helped Astra care for Sonji. He added a cloak, bedroll, and saddlebags. "The canteens and food are at the house."

They returned to the house and packed the food and canteens.

Astra tightened the caps for the two canteens. "Papa will meet me in Todros with fresh clothes. I should be all right for a few days."

The Creator shook his head. "Go to your room and clean up. You do not need to carry evidence of one journey into the next."

She left, and the Creator sat with Hamal in the front room. "I ask that you stay a day longer."

"Why?" Hamal fussed with his hair.

The Creator leaned forward. "Why do you think?"

"My father." Hamal tugged at his shirt collar, the room feeling warmer than before. "Sending Sonji away with Astra won't stop him from stealing from you. And aren't you worried for your treasure?"

"I overheard you confess to Astra that you now doubt your father's faults outweigh the good in him." The Creator leaned back in his chair, denting the pillows behind him.

Hamal remembered.

Astra clomped down the stairs in her boots. "Thank you, Grandpa." She wore a clean shirt and pants with her old boots while her other clothes were folded and tucked under her arm.

Hamal left his chair and moved for the door with Astra.

The Creator called from behind him. "The choice is yours, Hamal."

Hamal cringed and led the way out of the house.

Mo flew nearby and Sonji, reins looped over her neck, waited for them in the front yard.

Astra hurried to catch up to him. "Hamal, why are you in a rush?"

Hamal forced himself to slow down. "No reason."

Sonji and Mo followed.

They arrived at the gate fast, too fast.

"Do you want to ride double?" Astra patted Sonji's shoulder.

"I'm not going back with you. I need to stay a while. My father and I have a few things to talk about." He tugged at his shirt collar, the thing feeling too tight.

"Like his stealing my horse to open the Creator's treasury?" She lifted an eyebrow, her eyes full of kindness.

"Yes. And some other topics." He forced his hand from his collar and shoved it in his pants pocket.

She hugged him. "You're brave to face your fears. Perhaps you and your father can have a relationship after this."

"I never thought of that." He shrugged, stepping out of the embrace.

"Ham …" She fiddled with Sonji's reins. "You started to say something before Grandpa came over."

"Why do you call him Grandpa?"

She pushed sand with the toe of her boot. "I call him Grandpa because I always imagined my papa's father to be like him—strong, capable, kind. Besides, he told me that I don't have to call him the Creator or sir."

"Huh." He tilted his head.

"You were saying ...?" She stopped pushing the sand and looked him right in the eye.

His fingers itched to grab his collar. "You keep asking about Vivian and me, but we were nothing more than friends."

"Why? I mean, she's pretty and smart and kind. She really likes you."

"I doubt she likes me in the way you're suggesting. There was a stable boy she was sweet on when I worked for her father. And I never thought of her as something more. There's only one girl I've ever thought of that way. And she's you."

"You mean that?" She smiled, her eyes more beautiful than jewels.

"Uh-huh." He shifted, heat filling his face.

She planted a kiss on his lips, sweet and fast. "Good." She mounted Sonji.

"Wait." He stepped toward her.

She faced him. "What?"

"The Creator told me Sonji was never the literal key to the treasury, but that a key had been made to look like her. She was stolen because of a misunderstanding."

"Huh." She touched her chin. "Kind of like people exaggerating about the Creator's palace."

"Uh, I guess." He stuck his hands in his pockets. "The trick to getting in the treasury is befriending Mo and sending him through a mouse hole to fit the key in a special lock."

"Why are you telling me this?" She raised an ebony eyebrow.

He shrugged, desert flies buzzing in his gut. "I don't know. Because I thought you'd like to know."

"Thank you for sharing." She giggled. "Meet me when you're finished making amends with your father."

"Where?" His heart fluttered in his chest.

"Wherever you can catch me." Her giggle stretched into a beautiful smile.

"I will." He smiled.

Astra and Sonji trotted north, north for Desert City, Nahrot, and the race.

He touched his lips that tingled from her touch and whooped. She was the best thing to ever happen to him. *Creator, bless her.*

Mo circled his head as he returned to the purple house, his heart lighter than it had been in a long time.

CHAPTER 69

Astra and Sonji galloped for home. As they passed through the deserted village, she thought she saw someone wave to her from beside the well, but she passed by too fast to be sure.

At midday, she and her mare reached home.

Ehsan wrapped her in a hug. "You found her. You found Sonji. Where was she?"

Astra eased herself from the embrace. "I'm not sure you'll believe me."

"Try me." Ehsan slipped Sonji a slice of apple.

"How about I explain after the race, when we ride the train again?" Astra stepped away from her horse and peeked inside the house.

"Sure." Ehsan ran her hands over the tack. "This isn't yours. What happened to the old tack you've been using?"

"I think the saddle is still in the barn. I, um, lost the bridle in the desert." Astra eased her way over to the front of the house.

"Where did this new tack come from? And what are you looking for?" Ehsan raised a slender, dark eyebrow, her brown-gold eyes full of questions.

"I'll explain everything on the train ride. I promise. Where's Papa?"

"He went into town. That man, Mr. Rose, I guess he sent a shipment of wood when he learned Papa's shop burned down. It's supposed to be coming in."

Astra gaped. "How can a shipment get here so fast?"

Ehsan counted on her fingers. "The fire was about two weeks ago."

"How did Mr. Rose know so soon?" Astra's brow furrowed.

"I don't know. Maybe Papa sent him a message about not being able to fill an order and he happened to mention the fire? Why?"

"No reason."

"Why do you need to speak with Papa? What about the race?"

"Tell him I've found Sonji and returned to the race." Astra mounted her mare. "Tell him Hamal will be home in a day or two, and he might come with his father."

"Wait, so Hamal isn't with you? He won't be helping you resupply in Gefen? And he has a father?"

"No, I don't think Hamal's going to make Gefen. And, yes, he has a father."

Again Ehsan counted on her fingers. "Won't your supplies be getting low?"

"Probably." Astra patted her pocket and found a coin purse. "I have a little money. I can buy what I need."

"Are you sure?" Ehsan fussed with the end of her belt. "Papa and I can leave early tomorrow and try to catch a train to meet you in Gefen … you won't be getting any supplies in Camel's Head, though." She tugged her braid.

"Trust the Creator, little sister."

"I do. Your plans, though, seem to have gone to ruin."

Astra turned Sonji. "Everything will work out."

"Sure," Ehsan said. "Papa and I will watch for Hamal and his father, I guess."

"Thank you. I'll see you in Todros." Astra clicked her tongue. Sonji skipped her usual trot and went straight into a gallop.

Astra's heart leaped and her nerves zinged.

CHAPTER 70

Late afternoon sunshine warmed Astra's back. The shadows of the dunes stretched across the sandy valleys. Astra and Sonji trotted in the middle of the slower racers. The Palace of the Creator felt more like a fantasy than reality. Her newer, sturdier tack, her strengthened trust, and her new definition of herself—worthy, useful—counteracted the surreal feeling.

Mama, Papa, the *tollarb*—they were right to end their prayers with "*We trust in you.*"

Miles and miles of sand hid what lay ahead and what lay behind. Astra let Sonji set the pace. The familiar rhythm allowed her mind to wander ... and wonder once more why Mama was unsettled by her summons.

The first time she'd answered a summons, she'd contradicted the rumors by returning home. Didn't Mama believe she'd return a second time? Or could her trouble be that simple—she feared by answering again she would not come home? The Creator showered her in blessings, wished her good and not trouble, and loved her. Astra believed that as strongly as she believed her mother would return again.

Sonji's ears twitched.

"I kissed Ham. Not on the cheek, but on the lips. What if we're not meant to be more than friends?"

Sonji slowed to a halt.

Astra stood in her stirrups. She twisted forward, to the side, back, and to the other side. "What's wrong?"

Her mare whinnied and stepped to the left.

Astra gave Sonji her head.

Her horse's nostrils flared and she walked around a dune.

Astra strained to see in the deepening shadows.

Ahead, a dark shape appeared. The closer they drew, the better the shape of a rider and her horse formed.

Astra called to the pair. "Vivian, Midnight, are you all right?"

Vivian, her hair a mess and her sinar torn, urged her horse to walk. Midnight wore a bloodied rag on his front leg.

Astra urged Sonji to sidle up beside Midnight before she touched the girl. "Vivian."

"Huh?" She turned, revealing a cut across her cheek, dried and ugly, and her eyelids puffed as if she'd been punched. "Astra?"

"Why don't we stop for a snack?"

"Sure ... I guess."

Midnight stopped.

Sonji touched muzzles with him.

Astra slid from her mare's back and helped Vivian to her feet. "Let's sit over here where the sand is flat and there's some sunshine to keep us warm." She removed her new cloak from her saddle and wrapped it snugly around her friend.

Her friend? Yes, Vivian was her friend.

She checked the bags on Midnight's saddle. All four were empty and there was almost no water in the canteen.

Astra removed a wooden bowl from her bags and filled it. First, she watered Midnight. Then, she sat with Vivian, helped her drink, and tended to her cut. "What happened?" She brought out a dried biscuit.

"What happened ...?" Vivian chewed slowly on her biscuit.

Astra pulled some hay from her bag and separated it into two piles.

Sonji pushed her share to Midnight.

Astra returned to sit by Vivian, warmed by her mare's kindness. She wrapped an arm around her friend. "Vivian?"

"I left Nahrot like you told me to. Before nightfall, I reached the check-in, you know, the one before Gefen. Bandits attacked me and the other racers spending the night. They kept asking if anyone had seen a white horse. Do you know if there's any reason why anyone would be after your mare?" Vivian stared beyond and didn't pause for an answer. "Midnight and I managed to escape into the night. We tried to follow the race route, but I got lost. At first light, I stopped. We were both tired ... and I figured we'd ridden far enough to be safe."

She pulled apart the biscuit and nibbled. "I should have stayed in Nahrot and waited for you to return." She shivered. "I rode further after a nap. We finally reached familiar ground and Midnight startled. Something large and sand-colored, I think it was a desert cat, chased us. It outran us and charged. Midnight reared and I barely managed to stay on. The cat attacked. Midnight bolted. I remember shouting a prayer. The sun was setting by the time I managed to regain control. We were both exhausted. I used strips from my cloak to bandage him and camped in the wild. But I couldn't sleep. What if that cat was still after us?"

"Sounds terrifying." Astra rubbed her hands along Vivian's arms. "I'm glad Sonji and I found you two."

Vivian tugged the cloak tighter around herself and continued to nibble.

Astra moved away and dug through her saddlebags for medical supplies. "Sonji, can you help me with Midnight?"

Sonji bobbed her head.

"Thank you, girl." Astra gave Midnight's reins to her horse, and Sonji held them.

Midnight fussed until his good side pressed against Sonji's.

"I need to see your wound." Astra patted his sweat-dried shoulder before untying the blood-drenched fabric on his foreleg. The scratch looked ugly, but thankfully it was only a surface wound and nothing deeper.

"I'm sorry … this may hurt." She wetted a rag in a bowl of water and salt mix. Then, she washed, cleaned, salved, and wrapped the wound. "Hopefully my handiwork helps."

She put her supplies back in her bag and examined the rest of Midnight. She ran her hands over every inch of him and unsaddled him to rub him down. Besides his foreleg, she salved a small nick on his other front leg.

"One very blessed horse." She gave him and Sonji each a handful of grain. Then, she returned to Vivian.

A rider on a red horse passed them.

Astra knelt by her friend. "Seems the others are still on the move. How do you feel?"

"Tired. But better."

Astra downed a few dried apricots and offered Vivian a few, but she shook her head.

Astra held out her canteen. "Would you like another sip of water?"

"Yes." Vivian drank deeply, her hands steadier, her distant expression lessening.

Astra cinched the saddle back on Midnight and double-checked the bandage. "Bleeding looks to have stopped, and he doesn't seem to be in pain. I think you can ride him further."

Vivian kept the cloak on as she inspected Astra's handiwork. "Thank you. You're an answer to prayer."

"I'm not sure about an answer, but maybe a helping hand." Astra warmed. "How about I help you on? Sonji and I will ride with you to the next check-in point."

Vivian embraced her. "Thank you."

Astra uncomfortably patted her new friend on the back. "You're welcome."

The sun slipped below the horizon, and they traveled by starlight until torches illuminated an oversized puddle and a drafty-looking tent anchored to a couple of palm trees.

Astra dismounted.

"I'll set up camp." Vivian tied the horses.

Astra nodded and approached the check-in tent.

The youngest *jundiin* she'd ever seen sat beside a three-legged table. "We were attacked a couple of days ago." He pushed his turban off his eyebrows. "The bandits were after a white horse."

"Huh." Astra used a stubby pencil from the middle of the table to write her name beside Vivian's.

"Yeah, you haven't seen one, have you?"

"I own one." Her insides chilled and shriveled. Hamal's father no longer chased her for Sonji, but that didn't mean his men had dropped the hunt. How could she not have thought about further trouble? She forced her breathing to remain normal and lowered her hand into her pocket. No bell. And now that she thought about it, there was technically no guarantee that Kaseem had dropped his interest in Sonji.

The *jundiin* gripped the pommel of his sword. "You'd better be careful. These bandits aren't friendly."

"Thank you for the warning." Astra untied Sonji and Midnight and led them to the water.

The horses slurped for a long while as Vivian made a fire and pitched a tent by the palm trees.

Astra prayed—prayed for Vivian, for Midnight's healing, for safe travels, for the bandits to stop searching for Sonji.

CHAPTER 71

After days of worrying about shadows, trying to escape, and working to thwart his father's treasure plans, Hamal sat in the Creator's grassy backyard.

Men, women, and children of every skin tone, build, and hair color worked the garden beyond the sloped yard. Animals of every imaginable color and kind helped the people.

A small, dark-skinned boy rode a massive, gray beast with huge floppy ears and a nose longer than any desert snake. Bright-hued butterflies followed a girl with auburn hair through a patch of flowers while a man and a red horse collected oranges from a tree.

"Amazing."

Hamal turned, shielded his eyes from the late morning sunshine. His father perched in a chair, one hand pressed to his side.

Hamal frowned. "Did the Creator say you could leave your room?"

Kaseem waved him off. "The Creator never tells his creations much. He offers us guidelines. We are free to decide to follow or not."

Hamal's frown deepened. "So you left against his recommendation."

"He told me I can enjoy some fresh air as long as I am careful." Kaseem eased further onto the chair and leaned against the slanted back.

"Am I to believe you've left your old ways behind you since we are sitting here?" Hamal moved to the chair beside his father's.

"My old life won't go away because I've decided to change my habits, my son." Kaseem sighed and winced.

"What does that even mean?" Hamal's fingers curled. His old hurt tunneled for the surface like an angry scorpion, but he pushed it back and focused on the memory of his father facing the Destroyer for him.

"When I saw you three years ago" … Kaseem sat up and faced Hamal … "fear seized me. I couldn't be your father. I'd already missed so much. Your natural talent and charisma, though, caught the eye of my men, and if I showed you too much interest and let you leave, they'd drag you back. So, I stayed distant and hoped you could figure out your own way to escape. I didn't want you becoming me as I had become my father."

Something shifted in Hamal's heart.

"When I saw Willard's face and heard you'd vanished during our theft at the Roses' estate, I thanked the Creator like I'd never done before. You were free. I hoped you'd never return. Hoped we'd never cross paths again. You're better off without me."

Hamal didn't remember scooting closer to his father or placing a hand on the man's shoulder. But he did, and he squeezed tight. "A son always needs his father."

"You don't need me." Kaseem grabbed Hamal's wrist and moved his hand away. He stood and disappeared into the house.

The Creator sat in Kaseem's chair. "Give him time, Hamal. Your father sees his faults now. He's not ready to forgive himself and move on."

Birds chirped overhead. A bee buzzed by, followed by Mo. The air smelled of flowers and ripening fruit.

Hamal leaned back in his chair, the wood biting into his back and bottom. "Creator, where did the people and animals come from? I mean, are they like my mother, people you've summoned?"

"Some are." The Creator faced him.

"Only some? Then, why all the rumors about most not returning home after a summons?"

"There are many reasons. Think of your mother and what she faced."

Hamal nodded. "I have."

"Think if she had gone alone." The Creator clasped his hands and set them in his lap.

"I might never have seen her again."

The Creator leaned forward. "Are all people like her, willing to share a burden?"

"No." Hamal leaned toward the older man. "My mother showed me a cog with your mark on it. She wondered if the cog and the rest of the parts she collected with Fatima might be from one of those machines she saw in a tapestry in your front room where angels and Destroyers are fighting. Are they?"

"Maybe." The Creator stood. "The tapestry you speak of is an image of the Great War, and as I've said, the machines power the Veil."

Hamal's heart rate increased. "Are the machine parts why the Destroyer chased them?"

"Why do you suppose the Destroyer confronted you last night?"

Hamal rubbed his chin. "I don't know."

A red horse approached, bearing a man clad in purple. "Great Father, I am ready for duty."

The Creator handed the man a rolled paper tied with a purple ribbon.

The man tucked the paper in his breast pocket and bowed to the Creator. "Thank you for this honor. I will return to you swiftly." He mounted his horse and trotted around the house.

Hamal stood. "Before Astra left, you said you spoke to my mother in a dream, gave her a new summons—why not send her a new paper like you did for Fatima?"

The Creator said, "The needs of each of my children are different. I meet them in their need—not at my preference." Then he joined the people tending the garden.

CHAPTER 72

For the evening meal, Hamal sat at the kitchen table with the Creator. Fruit, warm bread, and roasted chicken spread before them.

Kaseem joined them after they'd filled their plates. His movements were stiff.

The Creator excused himself, saying he needed to tend to something outside.

Hamal watched the backdoor close, wishing he too had an excuse to escape.

Kaseem filled his plate and then pushed the food away. "Not long after your mother returned from her summons, I received a message from my father. He said he was dying, said he needed me. I promised your mother I'd be back after a few months because I didn't think my father had long to live. Months later, I learned the truth—he wasn't dying, and he didn't really need me. But by then, there was no way to escape. I couldn't get your mother a note and attempt to explain the trouble I'd landed in."

Hamal ate his dinner, unsure what to say in return.

Kaseem sipped his drink. "Years later, when you showed up, I kept thinking about following you home, but guilt over everything I'd done kept me from going." He sighed and pushed away his drink. "I've done more than steal, my son. I've killed people, some of them innocents."

Hamal tried to focus on the changes he'd seen in his father. The kindness, the bravery, the guilt. He scooted his chair closer to Kaseem's. "David, my mentor, says a man is more than his past. He is a creation of the Creator."

Hamal's father met his gaze. "You want to know why I've come?"

Hamal forced himself not to answer.

"Because now my father is dying, and I've come to grant his final wish." A tear dripped into Kaseem's tangled beard. "I've come to steal the Creator's treasure."

Hamal's mother's words about forgiveness being for himself, not so much for the offender pushed to the front of his mind. Perhaps forgiveness would help his father some even if the act benefited himself more. "Father, there is no sin in a son loving his father."

"Because of your grandfather, I stole your friend's horse, I abandoned you and your mother, and ..." Kaseem sobbed.

Hamal stood and hugged his father. "I forgive you."

Kaseem tried to push away, and then, he clung to Hamal like a drowning man clinging to a raft. "I don't deserve your understanding. I don't deserve you or Omaira."

Hamal strengthened his hold. "We deserve nothing we are given. I think that's why Mother insists we say thank you to the Creator at every meal, every time we wake in the morning, and as we fall asleep each night."

"Wise woman." Kaseem released Hamal and pulled a handkerchief from his pocket.

"Indeed." Hamal returned to his seat, an unfamiliar warmth spreading through him.

Mo flew around the Creator as he entered and set a key on the table.

Kaseem picked up the key. The bow was shaped like Sonji's head, the shaft her neck, and the pin featured three uneven bits.

Hamal's warm feeling faded.

The Creator stepped toward the backdoor. "Come, my child."

Kaseem's hand shook.

"Come."

Kaseem followed the Creator outside.

Hamal snuck to the door, and his gizmo hovered beside him.

Stars glittered in an ebony sky. The soothing sound of running water mingled with the soft sounds of animals roaming in the dark. Glow bugs fluttered in the trees. No one worked the garden. Where had they gone?

The Creator and Hamal's father walked to the bottom of the sloped lawn.

Kaseem stopped. "I don't need the treasure. Neither does my father." He gave the key back to the Creator. "I'm sorry for the pain I've caused. I'm sorry I came." He walked away from the house.

In a deep, loving voice, the Creator said, "You are forgiven, my child."

Kaseem dropped to his knees. Tears glistened on his cheeks. "Creator, I don't deserve your kindness, your forgiveness." He wiped his face and nose with the back of his hand.

The Creator crossed the lawn and embraced Kaseem. "No one deserves kindness or forgiveness. They are gifts."

Gifts, according to the *Creato*, were to be freely given and shared.

CHAPTER 73

Astra's worry over Vivian and the race did not keep her from a dream-filled sleep.

Bright afternoon sunshine revealed a canyon and a bridge. Mama and Omaira each had a bag tied to her belt that held machine pieces found in the sand.

Astra's mother stood and stretched her back. "Omaira, do you have any idea why we are collecting these metal pieces?"

"One, but it's not a comforting thought." Omaira wiped sweat from her face.

"Tell me anyway." Mama picked up several silver cogs.

"Do you know how the Veil was made?"

"Machines, from the look of the tapestry at the Creator's. Growing up I'd thought magic."

Omaira nodded. "Machines powered by the Creator's magic and maintained by his angels. One of which we were summoned to collect the pieces of. Why else do you suppose we've struggled to get here?"

Mama tied off the full bag at her waist and dropped it in the back of a wagon. "Because we're fulfilling the task we received by answering our summons?"

"I wish it were that simple." Omaira dropped her bag in the wagon. "By collecting the pieces of this destroyed machine, we are helping to restrengthen the Veil that keeps the Destroyers and their minions from coming in direct contact with us."

Mama fastened a fresh bag to her waist. "You can't be serious."

"I am." Omaira tugged an empty bag from beneath a stack of full ones.

"The *Creato* says more than the Destroyers and their minions live on the other side of the Veil." Mama shuddered.

Omaira nodded again. "I fear what the machine being down long will cause ... and I wonder who caused it to fail." She shuddered too. "And I fear what will happen if more of the machines holding the Veil should fail."

Mama took a step away from the wagon. "I don't want to think about it. I'd rather get this thing back to the palace and return home as soon as possible."

"Me, too."

A rumbling like thunder echoed from the ground.

Mama and Omaira grabbed the wagon. Their horses whinnied.

"What was that?" Mama's fingers were bone-white.

"Trouble," said Omaira. "Get in the wagon quick."

The women jumped in the wagon and slapped the reins on their horses' backs. The horses surged forward.

A dark, furry shape with red eyes materialized from a shadow and pounced at them. A sound between a shriek and a tiger's roar erupted from its throat.

The horses jerked at their harnesses.

Mama held on with one hand and jerked a necklace off her neck with the other. She raised a flower-shaped pendant at the creature. Magic burst forth, creating a huge shield.

The creature smashed into the shield and roared.

The dream ended abruptly, and Astra stared up at the face of her horse.

Sonji held in her teeth the saddle blanket Astra had used as a pillow.

Astra groaned. "This is why you sleep in the barn and not the house." She flopped on her face and covered her head with her cloak.

But Sonji stole the cloak.

"Sonji." She crawled from her bed and stumbled after her running horse. "Bring that back or no breakfast."

Sonji slid to a halt at the end of her tie-line, spun around, and pranced back. She dropped the cloak.

"That's better."

Sonji nickered.

Astra fed the horses, woke Vivian, served a simple breakfast, and packed up. She glanced at the sign-in sheet—many, many names filled the page—but there were no new signatures after her name.

The *jundiin* slept under his table, his stool pushed in a corner.

Astra and Vivian mounted and rode for Gefen as the sky changed from gray to pinks and oranges. Blue would be next.

Please, Creator, watch over me, the other racers, and my family.

An unfamiliar peace settled in Astra's core. *Thank you, Creator.*

She wove her fingers in her mare's silky mane and let the steady rhythm of pounding hooves ground her.

CHAPTER 74

Night beat Astra and Vivian to Gefen. They dismounted by the check-in table and a *jundiin*, sleeping in his chair.

Vivian rapped her knuckles against the table. "Hello."

An older gentleman jerked awake and lifted a stick shaped like a gun. "You can't take me." He blinked and adjusted his turban. "Oh, racers. Excuse me." He set his stick aside.

"You're excused." She wetted the tip of a quill and signed her name on the list. "Thank you for waiting for us."

Vivian handed Astra the quill.

"Waiting is my job. Glad you and your friend arrived here in one piece ... mostly." He gestured at Vivian and the horses.

"Me, too." Astra added her name to the list.

He looked at the paper. "You're Astra Paksim."

"Yes, sir."

"I have a couple of messages for you." He removed several papers from a jar and sorted through them. "There's this one and another. Let me know in the morning if you have any answers you need sent."

"Thank you. I will." Astra collected her messages and stepped away from the table.

Vivian pointed at the jar. "My name is Vivian Rose. Are there any messages for me—possibly from a Bartholomew Rose?"

The gray-haired *jundiin* again rifled through the papers in his jar. "No, I'm sorry. Might receive something in the morning."

"Thank you for checking." Vivian stepped back.

Astra glanced at her replies in the light of a torch. One was from Mrs. Zilfel saying she'd taken Hamal's place for supply help, and she was staying in an inn by the center of town called Gefen's Place. "Mrs. Zilfel has come to our rescue."

"Really?" Vivian yawned. "Did she arrange accommodations for us for the night?"

"No, I don't think so." Astra nibbled her lower lip.

"So how'd she come through?" Vivian yawned again.

"She has my supplies."

"Great."

They asked the *jundiin* for directions and walked to Gefen's Place.

Before Astra could knock on the front door Mrs. Zilfel answered. "Ah, my brave racers have arrived." She hugged them. "You can stable your horses around back. I'll order you some dinner." The door closed.

Vivian led the way around back where a stable boy about Ehsan's age hurried up to them. "I can care for your horses for you," he said.

Vivian patted Midnight's shoulder. "We can care for our horses. Thank you. But, um, which stalls can we use?"

The boy showed them two empty stalls. Astra and Vivian tended to their horses. Astra smiled, the promise of warm food and a possible bed circling her head.

Vivian yawned. "I might skip supper after the excitement of the last couple of days."

"I won't." Astra's stomach rumbled.

"You and your horse are bottomless pits."

The friends headed into the inn where Mrs. Zilfel waited for them at a table in the back.

A woman delivered drinks and bowls of stew with rolls. "I hope you enjoy."

Mrs. Zilfel paid the woman. "Thank you."

Astra and Vivian sat and joined hands with Mrs. Zilfel before praying over the food. Vivian finished her supper first, then followed Mrs. Zilfel's directions to a room at the top of the stairs. Astra got up to follow her friend.

But Mrs. Zilfel caught her arm. "Where is Hamal?"

"Um, I'm not sure. Why?" Astra eased her arm from the older woman's grip.

"His mother isn't doing well. He needs to get home quick." She walked away.

Astra sent up a prayer for Omaira, and then climbed the stairs to find Vivian plopped on a bed in her dirty clothes. "I guess you weren't kidding about being tired." Astra crawled onto the second bed and blew out the oil lamp on the nightstand.

Despite her worry about the bandits and Omaira, Astra managed to count Vivian's snores and slip into slumber.

CHAPTER 75

Hamal hoisted a small pack provided by the Creator onto his shoulders. He hugged the source of hope and healing before he joined his father on the path to the gate. They walked several steps before Hamal said, "Father, I'm sorry for the way I treated you three years ago and over the past several days. Please, forgive me."

"You are forgiven." His father embraced him. "Thank you for your forgiveness."

Mo wiggled in Hamal's pocket, and Hamal let him out, watching him zip ahead.

Multihued birds twittered the most beautiful music, flowers released an exotic perfume, and butterflies floated around Hamal and Kaseem.

His father lifted a hand toward a small bird with a needle-like beak. The tiny bird landed on his finger, perching for a mere second before darting into the sky. The bird's wings fluttered so fast they blurred, and it hummed instead of tweeting.

"This place is incredible." Hamal watched a giant yellow butterfly land on a flower.

"There's no place in the world like the Palace of the Creator," said his father.

"I almost wish we could stay." Hamal stopped by the gate.

"Your mother and I felt the same way when we visited years ago." Kaseem smiled, but his eyes were sad.

"What?" Hamal turned and faced his father.

"Before you were born and we were married, Omaira and I visited the Palace of the Creator. Both then and now I feel like I've lived a dream, even though I haven't."

"How were you called?"

"You know the difference between a call and a summons?" Kaseem's brow furrowed.

Hamal rubbed the back of his neck. "Astra told me. I guess her great-uncle saw her horse and explained the difference to her."

"Ah."

Mo zipped by father and son as they stepped into the desert.

Kaseem's lips tipped up and a knowing gleam lit his eyes. "You and Astra seem close—closer than friends."

"Closer than friends? No." Hamal shook his head and refused to meet his father's gaze.

Kaseem chuckled. "You'll figure out what's in your heart before long."

Hamal gave a noncommittal sound. "What happened to the caravan Astra and I found you with the first time we got Sonji back from you ...?"

"They continued on their journey without us." Kaseem frowned. "They weren't too happy to learn their new friends were thieves. And I'm sorry again for the trouble I've caused."

"You're forgiven. I was just curious." Another question burned on Hamal's tongue, but he swallowed it back. Guilt over upsetting his father soured his stomach.

They trekked across the sands and stopped in Desert City where Ruth and her camels waited by the village well, as promised. She forgave Kaseem for kidnapping her and assured him that her husband Zeb would not seek revenge. Then she handed each the reins for a camel and said, "Hamal, my husband sent me a message while you were away about your mother not doing well."

"Omaira." Kaseem breathed the name before leaping aboard his camel.

Ruth and Hamal hurried to mount theirs. Hamal's heart felt like it was stuck in his throat and beat faster than a bird's wings.

"Let's be on our way." Kaseem clicked his tongue and took the lead.

Hamal followed, with Mo beside him. His happiness from reuniting with his father and forgiving him fell away.

CHAPTER 76

At dusk, Hamal, Mo, Ruth, and Kaseem entered Nahrot. Kaseem hid the lower part of his face with the long tail of his turban.

Wisewoman Yasif stepped out of the *mople* and blocked their way. "Where have you been?" She waved her hands. "Don't answer. Doesn't matter. Hamal, your mother needs you."

Hamal dismounted, thanked Ruth, and headed for home with Kaseem and Mo hurrying after him.

Wisewoman Yasif yelled, "I'll be by soon with some medicine."

Hamal entered his home with his father and Mo. Mo dived into a pile of clothes.

Ehsan smiled from where she stood by the kitchen table. "You're here." She had dark circles under her eyes, and her hair was a mess. She needed rest.

"Yes." Hamal wiped sweat from his forehead. "Thank you for being with my mother."

She sat. "You're welcome. Your mom is like an aunt to me."

Hamal closed the door and reached for the shuttered window. "Father, why don't you sit with Mother for a while?"

Kaseem tipped his head and left the room.

Hamal opened the window and allowed inside the cool evening air. A breeze ruffled a shirt atop a pile of clean and freshly mended clothes by the door. "Do you need me to take the orders out?"

"Yes, that would be helpful." Ehsan fussed with the belt for her skirt. "But do you think you'll take long?"

He approached her, squeezed her shoulder, and assured her he wasn't leaving at the moment. He thanked her for her hard work and asked if she would like to take a nap or play with Mo, who was exploring the clothes by the door.

She released her belt, said she'd like to take a nap, and asked if she could use his bed. He told her she could, and as she headed for his room, she added, "The money people have given I put in an empty jar I found on the counter."

"Sure. Thank you." He watched Ehsan close the door to his room before he slipped into his mother's quarters.

He sat by Mother's bed in the chair someone had brought from the kitchen table while his father stood on the other side and held her hand.

She breathed deeply, her eyelids closed. Her inky black hair with hints of gray splayed over her pillow. Her face was clean, but she had dark circles beneath her eyes. And she was more slender than she'd been.

Tears dropped onto his hands, and he wiped his face. "Creator, thank you for my safe travels. Thank you for bringing my father back into my mother's and my lives. She was right. He'd not wanted to be away from us. Creator, we trust in you."

A commotion drew him to the front room.

Wisewoman Yasif slammed the door. "I came as I said I would." She gave him a vial of medicine. "Your friend Astra has not failed Nahrot. She's still in the race and she may make the finish line yet."

"Uh-huh." Hamal set the vial in a basket on the counter.

"I'm amazed she slipped by the sandstorm and the bandit attack. A few of the other racers didn't—they dropped from the race. Thankfully, no deaths so far. Praise the Creator." She leaned close. "How is your mother?"

"Asleep." *Or she was until you came.*

Wisewoman Yasif headed for his mother's room. "I should check on the dear."

"Wait." Hamal stepped in her way. "I need to know—if you saw my father again, what would you do?"

Her forehead furrowed. "Kaseem is here?"

He bit his tongue.

She lifted an eyebrow. "He is, and you've made amends. You're afraid I'll tell on him to the commander or report to his men." She patted Hamal's shoulder. "You have no need to worry. I won't report Kaseem to anyone."

This time his forehead furrowed. "Why?"

"I have worked as a wisewoman in many towns. My first job, I lived in the town where your father grew up. I treated many a broken bone and ailment for him over the years. He's a good person, maybe a bit lost." She patted Hamal's shoulder once more. "I'm hoping not too lost now, since you've grown protective of him."

Hamal stepped aside, struggling with what to say in return.

The wisewoman pulled her hand back. "How about I come by later? Give Omaira and Kaseem a moment alone?"

"Thank you," said Hamal.

She stopped by the front door. "Tell your father, his brother Willard is still around and healing all right. But his two men are gone. I suspect Willard gave them orders of some sort."

"I'll tell him." He opened the door for Wisewoman Yasif. "Thank you."

"You're welcome." She turned, scanning the room. "Where is Ehsan? I thought she was staying here."

"She's taking a nap in my room since I've been sitting with Mother." He glanced at the mostly empty street. "Thank you, Wisewoman Yasif, for caring for Mother and watching over her. May your home be showered in blessings."

"You're too kind, Hamal." She gave him a small smile. "And your home needs the blessings more than mine. I'll be praying."

She stepped into the night, and he closed the door behind her with a sigh as Mo peeked out from under the mended clothes.

"I need to tell Father about Willard and his men."

Mo burrowed deep in the laundry as Hamal returned to his mother's room.

CHAPTER 77

Sharp knocks woke Astra. She untwisted her clothes from around her and shook Vivian. "We need to go."

She cracked open the door of their room and peeked through the railing on the other side of the hallway to the front of the inn.

The solid-built woman who had fed them dinner, blocked whoever stood in the street. "I have no such guests. Please, leave or I'm calling the *jundiin* on you."

A man muttered something.

Her door slammed.

Astra rushed back to Vivian. "We need to leave. No more sleeping." She tossed back the drapes covering the window and saw the stable.

"Five more minutes, *Mutter*." Vivian rolled over.

Astra dragged Vivian from the bed. "We don't have five minutes, and I'm not your *mutter*. Wake up."

Blurry blue eyes snapped open. "What?"

"The bandits are here—after Sonji. They knocked on the front door, and the owner threatened to call the *jundiin* on them. I think she bought us a few minutes to saddle and leave. We can tend to Midnight when we're safely away." She grabbed her sack of supplies and hoped there was enough for two. "Help me with the window and supplies."

Vivian rubbed sleep-sand from her eyes and pushed the window open. "Wait, what about—"

"We'll send a messenger with payment."

Vivian pulled a purse from the pocket of her split-skirt and dropped a silver winkll on her bed. "There." She climbed into the tree by the window and grabbed the supplies from Astra.

Astra climbed onto a thick, gnarled tree limb and shut the window for their room.

They slid down the trunk and ran to the stable. Both horses startled from their sleep.

Astra thanked the Creator the thieves weren't in the stable. "Time for us to go." She pulled Sonji from her stall and saddled her.

Vivian did the same with Midnight.

They shoved the supplies into Vivian's empty saddlebags. Astra rolled her sack into a ball and tied it to her saddle.

Two burly men blocked the exit.

The man wearing a red band on his upper arm smirked. "One white horse."

The other man advanced.

Astra's heart hammered against her rib cage. "Quick, head for the back." Most stables had a second entrance.

Vivian shouted. "Astra!"

Astra froze.

Red Band yanked Vivian back and the bandit took Midnight.

Red Band snarled. "If you don't give us your horse, we will hurt your friend." His accent was sharp, like Vivian's.

Creator, where are you? We need help. Astra clutched Sonji's reins to her chest. "Why does your boss want my horse?"

"You're playing for time," said the other. He too spoke with an accent.

Red Band tightened his hold on Vivian.

Vivian squeaked.

"I'll—I'll give her to you." Astra stepped toward the men. "But I'd like to know why you have to have her."

"Boss wants her." Red Band didn't loosen his grip.

"Why does he want her?" She advanced another step.

"Don't know and don't need to know."

"Release the woman. You're under arrest." Several armed *jundiin* flooded the stable.

Astra sighed with relief. The owner had followed through on her threat.

The gray-haired *jundiin* from check-in approached them. "I'll need your statements at my tent before you can continue."

"Yes, sir." Astra forced her grip on Sonji's reins to relax. "Thank you for coming."

"I'm glad to be of service. And I'm sorry you had to deal with those brutes." He turned. "If you'll follow me, your delay will be shorter."

One of the *jundiin* listed the bandits' crimes. Neither of them smiled. They were headed to jail for a very long time.

Vivian leaned close to Astra as they trailed the older *jundiin*. "You don't suppose this kind of trouble will continue to follow us the rest of the race, do you?"

"I don't know." Astra patted her mare on the shoulder. "But the Creator answered my prayer, and we escaped. I trust he has our backs."

"Me, too."

But still, a cold dread blossomed in Astra's belly. When she'd spoken with Hamal, he'd mentioned his father and three men were after her horse. She'd left Kaseem at the Creator's with Hamal, and the other three were supposed to be at Wisewoman Yasif's. So how had these two men found Sonji? Were they part of Kaseem's crew? They had the accents Hamal described, but they spoke Dryzzian. He'd not thought they knew a second language. And what about the third man, the one Hamal called uncle and who wore an eyepatch—would he come for her again?

CHAPTER 78

Astra and Vivian rode for Angel Wings.

The Great Desert Race was Astra's dream. She'd escaped bandits, crossed the halfway point in Gefen, and visited the Palace of the Creator. Now she needed to try for the finish line.

"What are we looking for?" Vivian sipped from her canteen.

"What do you mean?" Astra shifted in her saddle, forced from her thoughts.

"My map says after Gefen we're to cross a canyon named Angel Wings. How will we know we've arrived? Is there a marker? A bridge? A sign?"

"A bridge." Astra shrugged. "At least that's what the commander back home told me. I've never ridden this far before."

The dunes mellowed and flattened to reveal a narrow bridge crossing a dark line in the sand, a line that on either side curved and widened. Astra thought the canyon looked like a smile with the lips pinched in the middle rather than the wings of an angel, but maybe her viewpoint was the problem.

Ahead, a couple of racers covered their horses' eyes and crossed the bridge.

"I guess we found Angel Wings." Vivian gestured to the canyon.

Astra nodded as they arrived and reined their horses to a halt.

Vivian dismounted and leaned toward the edge. "Midnight and I have walked over bridges back home, but nothing with a drop like this. No wonder they wrapped their horses' faces."

Astra joined her friend on the ground and peered over the edge of the canyon. "I've never crossed a bridge before."

A thousand-foot drop-off led to the bottom of Angel Wings. Rocks, sand, and broken bits of wood—perhaps lost cargo or previous bridges—littered the bottom.

She stepped away. "Maybe we should try riding around instead of crossing."

Vivian shook her head. "We'll be further behind taking the long way, and giving our statements for the *jundiin* because of Sonji's near-theft already cost us precious time."

Another rider joined them. He covered his mount's head with his cloak, and they walked onto the bridge.

"We're crossing." Vivian grabbed her torn cloak from her saddle. "And we'll not look down."

A cool breeze wrapped around Astra and whispered in her ear, "You are never alone."

She squared her shoulders. "All right. We'll cross."

"That's my girl." Vivian smacked her on the arm. Her blue eyes sparkled.

"Yup." Astra rubbed her sore arm and retrieved her cloak.

They covered their horses' heads and eased their way onto the bridge.

Astra walked beside Sonji and forced herself to gaze only at Vivian's backside. Thinking about the drop sent her pulse soaring—looking down would be the end of her.

She whispered whatever popped into her head to Sonji. Random comments about Ehsan's messiness, how she'd like her papa to not cook food too spicy, her hope to finish the race, how she missed Hamal—anything and everything that came to mind—she used as a shield against her fear.

Her foot hit soft, familiar sand.

She sighed. Wonderful dunes stretched as far as she could see.

Vivian stood a few feet away and removed her cloak from Midnight's head. "I knew we'd do fine."

Astra relaxed and freed Sonji of the cover. "We're past the bridge."

"Let's check in."

They approached the tent done in gold and tan and found no one there. A paper under a rock and a pencil in a heavy cup greeted them.

"Strange." Astra shivered.

They added their signatures to a page covered in the names of other racers.

"Maybe we should keep going." Vivian straightened her stirrup. "What do you think?"

"Sure. No one else has stayed." Astra tried to mount.

Sonji shied away.

"Sonji?"

Her mare tugged her toward the back of the tent.

A middle-aged man lay dead in the sand. Blood stained his uniform and his eyes stared without blinking.

The *jundiin*.

Astra gagged and backed away.

Sonji whinnied and jerked the reins from her hands.

Vivian screamed. Midnight whinnied.

A moldy but sweet-smelling beast with red eyes and razor-sharp teeth towered over the foursome.

CHAPTER 79

Hamal struggled to feel more than helpless as he sat by his mother the whole night.

Jabir had picked up Ehsan around dinner time. She returned in the morning and made breakfast for everyone. Later, she cleaned and attempted to mend customers' clothes.

Wisewoman Yasif and her cat visited. She tried to keep the cat from hunting Mo as she delivered remedies for easing Hamal's mother's fatigue and the deep ache in her muscles.

Father hardly left Mother's side.

In the afternoon, Ehsan sent Hamal out to deliver the mended clothes.

He'd paid close attention to her descriptions of where items went and the way certain folding or colored clothes separated orders ... but in his heart he lacked the drive to care. Clothes weren't people. Still, he hoped he did well.

Mo followed Hamal in a zig-zag fashion to his final delivery at the trading post where he zipped past Ruth and a tall man with a curled mustache sitting on the front steps to fly inside.

Ruth stood and greeted Hamal with a smile. "How is your mother?"

"Putting up a fight." He slipped his free hand in a pants pocket.

"Good, I'll keep praying for her." She took the clothes and hugged him before she gestured to the man. "Hamal, this is my husband Zeb."

"Nice to meet you, sir." He shook hands with the older man.

"Same." Zeb rested a long arm on his wife's shoulders. "Ruth mentioned you have a friend racing. Is she by chance the one everyone is betting on?"

"Yes." Hamal nodded.

"Must be a fantastic rider. The bets are heavy on her winning, but last I heard she was nearly in last place."

Hamal's lips curled up, and the heaviness over his heart lifted a little. "She's incredible."

Zeb tugged an end of his mustache. "Any idea why bandits have been looking for a horse like hers?"

There was something about her husband, and after everything she'd done for him, Hamal trusted Ruth, so he said, "How well can you keep a secret?"

Zeb leaned close. "I haven't spilled one yet."

Ruth smirked. "His word is as good as gold."

Hamal whispered, "She's riding Princess Gefen's horse."

Zeb's bushy, black eyebrows raised into his brown turban. "No wonder she's pursued—she's riding a steed as fast as the wind ... and worth a few winklls." He straightened. "I won't tell a soul about her horse."

Ruth handed Zeb the clothes. "Would you pack these, dear? I'll be along in a while so we can go."

"Sure." Zeb took the clothes and walked around the trading post.

Hamal shifted his weight from one foot to the other. "You're leaving."

"Yes," said Ruth. "We're needed elsewhere."

Mo zipped out of the trading post and hovered beside Hamal.

With his mother possibly on the edge of death, his heart squeezed at the idea of Ruth going. She'd become like a friend or maybe an aunt to him, thanks to their adventures. "Will I ever see you again?"

"Oh, I'll be back. This is one of Zeb's and my favorite places in Dryzza." She hugged him. "I will always cherish our paths crossing."

Hamal returned the gesture. "Even though we were kidnapped?"

Ruth released him. "More stolen than kidnapped. Zeb never received a ransom note, and he was frantic to find me when he'd learned I'd missed making a delivery in Urugha."

"You talked about the abandoned shack by Desert City ... you always said someone else lived there, but was that you?"

She nodded. "Yes. Zeb and I lived in the shack until the sandstorm buried the village."

Another question bubbled up. "You know a lot about calls, summons, and tasks."

"Zeb and I have experienced each. Our current task is why we travel so much. We are to lead the called to Desert City."

"How do you—"

"How do we know who needs to go? That's between us and the Creator."

"Oh." He nodded. "Thank you again for everything."

"My pleasure. And Zeb and I will keep your friend and your mother in our prayers." She touched his arm and inquired about his father.

"Yes," said Hamal, "my father is with my mother ... and I have forgiven him."

"I understand the hesitation. Past hurts crop back up at times, forcing us to forgive and let go again." She tapped his chest. "I am thankful the grace of the Creator has touched your heart. Trust he'll always be with you and help you carry your burdens." She wrapped him in a quick hug before backing away. "Zeb's waiting for me."

Hamal waved. "I'll pray for your safe travels."

She tipped her head toward him before stepping around the back of the trading post.

Mo dropped onto his shoulder and rubbed his neck. A whirring, purring noise echoed from him.

"I'm thankful you've stayed with me." Hamal sighed.

Camels grunted and kicked up dust. A few minutes later, the couple and their camels disappeared behind a dune.

Someone called to his left as Mo slid from his shoulder and flew ahead.

Hamal turned.

CHAPTER 80

Hamal forced himself to smile, forced his glum thoughts to the back of his mind. "Hello."

Isaac Zilfel waved from his front porch and approached Hamal. "I heard you'd returned home."

"Wisewoman Yasif is quick to spread news." Hamal stuck his hands in his pockets.

"She is." Isaac gestured to a saw and a stack of wood. "Jabir Paksim's friend sent me a shipment of materials while you were away. He told me I could pay him back by helping him widen his trading network."

"That's very generous of Jabir's friend."

"Very. I'm hoping to start rebuilding tomorrow. If David gives you extra time off, would you consider loaning me a hand?"

David. Hamal had forgotten about checking in with his mentor. He backed away from Isaac. "Sure. I need to get going."

"Understood. Peridot and I are praying for your mother."

Hamal left, not to speak with David or return home, but to slip into a quiet alleyway. He pressed his back against a rough wall and inhaled several deep breaths, let each out slowly. The Creator loved his mother, his neighbors loved her, he loved her—but why had she been bitten by the Destroyer and become so sick? He yearned to scream, yearned to kick something, but held the urges in. He did not want the attention an outburst would draw.

Mo zipped back to him as if asking what kept him.

He waved Mo onward. "Not now."

Mo flew ahead again, Hamal stepped into the evening light, and they traveled up his street.

Jabir, covered in sawdust, stood in front of Hamal's home. Ehsan exited the house before Hamal could ask him about the dust.

"Papa," she said, "did you make lots of progress on your workshop today?"

"I did." Jabir nodded. "I did. How is Omaira today?"

"Tired, but I think the extra rest she's gotten lately has helped."

Jabir rested a hand on his daughter's shoulder. "Rest is one of the best medicines for the ill. There's a hidden power placed in slumber that banishes the evil and restores the good—at least that's what your grandmother always said." He tipped his head and wished Hamal a good night before walking away.

"Good night, Jabir, sir." Hamal eased a step closer to his front door.

Ehsan opened and shut her mouth, and bounced on her toes. "Papa and I will be going to Urugha tomorrow to catch the train. Astra should be reaching Todros soon." She stilled. "Would you like to come with us?"

"Can I answer in the morning?" He'd forgotten until now he'd promised Astra he'd meet her at the finish line—promised the day she told him and Omaira her racing plans.

"The morning works. Good night and rest well." She reached up on her toes and kissed his jaw before sprinting after her father.

Hamal smiled.

Someone cussed inside.

His smile vanished and he entered the house. "Father?"

His father rinsed his hand in a bowl of water on the counter. "I've broken the vial of medicine Wisewoman Yasif dropped off."

Broken glass littered the sandy floor by his feet. Dark liquid soaked into the ground.

Hamal crossed the room. "Let me take a look."

Father kept his injured hand in the bowl and with the other waved Hamal back. "I'm all right. You should go see if the wisewoman has any more medicine." Dark circles and a scraggly beard revealed too much time spent worrying. "But be careful. Willard is probably still in her care and upset."

"Father, I'll be careful." Hamal shifted his weight from one foot to the other. "If Mother is sleeping, maybe you should nap for a while? You look almost as ill as Mother is."

"Feels like the pot calling the kettle black." Father chuckled.

"Maybe." Hamal sighed. "There's a small jar of healing cream and some bandages at the end of the counter if you want to treat your cut." He advanced toward the door. "I'll go to Wisewoman Yasif's."

"Thank you."

Hamal found Mo outside hovering by the door. The beetle-powered gizmo led the way up the torch-lit street as he glanced at the lanterns glowing in the windows of homes. Night unrolled overhead and the horizon deepened from gray to black.

Children played, dogs chased cats, and men and women walked home from work. A few people approached Hamal and promised to pray for his mother. They offered to help his family in any way they could. He thanked them and kept walking.

When he arrived at Wisewoman Yasif's house, he found someone had left the front door ajar.

Mo hovered by the front window. The drapes were drawn.

"Hello?" Hamal pushed the opening wider. "Wisewoman Yasif? Hello?"

A hand covered his mouth, and an arm pinned him against a muscled chest.

CHAPTER 81

Stars lit a dark blue sky as Astra wished for a moon and held one of the torches for the check-in tent.

Vivian held the other one on her side of the horses.

The Destroyer circled them, taunted them.

No one had come by since they found the body of the *jundiin* and been cornered. No one. Didn't the dead man have to report to a commander? Wouldn't the commander be worried if he heard nothing?

Astra yearned for the deep peace and awe she'd felt at the Palace of the Creator. More, she yearned for the Creator to save them.

A gravelly voice spoke into the unnatural quiet. "You smell vaguely familiar." Red eyes stared at Astra.

A warm breeze pushed back the chill of night. A feminine voice whispered in her ear. "You are not alone."

Astra kept her eyes on the beast. "I've never met you before. I doubt you know my smell." Thanks to the voice, her fear slackened, and her courage lifted.

The Destroyer's eyes narrowed. "You are one of hers."

"Her who?" said Vivian, her voice squeaked.

The Destroyer circled the girls and their horses. "A child of one of the women who collected the pieces of the machine. The one who burned me with her pendant."

The machine. Astra's dream of her mother and Omaira visiting Angel Wings pushed to the front of her mind. Was this the same Destroyer who had chased them? And if this was the same one, how had Mama's pendant burned the Destroyer?

Again the feminine voice whispered in her ear. "You are not alone. Seek me and your path shall be made clear."

Astra pressed her hand to her shirt, felt the flower pendant, and pulled it free. "Are you talking about this?"

The Destroyer growled. "You are her daughter."

Vivian's torch wobbled. "What's your *mutter* have to do with our trouble? And what are you holding?"

"I'll explain later." Astra swung the pendant toward the Destroyer and kept hold of the necklace.

The Destroyer leaped back.

"Vivian," Astra called. "Get on your horse."

"Are you mad?" Vivian squeaked again.

"No." Astra pulled Sonji close. "Now get on your horse and when I say to, drop your torch."

"You are mad." Vivian gave a high-pitched laugh. "But I think I like it." She swung up on Midnight. He pranced beneath her.

Astra shoved the head of her torch into the sand and mounted Sonji.

The Destroyer launched at her.

Astra held her pendant high and a thin, glistening shield exploded forth.

The Destroyer slammed into the shield and screamed.

"Now, Vivian." She squeezed Sonji's sides, and her horse burst into a gallop.

Vivian dropped her torch, then galloped after them.

The Destroyer roared and gave chase.

Astra glanced back. Something silver glistened by the torch. What if it was a piece of the machine? "Keep going," she hollered. Then, she leaned close to Sonji's ear. "We have to go back."

Sonji spun around.

Astra lifted her pendant and pressed it to the cold, hairy side of the Destroyer.

It screamed, a sound between animal and human.

She released her knotted reins, looped the necklace back around her neck, and leaned for the ground. She prayed her shifting weight wouldn't toss Sonji over.

Her mare stayed up.

Astra grabbed the silver object as Sonji spun and galloped after Vivian.

They passed the Destroyer.

It screamed and pounced.

"Creator, protect us—" Astra yelled.

A hot wind whooshed by her.

The Destroyer roared, but came no further.

"Thank you, Creator." She clutched the metal object to her chest and picked up her reins.

CHAPTER 82

Hopefully a safe distance from the Destroyer, Astra and Vivian slowed their mounts from a gallop to an easy trot.

Vivian called out. "You don't suppose the Light—the Creator, as you call him—was why we escaped that thing, do you?"

Astra felt the truth in the pit of her stomach. "I believe he is." She slipped her find into a saddlebag.

The glow of torches and the gonging of a clock disturbed the night. Astra leaned forward in her saddle and Sonji shifted to a canter. Vivian and Midnight kept pace.

Soon the eastern horizon lightened, and they found a tent on the outskirts of Camel's Head, one of their check-in points. The friends rode up to it and dismounted.

A woman *jundiin* sat in attendance. She sharpened her sword. "Hello, ladies. Get any rest recently?"

"Not really," said Vivian as she signed her name.

"Vivian Rose. I have a message for you." The *jundiin* slid a paper across the table.

Astra signed her name and kept a tight hold of Sonji's reins. They might have escaped a Destroyer and two of Kaseem's bandits, but what about the third man?

"Paksim. I have a message for you too." The *jundiin* slid a second paper across. Her sword shone in the early morning light.

Astra accepted the note and leaned close to the torch: *I'm staying at the Camel's Head Tavern and Inn by the clock tower. Jabir gave me your supplies for here. Mrs. Zilfel.*

Vivian sidled up to her. "My father will meet me in Todros. Said he had shipments to Nahrot which have kept him from meeting me in the other towns. He sent my supplies with Mrs. Zilfel."

She tucked her paper in a pocket of her skirt and whispered, "Astra, should we mention the dead man?"

"We should." Astra put away her own note. She should have replied to the last note from her father and read the second message already.

"What if she requests we fill out statements? I don't like being slowed down further."

"The man had a family. They need to know what happened to him." Astra moved closer to the table. "Ma'am, we have news about the check-in point by Angel Wings."

The *jundiin* sheathed her shiny sword. "What news?"

Astra and Vivian explained what they found—the Destroyer and the dead *jundiin*.

The woman *jundiin* shook her head. "I knew we were doing too well. Someone always winds up dead—especially there." She pushed two large pieces of paper forward. "Write down what you've told me and sign. Then, I will need you to lead my commander and me to the body."

Vivian fidgeted. "Do we have to face the beast now? I mean, couldn't we show you the body after the race?"

The *jundiin* tapped the papers. "The sooner you finish writing, the sooner you can continue racing." She leaned across the table. "Procedure dictates you take us, but I will let you slide if you leave your contact information and promise to be available if there are questions. Otherwise, we leave now."

Astra gently elbowed her friend. "I thought you were racing for the challenge, not to win."

Vivian bounced on her toes. "I'm not ... but being so far behind is uncomfortable. I'm not used to losing so badly."

"Then, let's write quickly." Astra faced the woman. "We'll be sure to answer any questions that arise later."

"Good." The *judiin* leaned back in her chair.

Astra and Vivian picked up their pens and wrote down everything they could remember. They pushed the papers back across the table and hurried to the tallest, thinnest building in Camel's Head. Their horses trailed after them.

Mrs. Zilfel waved from where she sat on the steps of the clock tower. Two bags rested at her feet.

Astra and Vivian hurried over.

Mrs. Zilfel stood. "I've rented a room at the inn if you want a short rest before heading on."

Vivian twisted the end of her braid around her finger. "Are you suggesting our late-night jaunt shows?"

"A bit." Mrs. Zilfel held up her hand, her thumb and pointer finger close together.

CHAPTER 83

Clang.

Hamal cringed—the sound of metal-on-bone grated on his ears—as Willard dropped to the ground. He turned and found Fatima with a metal pan held high above her head.

She smiled. "You needed help, right?"

Mo flew behind her and over the head of an older gentleman Hamal knew, but couldn't place.

The man squeezed by Fatima and tied up Willard before leaning his unconscious form against a wall. "Well, that ought to hold him for a while." Then he lit a couple of oil lanterns on Wisewoman Yasif's cluttered kitchen table.

"Astra's great-uncle." Hamal hadn't seen the man since before Fatima's mother died. He'd grayed and wrinkled a bit since then.

"And you're Astra's friend, Ham, or something." The man pushed a pair of spectacles higher on his nose.

"Uncle Trev," said Fatima, "would you mind looking around for the wisewoman? I've recommended more than once that she lock her doors. Everyone comes to her house, whether she's here or not."

Uncle Trev picked up a lantern and tugged an end of his mustache. "I don't mind looking. But why do you think I need to?"

"I'm not sure her guest garnered help for his injured leg in a respectful fashion."

"Ah." Uncle Trev ducked into one of the other two rooms.

Hamal massaged his jaw and neck. "Why'd you come here? Where did you come from?"

Fatima sat at the table and set down the pan. "Uncle Trev and I came from Sultan's Elbow. We stopped by here because the door was open and there weren't any lights. I thought a thief had snuck in, and Wisewoman Yasif might be in trouble."

"Oh." He took a seat by Fatima.

Mo stayed by the door.

"Lucky for us she has her counter and cooking supplies by the door." She pointed to the pan. "Do you have any idea where the wisewoman is?"

"No." He moved some of the stuff on the table. "Father broke a vial of Mother's medicine. I came to see if Wisewoman Yasif had any extra."

"Kaseem Nuru is here?" She stared at him.

"He is." Hamal dropped his gaze from hers.

Fatima patted his arm. "I won't tell the commander. But after all these years … I'd thought something horrible had happened or he'd died for him not to return to Omaira as he'd promised."

"My grandfather tricked him, and years of guilt held him hostage."

"Guilt can do that."

A clunking and clattering came from a room, and Fatima left to check on her uncle.

Mo landed on the table and rolled amongst the mess.

Willard groaned and his dark eyes opened. "What bloody happened?" He struggled against his bonds.

"My friends came to my rescue." Hamal stayed by the table and hoped none of his uncle's knives were within easy reach.

"We used to be friends."

"We used to be." Hamal remembered his father's brother teaching him how to throw knives and the stories he'd shared of thefts gone awry. But his neck still throbbed, and his heartrate had barely returned to normal. And there was the scar on his uncle's face.

"I saw you and your father ride into town. No white horse." Willard's eyes narrowed.

"There was a sandstorm." Hamal's mouth dried.

Willard's eyes narrowed further. "Your father can figure direction in a sandstorm better than a bird knows how to fly south for the winter."

"Why did you attack me, Uncle?"

"I'd helped your father capture the white horse and knew he'd ridden for the Palace of the Creator. When I saw you back ... and no horse ... I figured the old story was true, and he'd left the key and hidden the treasure ... and we'd be going to haul it north together. But your father's never come for me." Willard turned his face away.

"You hoped if you had me, my father would come." Hamal's heart ached for his uncle. "But he never stole the treasure ... and he's with my mother who is gravely ill."

Willard harrumphed.

Fatima and her uncle Trev returned. She knelt beside Willard. "I see you're awake. Glad my handiwork doesn't seem to have caused any permanent damage."

Uncle Trev fashioned a gag on Willard. "Sorry, sir, but we can't have you getting it in your head to make a big fuss on the way to the jail."

Willard glared.

"Wait." Hamal stood.

Fatima turned. "Why?"

"He's my uncle, my father's brother."

Uncle Trev faced Hamal. "So? Because when we found you, your uncle looked ready to strangle you."

Hamal stepped toward the door. "He's desperate, and he's hurt. Please, at least let Father speak with him before he goes to jail."

Fatima and Uncle Trev agreed.

Hamal ran from Wisewoman Yasif's to his house with Mo flying after him

CHAPTER 84

Hamal sat beside his mother and held her tiny, fragile hand. He rubbed his thumb across her bony knuckles and noted the ends of her nails were chipped. "I asked Father to go to Wisewoman Yasif's to talk with his brother. Seems we weren't the only ones who needed Father. Uncle Willard tried to kidnap me so he could remind Father about the treasure."

Mother slept, her eyes closed and her breaths even.

His beetle-powered gizmo rolled around the bed.

Hamal released her hand and pushed his bangs off his face. "Fatima and her uncle saved me from Willard. They plan to send him to jail, but if they do he'll lose his hands— he might even lose his life."

He dropped his hands to his lap. "I wish you were well and awake so we could talk. Willard's not all bad. He's lost. The way my grandfather raised him and Father, they didn't have much of a chance to walk the right side of the law ... to see money doesn't make life fulfilling."

Mother stirred and reached for him.

Hamal grasped her hand.

"Trust your Creator, my son. His ways are higher than ours."

"But if Uncle Willard goes to jail, won't Father wind up there too? We just got him back. I just forgave him, Mother."

She squeezed his hand. "Trust the Creator."

A knock came at the door to her room.

Hamal stood, his hand slipped from Mother's. "Fatima."

"Kaseem has asked for you." Fatima entered the room. "I'll stay with Omaira."

Hamal kissed his mother on the forehead. "I'll be back shortly."

"Take all the time you need, my son." Mother smiled.

Mo bounded from the bed, his wings clicking free and flapping.

Fatima took his vacated seat. "We'll be all right, Hamal. Don't worry."

Hamal and Mo hurried to Wisewoman Yasif's. The older woman still wasn't home.

Uncle Trev sat at the kitchen table playing cards. "Willard and Kaseem are in the spare room. Kaseem insisted on tending to his brother's bite wound."

Father met Hamal in the doorway of the room. He leaned close. "Willard's not a man to be trifled with."

"I know," said Hamal.

Father patted his shoulder. "I know you know, but a reminder never hurts." He stepped aside. "Willard wanted to talk with you before ..."

"Father, you wouldn't." Hamal's stomach roiled.

"Let's take matters one at a time." Kaseem sighed and rubbed the back of his neck.

Hamal caught Mo, disabled the wings, and stuck him in his pocket. He entered the room.

Willard massaged his leg. "I wasn't sure you'd come back ... and I wouldn't have blamed you for staying away."

"Why the change of heart?" Hamal stayed near the door.

"Even after everything I've put you through, you protested your friends dragging me off to jail, and you gave me a chance to speak with Kaseem." Willard shook his head. "Amongst my fellow thieves, I was as good as done. Why do you care?"

"You're my uncle." Hamal shrugged.

Willard harrumphed. "A poor excuse and we both know it."

"You taught me how to throw knives and skin an apple without cutting myself. You kept the others from giving me too hard a time when my father wouldn't acknowledge me. You cared for me when I was seasick on the voyage north. You challenged me and always believed I'd make the cut. You're a good man, Uncle Willard. You've just made a few poor choices is all."

"You know I'm not your blood uncle, right?" Willard turned his face away, giving a better view of his scar.

"My father has always called you a brother." Hamal crossed the room. "That's good enough for me."

"Your real grandfather was a commander of some *jundiin* in a city by the northern border. He let your great-uncle, a thief, escape during a raid. The next morning, your great-uncle learned that his brother died during the raid. Your grandmother had died giving birth to your dad. Rather than let your father end up in an orphanage, my old man brought him into the fold." Willard drew a dagger from his belt.

Hamal forced himself not to back away. "So, you're cousins. That's not how my father or I feel toward you."

Willard flipped the dagger and caught it by the blade. He held the pommel out to Hamal. "Here."

Hamal stared at the detail work in the blade and the pommel. "Where did—"

"I made the bloody thing. I was going to give it to you the night we robbed that rich trader up north, but we wound up fighting, and you disappeared." He shrugged. "Take the dagger before I change my mind."

Hamal accepted the weapon. "Thank you."

"Think nothing of it. And send your father in." Willard sighed. "I need to face up to my crimes."

"What's going on in here?"

That voice sounded a lot like Wisewoman Yasif.

Hamal left the spare room. "Wisewoman."

"That's me. What are all of you doing in my house?" Wisewoman Yasif glanced around the room. "My clock reads four in the morning. Don't you have beds to be in?" She dropped a basket overflowing with bloodied rags by the door.

Her cat trotted past her and into the second bedroom.

Nabila, Isaac's apprentice, snuck in behind the older woman and dropped off a second basket. "Good night, Wisewoman."

"Huh?" Wisewoman Yasif turned around. "Oh, Nabila, good night. Tell your grandma to soak those clothes in cold water and soap them up before hanging them in the sun. Most of that blood should come out pretty good."

"I will." Nabila vanished in the dark.

Fatima's uncle Trev gathered the playing cards. "Where'd the blood come from, ma'am? Are you hurt?"

"Hurt?" Wiswoman Yasif scoffed. "Peridot Zilfel went into labor. Had a healthy baby girl and made a mess." She planted her hands on her hips. "Now, is anyone going to explain why you're here instead of at your own homes?"

Father stepped from a dark corner by the back door. "Thought we'd pay Willard a visit."

"You're worried about Willard? He's mending fine. You should be with Omaira."

Hamal cleared his throat. "That's the second reason we came. We need some more medicine because the vial you gave us broke."

"I'll bring you a new one after I've had some shut eye. If she needs something to tide her over, have her chew on some Dryzzian mint leaves." She yawned. "Now leave."

Kaseem poked his head in the spare room.

Wisewoman Yasif smacked him on the arm. "I can take care of your brother."

"No, you can't." Kaseem disappeared into the room. "Willard's gone."

The wisewoman followed him and exited the room a moment later. "Did he mention any travel plans to any of you?"

Hamal slid the dagger behind his back and hooked it on his belt. "No."

Fatima and her uncle shook their heads.

Kaseem returned to the main room. "The sun is soon to rise. Wisewoman Yasif, I'll pay you what I owe for my brother and men when you come by with Omaira's medicine. And thank you."

She sat at the table. "That fool left. Hope he doesn't tear the stitches."

"Wisewoman?" Kaseem rapped his knuckles on the table.

She looked up. "Hmm? Payment? Medicine? Yes, we can settle them later." She yawned. "I'd best get some rest." She stood and stretched. "See yourselves out." Her bedroom door slammed.

Kaseem covered his face with the end of his turban. "Time to go home."

CHAPTER 85

Late in the morning, Astra saddled her mare. "One more night in the desert and we'll reach the ocean." Her nerves tingled.

"I've never seen the Southern Ocean." Vivian tightened the main cinch of her saddle.

"You mean you've seen the Northern Ocean before? I've never seen any ocean." Astra snuck a peek at the device she'd grabbed last night. It was the size of a thick book and made of metal and wood like one of Hamal's more complicated inventions. She wrapped it in a spare sack and hid it at the bottom of a saddlebag.

"I have. My family home is an hour's ride from the beach. We used to visit the water often."

"Used to?"

A tear slipped off Vivian's chin. "Before my *mutter* died. From the time I was little, we connected over three things— horses, the beach, and travel." A second tear slipped off.

Astra pulled a wrinkled handkerchief from her pocket. "Here."

Vivian accepted the offering and wiped her face. "My *mutter* told me once the view of the Southern Ocean is glorious. I don't know how she knew I'd get to visit there." She returned the handkerchief to Astra and removed an envelope from her pocket. "My *vater* gave me this note from my *mutter* the first day of the race. She wrote this on her deathbed. I can tell because of the slight shakiness to some of the words. Her encouragement, her belief in me ..." Her voice cracked. "When she became sick, I struggled sitting with her. She'd wasted away to someone so fragile I hardly recognized her."

Vivian pulled out a handkerchief and blew her nose. "How did she ever find the strength to write me? To tell me about the Southern Ocean and her love for me? Her final week ... I sat at her bedside only when my *vater* was too tired to be there. But she forgave me for my weakness."

Astra struggled to find words to soothe her friend and finally decided saying nothing was best.

Vivian put away the note. "I wish you and Hamal had had the chance to have met her. I'm sure she'd have liked you both."

"And I'm sure we would have liked her." Astra tested her ties and cinches.

Vivian checked the fresh bandage on Midnight's leg. "Thank you for helping me care for my horse and riding with me. I've had the most awful homesickness."

"I haven't had much time to be homesick." Heat filled Astra's cheeks and she recalled the last time she'd seen her home.

"I guess not, with bandits and sandstorms and me harassing you." Vivian smiled.

"I guess." Astra faced her friend. "Vivian ..."

"Yes?" Vivian stood and turned.

"Why were you at the abandoned shack?"

"Not long after my *mutter* passed, I was called in a dream to visit the Palace of the Creator. I didn't have the courage to go until this year, until I was almost due for the race."

"How did you know where to go?"

"My dream. I was given a map, and when I awoke, I drew what I remembered of the map." She pulled a crinkled paper from her pocket.

Astra glanced at it. The writing was in a foreign language, but the landmarks were familiar. "You're good at drawing."

"Thank you." Vivian folded her map and headed for the door. "Are you ready?"

"As ready as I'll ever be." Astra let Vivian slip out ahead of her and opened her second message from Gefen. *Astra, I hope to see you after the race, before I answer my summons. Thank you for sharing your courage and comfort. Wishing you the best. Mama.*

Astra put away the note and hurried after Vivian.

In the town square, they thanked Mrs. Zilfel for watching over their horses and supplies while they ate and napped.

"My pleasure." Mrs. Zilfel hugged each of them. "Take care. I'll be praying for you both."

Vivian swung into her saddle. "Will we see you at the finish line?"

Mrs. Zilfel shook her head. "No. I have a grandchild due any day."

"I wish you safe travels and congratulations in advance." Astra mounted Sonji.

"Same." Vivian nodded and turned her horse around. "Let's ride." She clicked her tongue and Midnight trotted away.

Astra and Sonji followed. The blue sky and the openness of Camel's Head reminded her of Nahrot. Between buildings and then dunes she spied train tracks to the north. From here on they'd guide her to the finish line.

Her heart fluttered. The fulfillment of her dream was within her grasp.

CHAPTER 86

After a couple of hours on the trail, Astra and Vivian joined a group of slower racers.

A man on a black and white pinto told them more than half the racers had dropped from the race. "Too much upset this year. First a sandstorm, then an attack by a group of bandits, and something was spooking the horses at Angel Wings. I heard later the *jundiin* for the check-in point was found dead. *Jundiin* hardly ever die out here. Usually the racers are more prone to die—someone always does something stupid."

Vivian asked him how many years he'd raced.

"This is my tenth run." He patted his pinto's shoulder. "Riding the son of my first mount. He's been as surefooted as his dam so far."

Astra mulled over the information. If a few more than a hundred had started the race, perhaps fifty or less were finishing. "Have there ever been so few racers at this point?"

"One other time," said the man.

"Do you remember why?"

"I doubt anyone knew why. But I suspect the high number of dropouts and a few deaths were tied to some creature following us."

Vivian paled. "A creature?"

"This is the Dryzzian desert. Legends are more alive and deadly out here than anywhere else. And you can't predict what will stir some of them awake." He eased his horse away from them.

Vivian shivered. "Reminds me of that beast we encountered by the canyon."

Astra agreed. "But why? Why are they appearing now? According to the *Creato*, the Veil has worked since the day it was finished, since the end of the war."

"I doubt the Destroyers took their loss very well."

"So they're destroying the Veil piece by piece?" Astra closed her eyes tight. Her mother needed to complete her summons. She needed to take all the pieces of the machine back to the Creator, so he could rebuild it. If the Veil failed ... Astra pushed the thought aside and forced her eyes open.

"I surely hope we're wrong." Vivian shivered a second time. "I can't stand the idea of them up to such evil."

"Me neither."

They arrived at the check-in point as the sun finished disappearing behind the western horizon. Almost everyone Astra remembered seeing at the starting line was camped here.

When she and Vivian signed in, they asked why the other racers were here.

"New rule," said the *jundiin*. "All racers are to gather here because the sultan wants to give everyone still racing a fair chance at winning. Once the last one is accounted for, you'll be released to run for Todros."

Vivian curled the fingers of her left hand and rubbed the pad of her thumb over the nails. "Is everyone here?"

He checked the list in his lap to the sign-in sheet. "You two were the last. Since the sun's down, I'll start everyone off at first light."

Astra and Vivian left the check-in and set up their camp. Both wondered why the new rule, why the chance to win, and agreed, if either should win, she'd ask the sultan for the answer.

A campfire tossed light and shadow on Vivian's face. "Astra, you seemed like you wanted to say something extra when I brought up my *mutter*'s letter. May I ask what was on your mind?"

Astra wrapped her cloak around herself. "Something I'm sure you already know—that your *mutter*'s beyond her pain and watching over you from somewhere in the stars."

"I know. Thank you for wanting to make sure my heart is at ease. You're a solid friend." Vivian squeezed Astra's shoulder. "I'm going to turn in."

"Vivian, thank you for letting me use your extra line for a second time."

"You're welcome." Vivian disappeared in her tent.

Before bed, Astra visited Sonji.

Her mare stood at the end of the rope and glared at it.

"I'm sorry, Sonji-girl. But after the thefts and the craziness, I needed to know you were close. Hopefully once we're home I won't ever have to tie you like this again."

Sonji snorted and rubbed her head on Astra's arm.

Astra braced against her horse's rubbing. "I'll take this as you forgiving me a little."

Another snort, and she poked at Astra's pockets.

Astra patted Sonji's neck. "You can have a treat in the morning." She crawled into her tent and fell asleep to the sound of Vivian's snores.

CHAPTER 87

A sleepy Hamal made sure he had Mo in his pocket and exited his home with a hastily filled pack. Ehsan and Jabir greeted him in the street. His mother had promised not to die, to hold on while he was away. His father, Fatima, and her uncle promised to stay with Mother at all times. Still, Hamal wanted to rescind his promise to Astra.

Ehsan grinned. "I'm glad you decided to come."

Hamal offered a non-committal sound.

Jabir chuckled. "We won't be gone long, and mothers are stubborn." He led the way toward the trading post.

Hamal grunted and followed until his mentor exited the blacksmith shop and wiped his hands on a rag. Heat flooded Hamal's insides. "David, sir."

"Hamal, I'm sorry I couldn't keep my promise."

Jabir and Ehsan kept walking.

Hamal swallowed, tried not to gulp. "What promise?"

"To keep an eye on your mother and the Paksims while you were off." David wiped his brow with the back of his hand. "The *amir* needed his order delivered right away because the sandstorm early in the race kept him from reaching Nahrot."

"Delivered?" Hamal vaguely remembered Ehsan coming into the blacksmith shop and playing with a specially fashioned dagger. There'd been some comment about an *amir* ordering it.

"I tried to convince him to wait a few days, but he wouldn't have it." The space between his eyebrows looked pinched. "Said he'd get what he wanted from another smith if I didn't deliver as soon as possible."

Hamal nodded slowly. "I see." He didn't, but he'd play along.

"I heard about your mother's condition worsening. I'm sorry. I'll keep her in my prayers. And return to work when you're ready." David backed toward his shop.

"Thank you, sir." Hamal struggled to remember if he had anything else to say before his mentor disappeared inside the blacksmith shop, but he missed his chance and had to jog to catch up with Jabir and Ehsan.

Isaac talked with Jabir by the trading post while Ehsan buzzed around an older gentleman packing goods on three camels. Four more camels waited in saddles.

Jabir crossed his arms, his gaze clearly on his daughter. "How is your wife, Isaac?"

"My Peridot is doing well ... and so is the baby."

"Congratulations. Boy or girl?" Jabir patted the trader on the back.

Isaac Zilfel smiled big as the moon. "Girl. I now have three best days of my life—the day I married my wife, the day my son was born, and now my daughter's birth. The Creator has blessed me."

A woman hollered from across the street. Isaac backed up several steps. "I need to go. May your travels be blessed." He hurried away.

The camel man hollered for them as Jabir tipped his head toward the Zilfels' home. "He's a happy man, if I ever saw one."

"He is," Hamal said.

CHAPTER 88

The train station in Urugha stank of livestock, over-ripened fruit, unwashed people, and cooking meat. Hamal tried not to retch. His gag while he was kidnapped smelled better than this place. He held tight to Ehsan's hand as Jabir led them through the thick group of people, animals, and cargo. Hamal's trip on the train to Latif City three years ago had been less crowded than this.

Ehsan tugged and wiggled her fingers. "You don't have to hold me so tight, Hamal. I'm not going to sneak away."

He glanced at their hands and loosened his grip. "I know. I'm sorry."

"You're forgiven."

Jabir directed them onto the train and to their seats.

Hamal stared out the window. A man and his dog performed tricks while people tossed coppers in his cap. A woman carried a basket of food and shouted prices. Boys his age and younger loaded animals and luggage onto train cars.

Ehsan tapped his shoulder and pointed to a tall man carrying scarves. "I think he's the man who sold me my new sinar. I didn't know he lived here."

Hamal pulled Mo from his pocket. "The world is a bit smaller than we think."

She sat next to him and nabbed Mo. "Bumping into people in unexpected places has nothing to do with the world being small. The Creator has more influence than we give him credit for."

Ehsan opened the top of her pack, fluffed her spare sinar, and settled Mo there. "Hamal, have you ever seen the ocean?"

"I have." He wasn't sure about seeing it again.

"Does water really stretch to the end of the world?"

He chuckled. "The world is round. There is no end."

She petted the gizmo like he was a tiny cat in her lap. "But you can sail so far all you see is water for miles, right?"

"Sailors claim so. I've never seen it for myself." He faced her. "Do you want to sail?"

"Yes." She met his gaze with soft brown eyes. "When I go, can I take Mo with me?"

"Sure. But keep him away from the water. He might rust and I'm not sure his joints will do well with the salt water."

"I'll be careful." She untied her cloak from the bottom of her pack.

"I know you will." He turned back to the window.

On the platform, a conductor called, "All aboard for Todros. Last call. All aboard."

"Hamal, do you think Astra and Sonji have a chance at winning?" She set her pack between them.

"Sure. Why do you ask?" The space between his eyebrows pinched.

"I bet a copper on her and I'd like to get it back." She snuggled down on the bench and used her cloak as a pillow. Her soft snores joined the noises of the other passengers.

The train whistled and chugged down the track in the direction opposite of Latif City.

Shortly before dusk, the train stopped in Camel's Head. Food vendors weren't allowed aboard, so Hamal and Ehsan disembarked to purchase some dinner.

They waded through the crowd to a woman with a basketful of sandwiches. Hamal handed her a coin, and Ehsan grabbed their food.

A familiar dark turban bounced between others.

Hamal pulled Ehsan through the throng.

"Hamal, where are we going? The train is the other way."

"We'll be back in time."

"Hamal. Ugh." Ehsan kept hold of his hand.

He wriggled between folks and popped out on the far side of the station. The turban bobbed not too far away. He chased after it, and the outline of a man grew more distinguished. With his free hand, he spun the individual around.

Not his uncle.

"Sorry, sir." Why'd Hamal think Willard was here? If he were found and identified, Willard would go to jail and lose his hands. Better to leave the man alone and not search for him. So, he prayed his uncle was somewhere safe and staying out of trouble.

"Can we return to the train now?" Ehsan gulped air. "And why did we run after that man?"

"He reminded me of someone." He turned. "I'm sorry I dragged you out here. We can go back."

They boarded and found their seats by Jabir.

Ehsan handed her father a sandwich and sat beside him. He looped an arm across her shoulders, and they prayed over their food before she devoured her dinner and fell asleep.

Jabir ate more slowly. When he finished, he gently turned. "In Latif, I bumped into a friend of mine. He said years ago he'd worked with a boy from Nahrot, and the description he gave me matched you."

"Oh?" Hamal wiped the crumbs from his sandwich off his clothes.

"My friend is Bartholomew Rose."

Icy tingles spread along his spine and arms. "Uh-huh." Hamal might have started to mend his friendship with Vivian, but he wasn't sure how her father felt about him.

"Have you ever worked up north training horses?"

"Um ..."

"If you have, I think you should visit with Mr. Rose." Jabir eased himself back around. "He's going to be in Todros to see his daughter."

"Uh-huh."

The sun sank below the horizon. Lights flickered on above the seats, and after a while, they dimmed to a warm glow. An ink black sky full of diamond-bright stars stretched over the desert. The constellation of Princess Gefen filled the window. The train jostled.

And Hamal lost sight of the image.

Campfires dotted the dunes. He searched for Astra or her white horse, but the train traveled too fast.

Strange to think Astra rode the same horse Princess Gefen rode when she saved Dryzza from the tyrant sultan hundreds of years ago.

He grinned. The Creator cared for individuals like himself and Astra as much as he cared for whole nations. Amazing, so amazing it felt almost unbelievable.

The train slowed to a halt, and a conductor walked through the car hollering, "Last stop—Todros!"

People shifted in their seats and grabbed their bags.

Hamal grabbed Mo from Ehsan's pack and dropped him in his pocket before handing Ehsan her pack. He followed Ehsan and Jabir onto the platform and into Todros.

The roar of waves echoed up the streets, and the salty, fishy smell of the ocean slapped him in the face. Hamal's short time aboard ship flashed to the front of his mind. His stomach roiled.

Jabir led the group to an inn.

Behind the counter sat a woman even older than Wisewoman Yasif. Her shoulders were hunched, her back curved, and her glasses magnified her dark brown eyes. "Hello." Her voice sounded bad as a creaky door. "How can I help you?"

"We'd like two rooms," said Jabir.

She reached in a drawer and dropped two tarnished keys on the counter.

Hamal reached in his pocket.

Jabir settled a hand over his. "I've got the tab tonight."

Hamal's mind flashed to the burnt furniture shop, the lost income. He'd repay Jabir somehow.

CHAPTER 89

Astra and Vivian lined up with the other racers in the gray of the predawn hour. Her muscles ached and fuzz dotted her brain after a restless sleep. She held tight to Sonji and trusted her footing in the sand.

A *jundiin* stood atop a table, raised a pistol, and fired.

A few of the horses whinnied, two shied, and the others leaped into a gallop.

The miles passed in a blur. Dunes rose and dropped away. They passed an oasis and a cluster of houses.

The sun rose high in the sky and the cool of the morning turned to sweltering heat.

A few of the racers slowed, their mounts sweaty.

Astra continually checked her mare for sweat and never found a drop. She also listened closely to Sonji's breathing and never heard a sign of trouble. She thanked the Creator for her special horse.

More horses fell back.

Vivian and Midnight kept pace.

When they reached the finish line, if Hamal was there, Astra needed to keep her promise and help him connect with Vivian.

The sun began its descent.

Astra's stomach growled and her throat felt as dry as the land around her.

Some of the racers eased to a slow canter while most, including Astra and Vivian, slowed to a trot.

Astra sipped from the canteen tied to the pommel of her saddle, and her throat rejoiced in the cool, wet relief.

From her bags, she removed a few dried dates and ate them. The heat had brought out the natural sugars in the dates and made her fingers sticky. She licked as best she could, but riding and eating, same as riding and drinking, did not work well together.

Dunes mellowed to reveal a town—and beyond it, something blue glittered all the way to the western horizon.

"Did we reach the ocean, Sonji?"

Her mare kept her steady rhythm and flicked her ears back.

"The water, it's beautiful." Her breath caught.

Vivian and Midnight raced for the lead.

Astra shrank herself in her saddle to keep out of the wind. "Let's give our new friends a challenge, girl."

Sonji ran faster. She passed Midnight in a few strides and kept going.

A joking holler echoed on the wind.

Astra smirked. She was where she belonged, atop a fast horse and racing across the desert.

Stretched between a pair of tall poles was a banner. Thick, black letters proclaimed the finish line. Beside each pole stood a representative dressed in off-white and gold. Behind them and out of the way, crowds waved flags and shouted.

Her courage shrank—so many people. She forced herself not to jerk on the reins and slow Sonji.

Not far ahead a gray horse and two red ones galloped for the finish.

She whispered to Sonji, "Let's show them how a real horse runs."

Every hoofbeat ate up the distance. They passed the red horses. Each stride drew them closer to the gray.

They passed the town.

Astra could win. The finish line waited half a mile ahead.

Sonji drew beside the gray and his rider.

The man bared his teeth.

Astra didn't bait him. She gave her mare her head and focused on the finish. The crowd faded to a blur of colors.

They crossed the finish line and ran right into the ocean. Salt water sprayed her in the face. Astra screamed and hollered and cried. She'd survived desert storms, bandit attacks, and more … and she'd won. Not just finished. But won. *Thank you, Creator.*

She wrapped her arms around her horse, who swam for shore.

"Thank you, Sonji-girl. Thank you."

Sonji shook herself like an oversized dog.

Astra laughed and held on. "I guess getting wet isn't your favorite."

Sonji snorted.

Other racers followed them into the water and back to the sandy shore. People crowded around, and several *jundiin* hollered.

Astra couldn't stop laughing. "We finished. Oh, my wonderful Creator. We finished."

Papa, Ehsan, and Hamal stepped from the crowd.

Astra jumped from her saddle. "You're here."

Her sister smooshed her in a hug. "We promised we would be."

"Where's Mama? Still in Sultan's Elbow?" Astra embraced Papa and Hamal.

Ehsan caught Sonji's reins. "Mama's at home with Great-Uncle Trev. They're watching over Hamal's mom."

Astra's joy diminished. "What?"

Hamal fussed with pieces of metal in his hands. "Mother's illness has worsened."

"Let's not focus on trouble—at least for now," said Papa.

"Agreed." Ehsan again wrapped her arms around Astra. "You won. I can have my copper winkll back from Wisewoman Yasif."

"You bet on me?"

"You're my sister. I know you better than anyone. And I know Sonji." She winked.

Astra squeezed her little sister. "Thank you for your faith in me."

A *jundiin* approached. "You are to return to the beach at dusk, so the sultan may reward you for your win."

CHAPTER 90

She had an hour until dusk. Astra hurried her family and her friend to their inn, but stopped by the steps to the porch because nailed to one of the porch posts was a wanted poster for Kaseem Nuru. She glanced at Hamal.

Ehsan grabbed Sonji's reins and tugged the mare up the alleyway with the threat of giving her a bath. Papa followed them.

Hamal yanked down the poster and wadded it up. "I'll see you in a while, I guess."

"Yes." Astra nodded. "Come with us to the beach."

"I will." The right side of his mouth lifted.

She rushed inside and took the fastest bath of her life. The whole time, her mind swirled with something Hamal had said. *The bounty on his head—dead or alive—is five hundred gold winklls.* Why five hundred? Was that the amount he'd stolen? And if so ... Hmmm.

She dried off and reached for the clothes she'd tossed on the privacy blind of the room she shared with Ehsan. She pulled down the same soft shirt and leaf-green skirt she'd worn the day Mrs. Zilfel paid her the gold winkll. She didn't remember packing the outfit. And Ehsan's blue, flower-patterned sinar stuck out of the skirt's pocket. She slipped on the outfit and stepped around the blind.

"You look beautiful." Papa sat on a chair by the door.

Ehsan grinned. "You're as pretty as a princess."

Heat flooded Astra's cheeks, and she thanked them for the compliments and outfit.

Papa admitted a beaming Ehsan thought to bring the clothes before hurrying her off to take a bath. He crossed the room to stand beside Astra. "You remind me of your mother at your age—beautiful and strong as a desert flower."

"I wish she were here." Astra traced the swirls and flowers her mother embroidered along the collar of her shirt.

"She wanted to be here, but she was needed back home." Papa cupped her cheek. "Your mother and I are proud of you."

"Thank you, Papa, for supporting me and letting me race."

"You're welcome."

Loud splashing interrupted the moment, and Ehsan hummed a tune from Shabbos gathering.

"Ehsan," Papa called. "Hurry."

"I am, Papa."

At dusk, Astra stood on an empty beach with Papa, Ehsan, Hamal, and Sonji. The racers and others celebrated in Todros.

Strong, calloused fingers twined with Astra's, and she turned to find Hamal beside her. Heat flooded her cheeks as she looked into his warm, brown eyes.

Papa cleared his throat, and Astra and Hamal dropped hands.

Three *jundiin* approached. One wore a sash full of medals across his chest. A creamy-white feather pinned by a gold button decorated the front of his turban.

Astra gripped the sides of her skirt, ready to curtsy if told to. She wasn't sure what else to do.

"Hello," said the fanciest of the *jundiin*. "I saw you win. One of my *jundiin* says your name is Astra Paksim."

"Yes, Your Majesty." Astra curtsied, certain only the sultan would say 'my' about a *jundiin*.

He tipped his head to her.

When he straightened, she noticed he had one blue eye and one brown. He wore his beard and mustache shorter than most men did, but there was still a curl on each side of his mustache. And his ebony hair was trimmed short.

He smiled. "Would you like to be sketched with me?"

"Sure—I mean, yes, Your Majesty." She stepped closer.

"Let's have the whole family." He waved Sonji, Ehsan, Papa, and Hamal closer.

One *jundiin* set up torches, and the other pulled a sketchpad and pencil from inside his uniform coat. Soon the pencil of the second flew across his pad.

"I've never been sketched before," said Ehsan. She stood near the front and held Sonji's reins.

Astra couldn't remember ever being sketched, either.

The sultan smiled bigger than before. "I'm honored to be part of your first sketch."

Ten minutes later, the *jundiin* showed them his sketch.

The sultan lifted half-moon spectacles from a breast pocket. "Fine work. I'll need copies made—one for Miss Paksim and the rest for the announcements I'll release."

The *jundiin* flipped a blank page over the sketch and slid the pad of paper inside his coat. The other extinguished all but one torch. They waited off to the side.

She'd get a copy of her sketch, and she'd be on an announcement. Astra nibbled her lower lip. Her sister elbowed her and vaguely shook her head.

Astra released her lip. "Thank you, Your Majesty." Hamal and her family added their own thanks.

The sultan clasped his hands behind his back. "Now, the matter of your prize."

Astra held up her hand. "Your Majesty, when I reached the last check-in, all the racers were told to wait until the stragglers caught up, but I don't remember reading about such a rule before ... or the inspection of the mounts."

His eyes twinkled. "A voice on the wind told me of a young lady racing a certain mare. Rather than have her horse reveal how special she is to the world, I adjusted a few rules."

"But me winning—"

"You winning by a few strides surrounded by other racers who've had to travel the same distance as you after a night's rest doesn't look strange. You crossing two days' worth of desert in a day and winning would have drawn unwanted attention."

Sonji bobbed her head.

Astra's eyes watered. "Thank you, Your Majesty."

He tapped his nose and winked. "You and Sonji are welcome." He removed a coin purse from his belt. "Now, about your prize." He placed a bulging bag of gold winklls and jewels in her hand. "Usually I give several bags of gold, but since we're doing this in Todros instead of Latif City I felt a single bag of equal worth smarter."

Astra stared at the money and jewels. She'd never seen so much wealth in her life.

Ehsan leaned close. "Thank you, Your Majesty."

"Yes, thank you, Your Majesty." Astra recalled the night in the desert she spent with Vivian and how Vivian helped her search for Sonji. She also remembered Vivian's promise that if she won, she'd split her winnings with Astra.

"You're most welcome. May the Creator abundantly bless you and your family."

Papa settled his hand on Astra's shoulder. "And may he bless yours."

The sultan and his *jundiin* turned.

"Wait, Your Majesty." Astra tied the money purse to her belt.

"Hmm?" He faced her.

She dipped into a curtsy. "Um, Your Majesty, can we speak in private for a moment?"

A dark eyebrow lifted. "We can." He waved to his men, who stepped back.

She led the sultan a short way from her family and spoke with him in whispers before giving him five hundred gold winklls' worth in a few jewels.

The sultan pocketed the money. "Kaseem will be free to roam in Dryzza, but I cannot promise elsewhere. The only reason I'm considering dropping charges against him—besides your payment for his thefts—is because I don't know of him killing anyone in my borders." He leaned close. "Please, strongly encourage him to never steal and to never leave Dryzza. Many seek his blood."

"I will." She shifted from one foot to the other. "Your Majesty ... why did you help keep the world from finding Sonji? Why don't you want her for yourself?"

"My parents taught me real treasure is not gold and jewels, but love freely given."

Astra struggled with a reply. Finally, she said, "You don't need the Creator's treasure, so you don't need my horse?"

He chuckled. "The Creator's treasure is love. He gives his love to everyone, no strings attached. So, no, I don't need your horse. I already have the treasure."

His tone grew more serious. "My brother, the *amir*, does not see this truth as I do. You are lucky the sandstorm stopped him from racing alongside you—and that my men caught the bandits he sent after you. I recommend you not race again."

"Oh." She caught her lower lip in her teeth, released it. "Why the change in treatment of outcasts?"

He rubbed his chin and leaned close. "Why do you suppose?" He smiled and his mismatched eyes twinkled.

And the reason dawned on her—because he was one, he cared about everyone.

The sultan waved his men to his side and left.

Papa headed for the town, and Ehsan and Sonji followed him.

But Astra stayed back and caught Hamal's arm. "Thank you for coming."

"You're welcome." Hamal lifted the right side of his mouth.

She released him and soaked in the warmth offered by an ocean breeze. "I spoke with Vivian during the race, and she mentioned you working for her father. I think you should talk with her and him. You might be surprised in a good way."

"Astra ..." He pulled off his turban, ruffled his hair, and smooshed his hat back on.

"Please, Ham, if you get the chance to talk to them do so—for me." She pouted her lips and lifted her eyebrows. "Vivian's become a good friend. I don't want my two closest friends ill at ease with each other."

He sighed. "I'll try."

"Thank you." She kissed his cheek, lifted her skirt, and ran after her papa.

Hamal chased after her.

CHAPTER 91

Music, shouting, and laughter shook the town. People spilled out of taverns and restaurants. Horses and camels were tied to hitching posts and porch railings. The scent of alcohol, dirty people, and fish mixed with the briny sea air.

Hamal tried to ignore his sick feeling and keep Astra's family in his sight. Jabir held onto Astra, and she held onto Sonji's reins, and her sister rode the mare.

A figure emerged from a shadowy alleyway, and a familiar voice spoke to Hamal. "Your great-uncle claimed possessing the treasure would fix all his troubles and fulfill all his dreams."

He stopped. "Uncle Willard ...?"

His uncle turned his eyepatch to him and raised a walking stick. "Your father knew better and tried to convince me of the truth for years, but I never listened." He walked. "Treasure doesn't solve a man's problems, and it doesn't love him."

"What are you doing here?" Hamal lost sight of Astra, but he didn't panic because he knew she and her family were heading to their inn for dinner.

"Correcting a few wrongs."

"How'd you get away?"

"A smart thief never reveals all his secrets."

They stopped in front of the inn Jabir had booked.

Willard reached in his pocket and pulled out a paper. "Give this to your father and tell him I'm sorry for leaving like I did ... and for the fires I started against his orders."

Hamal took the paper.

"Tell your girlfriend she'll never have to worry about her horse being stolen again. I've seen to that." Willard patted Hamal's shoulder. "Take care, nephew."

"Will I ever see you again?" Hamal's heart weighed heavy in his chest.

"With any luck, no."

He hugged his uncle.

The man stiffened, then slowly relaxed, and pushed out of the embrace. "I'll ... um, miss you too." He backed away a step. "Take care." And then he blended into the crowd.

The door to the inn opened and Jabir stepped out. "Hamal, there you are. Have you seen Vivian or Bartholomew Rose? They're supposed to join us for a late dinner."

Hamal frowned. "No."

"Jabir." A heavily accented voice called.

"Bartholomew." Jabir waved.

Mr. Rose and his daughter squeezed free of the throng in the street. Vivian wore a blue dress and a matching shawl. Her father wore a brimmed hat and a vest over a nice shirt.

Hamal's past had snuck up on him.

The men exchanged news as Vivian paused beside Hamal.

Hamal wanted to eat his promise to Astra. Sure, he and Vivian had come to some understanding before she left Nahrot. But ... that didn't mean everything was good between them, that what she said wouldn't reawaken his deep guilt over running away.

Vivian smiled. "You look well."

"You, too." To be able to melt into the floor would be wonderful.

"My *vater* would like to speak with you." She touched his arm. "Do not be afraid. He bears good news." She pulled her hand back.

Jabir invited her inside.

Hamal heard Astra and Ehsan laughing. He stuck his hands in his pockets and wished he were with them. The fingers of his right hand brushed Mo. "Hello, Mr. Rose." He felt fourteen again.

"Bartholomew." Bartholomew Rose held out his hand. "We're both men. You can call me by my first name."

Hamal shook the hand of his former boss. "Bartholomew."

Bartholomew pulled a coin purse from his pocket. "I believe we have some back pay to discuss."

"Back pay? I ran out on you, sir, without warning."

"Vivian mentioned your father and why you left." Bartholomew opened the purse. "I hold none of that against you—you are forgiven. But that doesn't excuse me from paying you your dues. Your work with my daughter's horse and my stock was sound."

Hamal stared.

"How much do I owe you?"

No words would form.

Bartholomew gripped Hamal's shoulder with his free hand. "I remember a training session when you told Viv, 'Your colt has the fire of the desert in his veins. He'll be a fine racer.'"

"I don't remember." Hamal stuck his hands back in his pockets.

"I do. And when I watched my Viv take third place today, I knew you'd spoken the truth. Your faith in her and that long-legged yearling were spot-on." Bartholomew released him and he opened the purse.

"Vivian and her colt came in third because of her faith, not mine. I just gave her a few pointers. She's a natural with horses."

"She takes after her mother that way." Bartholomew counted out a fistful of winklls and handed them over.

"Thank you, sir." Hamal stuffed the winklls deep in his pockets. The money would help him pay Wisewoman Yasif for his mother's medicine. His work in her yard hadn't paid for the more obscure ingredients she'd needed.

"You're welcome." Bartholomew patted him on the back. "Now, let's join the others for dinner."

CHAPTER 92

An hour before dawn, Hamal slipped from the room he shared with Jabir.

A cool wind dusted through the town.

No torches burned, no loud music played, and no crowd pushed against him on his way to the beach. He removed his socks and shoes and rolled the cuffs of his pants. The cold ocean water shocked his system in the best of ways. Seagulls flew overhead and waddled along the shore.

Mo wiggled in his pocket, then quieted.

Mo, not a gizmo come to life but a magic metal beetle that had moved into Hamal's gizmo. Amazing. Hamal thought about the beetle shedding the round invention like a second skin and flying with his shiny little wings. Mo looked kind of like the little creatures in the tapestry depicting a battle between good and evil. Perhaps they were magic metal beetles. The Creator had said that Mo's brethren cared for the machines that held up the Veil, an invisible line shown in the tapestry that seemed to stretch forever. He wondered what happened to the beetles when a machine failed.

A dark chill crawled up Hamal's spine.

He turned, sensed something watching.

A dark shape moved in the shadows and disappeared down an alleyway. If that was a Destroyer or one of its minions … well, he could hardly wait for the Creator's device to be fixed and the Veil strengthened.

He sent up a quick prayer for protection, pulled on his shoes, and headed for the inn.

At the front desk of the inn, the old woman slumbered in her chair. Her purple creation stretched even further than before. At the bottom of the blanket, in dark purple thread, was stitched a flower bearing three petals.

He paused. The intricate work reminded him of Astra's miniature tapestries, her needlework as she called it. The last one featured Princess Gefen and Sonji. The princess had had to face her father, a man touched by darkness, to save her people. And the Creator had said that the darkness drew people to do more than be wicked to each other … sometimes it convinced them to break the machines powering the Veil.

Please, Creator, don't let the Veil fail and allow the Destroyers to ravage the land.

The floor above him creaked.

He heard a man's and two girls' voices whispering—probably Jabir, Astra, and Ehsan.

Jabir descended the stairs. "There you are. Ready to go home?"

"Yes." Hamal missed his mother. He wished she'd been able to come, to meet the Roses, to cheer on Astra, and to dip her toes in the ocean. *Creator, please continue to watch over my mother. Please heal her.* He pushed his crawling gizmo back in his pocket and his wandering thoughts to the back of his mind. *Thank you for now.*

CHAPTER 93

Astra sat beside her sister on the train ride home. Ehsan slept, wrapped in the purple blanket made by the innkeeper. Astra marveled at the kindness of the old woman and her mastery with knitting needles. The stitches were tight and perfectly even.

Sand stretched for miles. Villages appeared and vanished. Sometimes an oasis disturbed the scenery.

Astra reviewed the last few weeks: Her visit to the Palace of the Creator, her returned yearning to be a wisewoman, realizing she wasn't an outcast, getting to be sketched with the sultan, his knowledge of Sonji shielding them from trouble, her kissing Hamal on the lips, and making friends with Vivian Rose. She'd cherish every memory forever and more.

Hamal fiddled with some metal pieces.

Her happy moment sagged. Ever since Papa had asked if they were ready to go home, Hamal had distanced himself from her. And she understood why. He worried about his mother.

Astra leaned her head against the wooden back of her seat and prayed.

A cool breeze slithered through the stuffy train.

She tugged a corner of Ehsan's blanket over her.

A feminine voice whispered in her ear. "All of my children are special. None need win battles or save countries to be remembered by me."

Thank you, Creator, for everything—even the hard moments.

Astra rode Sonji into Nahrot. Papa, Ehsan, Hamal, and an old trader followed on camels.

Villagers threw streamers, yelled her name, and played the Dryzzian anthem. A banner reading "Congratulations Astra" hung between the House of Citizens and the inn. The sweet scent of honey rolls and candy mixed with roasting meat and cooking vegetables.

Someone shouted that she should be honored with a song like Princess Gefen was.

Astra's cheeks flamed. Her nervousness over crowds stretched her nerves. A soft wind wrapped around her, and a feminine voice whispered, "You are not alone." Astra relaxed.

Sonji ate treat after treat, and someone slipped a wreath of silk flowers over her head.

Mama pushed her way to the front of the crowd.

Astra leaned down in her saddle and embraced her mother. The villagers pressed too close for her to dismount.

Her mother whispered in her ear, "I'm so proud of you. You chased your dream."

Astra tightened her hug. "I've missed you, Mama. And thank you for the pendant and letting me race."

"You're welcome." Mama pulled back and patted Astra's leg. "I've missed you too. I'll see you later at Omaira's." She let the crowd push her away.

Astra accepted a silk flower bracelet from a villager. "Thank you. Thank you," she yelled. "I'm honored by your kindness. But I'm no more special than any of you. All I did was follow my dream. Any of you can, too."

Astra glanced over her shoulder to her sister, papa, and Hamal—only to spy Ehsan sneaking something from Hamal as he talked with Papa. Why?

The village clock dinged two in the morning when Astra escaped the still-celebrating crowd to stable Sonji. She found her sister and father asleep at home before she snuck to Omaira's to visit her mother.

"Mama?" Astra whispered when she entered the Nurus' home.

Mama set aside the shirt she mended and got up from her chair beside the kitchen table. She crossed the room, kissed the top of Astra's head, and held her close. "My blessing, I'm happy to have you home safe."

"I'm happy to be home." Astra clung to her mother, she'd missed her more than she missed home. "When did you return to Nahrot?"

Mama explained that she'd come home with Great-Uncle Trev shortly before Papa left for Todros. Hamal had loaned the old man his room as a thank you for his help and because he couldn't stand to leave his mother's side for very long.

"Is ... is Omaira doing any better?"

"No." Mama returned to her seat and moved a pile of clothes off a bench to the table. She patted the bench. "Come, sit with me a while."

Astra sat and leaned against her mother. "I won."

Mama rubbed Astra's back and rested her head on hers. "You did. Wisewoman Yasif received word by pigeon yesterday and spread the news faster than fire."

"I split my winnings with a friend I made during the race. She helped me finish what I started."

"That was very generous of you, and she sounds like a good friend."

"She is." Astra lifted the pendant that hung around her neck. "Mama, why'd you leave?"

"I was scared to answer my summons."

"But you're not now? I mean, what changed? Why did you come back?"

Mama straightened and held Astra's hands in hers. "I'm still scared, my blessing. But seeing the person you were becoming by facing your fears convinced me to face mine."

Astra pulled off the pendant and slid the necklace over her mother's head. "I want you to take this with you."

"It's your birthday gift." Mama touched the flower, her eyes brimming with tears.

"And I want Sonji to go with you."

"Astra, no"—Mama shook her head—"she's your horse. And you've just returned from racing."

"Sonji's special—she'll help you." Astra squeezed her mother's hands. "I know you and Omaira were asked to collect the parts of a machine for the Creator." She met her mother's gaze. "And I know the machine is important."

"How do you ... know?"

"Odd dreams, a few comments by different people." Astra shrugged. "I found a piece of the device at Angel Wings, and a Destroyer gave me a hard time, but the pendant helped me escape."

"My brave girl." Mama hugged her. "I'll answer my summons at sunrise."

"I'll be there to wave you off, and I'll pray for you." Astra pressed her face into her Mama's shirt and inhaled the scent of baked bread and honey, the best scent in the world.

CHAPTER 94

After a couple of hours of sleep, Astra saddled Sonji and filled the saddlebags. "You'll take good care of Mama, won't you, Sonji-girl?"

Her mare snorted and flicked her ears.

The flower pendant hung from Mama's neck as she exited the house. She tucked a sack of clanking parts at the bottom of one of the bags.

Astra hugged her mother.

Ehsan hid something behind her back, snuck behind Mama, and slid a familiar metal ball into a saddlebag. She lifted her finger to her lips.

Astra narrowed her eyes. So that was what Ehsan had stolen. But why?

"I'm going to miss you." Mama released Astra and pulled Ehsan into an embrace. "And I'm going to miss you."

Papa stepped out of the house and handed Mama a cloak. "I don't want you catching cold."

Mama hugged and kissed him.

Ehsan covered her face. "Ew."

Papa chuckled and led the way to the back gate. He kissed Mama's forehead. "I'll be praying for you."

"And I for you." Mama led Sonji out and mounted. They disappeared behind a dune.

No one moved for a long time.

Please, Creator, watch over Mama, Sonji, and Mo. And send them back to my family. Astra wiped a tear from her face.

Papa closed the gate and headed for the house.

Ehsan slipped her arm through Astra's. "Do you want to see what Papa and our neighbors have been doing while you were racing?"

"Sure."

Ehsan led her to the furniture-making shop and through the back door. "They made the inside bigger, and now Papa has two spare rooms to store his furniture." She pointed to a set of shelves built under the workbenches. "I made those."

Astra removed her arm from her sister's hold so she could touch every workbench, stool, shelf, and cubby. "Ehsan, this is amazing."

Instead of the smell of ash, the aroma of freshly cut wood permeated the space.

Ehsan grinned. "The Creator is good."

"Always," the sisters said in unison. They decided to thank everyone with a lunch at Mr. Zilfel's trading post.

Before Astra could ask about Mo, a sharp knock drew her and her sister to the yard. Papa stood beside the back door of the shop. "Astra, the wisewoman is here to speak with you. She's at the front gate."

Astra hurried to the front.

Wisewoman Yasif waited with her cat. "I wanted to offer my personal congratulations ... and offer you an apprenticeship."

"An apprenticeship?" Her pulse raced.

"While you were busy racing, Isaac and Peridot had their baby. Nabila, sweet girl, tried to help me, but kept turning green. Peridot mentioned you had helped with her first child and had been studying under your grandmother."

"I did." Astra's hopes lifted. "Are you serious?"

"I am. But you need to understand I've never had an apprentice before, and I don't like repeating myself."

Then why do you spend so much time gossiping? "I'll make sure to listen closely and keep a notebook handy."

"Good. You can start now. I need help with Omaira. Your great-uncle is sweet but he's not much of a caretaker." Wisewoman Yasif opened the gate.

"Wait, you mean *now*?"

Wisewoman Yasif harrumphed. "Yes."

"Let me tell Papa, and I'll be right with you." Astra darted into the house and grabbed a satchel, a notebook, a pencil, and her latest needlework. She found her father and Ehsan entering by the side door and told them about her apprenticeship before she ran to catch up with the wisewoman.

CHAPTER 95

An old kitchen chair dug into Hamal's backside as he sat in the dark and listened to his mother's steady breathing. The travel and celebration exhausted him, but his restless worry for his mother kept sleep at bay.

She stirred, but did not wake. "Fatima?"

"Mother?" He tried not to yell.

Father jolted awake in his chair. "Yes?"

Hamal reached out to her.

Mother arched her back and fell onto her pillows. "Fatima beware." She caught Hamal's arm, her grip stronger than steel.

"Mother." He tried to break her hold. "Let me go."

"Return. Return." She released. Her normal, steady breathing returned.

Father reached for her hand and rubbed her knuckles with his thumb. "Don't worry, Omaira. Fatima is returning the last of the machine parts. Your summons is almost complete."

Hamal rubbed his arm and scooted his seat out of reach. Why the sudden, intense dream? He adjusted the blankets and pushed her tangled hair away from her forehead. "Everything is all right, Mother."

Father yawned. "My son, you look tired. Why don't you try to get some sleep in your room? I'll stay here with your mother, and Trev is available to help me if anything comes up."

Hamal tried to collect his scattered thoughts—Trev was an uncle. Hamal had seen his uncle Willard in Todros. He removed a wrinkled paper from his pocket. "I crossed paths with Willard while away. He gave me this for you."

His father took the paper from him. "Thank you. Now try to get some sleep."

"I'll try." But he couldn't sleep. He tiptoed past his room, where Astra's great-uncle Trev slept soundly, and into the night.

The clock on the House of Citizens struck four. Astra and her mother had left for home at two-thirty. An eerie silence floated over the village. Not a torch burned or oil lantern glowed at this hour.

A deep, unsettling cold knotted his insides.

He snuck inside the *mople* and bumped into a pew. A loud thud echoed through the space.

He cringed.

The man sleeping in the front pew gave a horrible snort and called, "Who goes there?"

"Hamal."

"Hamal Nuru? Welcome, come forward." The man stretched, his joints audibly groaning in the open room.

A flame spurted to life.

"Seems my candle burned out. Troublesome things always need tending." The man—Tariq Ke'ev—turned.

Hamal proceeded toward the front. Stepping inside the Palace of the Creator hadn't made him as nervous as he felt being in the Nahrot *mople*. "Hello."

His beard and mustache trimmed, his nice clothes wrinkled, the *tollarb* set the candle on a pew. "I heard you've been up to some wild adventures."

Hamal managed to nod.

You have no need to fear me. I promise." *Tollarb* Ke'ev scooted over on the pew, nearly bumping his candle, and motioned to the emptied space. "Wisewoman Yasif mentioned why you are uncomfortable with *tollarbs*—that the previous one gave you a hard time for missing Shabbos gathering. I'm sorry he did that."

Hamal stood in the aisle, unsure about sitting so close to the spiritual leader. "Why don't you ever ask me about my poor attendance? Or question why I've come here so early in the morning?"

Tollarb Ke'ev said, "We each come to the Creator when we are ready—not before."

His statement reminded Hamal of a previous one. "Why did you tell me never to be afraid to place what I don't understand in the Creator's hands? You commented about having a feeling, but that doesn't really explain why you told me what you did."

The *tollarb* chuckled. "Even after recent experiences, you still question the why of everything." He stood, tried to straighten his clothes. "Again, I'll say, never be afraid to place what you do not understand in the Creator's hands."

"Mm-hmm." The repeated answer didn't really help Hamal.

Tollarb Ke'ev gave up trying to straighten his clothes. "Perhaps when your mother is feeling well, I'll ask her about how to get rid of wrinkles." He hummed off tune as he patted Hamal on the shoulder and exited the *mople*.

Hamal sat in the front pew beside the candle and soaked in the peaceful silence despite what the *tollarb* having said stirring up more questions than answers.

An hour later by the chime of the bell, Hamal blew out the candle and left the hall. The sun peeked above the horizon.

Up the street, David exited his home and fed his donkey.

Hamal jogged over to him. "David, sir, thank you for your understanding and prayers."

The donkey brayed, and he patted the old work animal. "And thank you for letting me borrow your donkey."

"You're doubly welcome." David rubbed his chin, his brown eyes gleaming. "I understand the need to follow a trail while it's fresh, but, if I remember right, you didn't ask to use the old boy to chase down Astra's horse." He chuckled.

"I'm hoping to be back to work soon. Let me know if you need anything." Hamal slid his hands into his pockets. No Mo. Where'd he lose him? Or had Mo escaped?

David inched toward his shop. "I need to finish Jabir's order of replacement tools."

Hamal moved back. His mind circled to the list he'd seen after the fire at the furniture shop. "Is that the order I started to help you with a couple of weeks ago? Something about a shovel and a pair of pliers and screws and something else?"

"Yup. I've finished part of the order, but getting enough screws created takes time."

"I didn't know Jabir used screws."

"Said he'd heard somewhere about them being used now. He's got a project in mind he wants to try them on." David shrugged. "He's always trying to keep on top of better ways to build." He placed his hand on the doorframe of his shop.

"I can deliver the order for you when it's ready."

"Sure. I'll see you around, Hamal." He disappeared inside his shadowed shop.

CHAPTER 96

Hamal returned home and found his father in the main room with Trev. The men were playing a card game.

Hamal stepped toward his mother's room.

Kaseem set a card on the table. "I wouldn't go in there right now, son."

"Why?" Hamal paused.

Kaseem set another card on the table and lifted one from the deck. "There is much to learn about life. And something I've learned is when women shout for a man to leave a room and they pull out the soap—he'd best leave."

Trev adjusted his oversized spectacles. "He means my great-niece and your busybody wisewoman are giving your ma a bath."

"Oh." Hamal sat on the bench next to Trev.

An hour later, Astra and Wisewoman Yasif came from his mother's room.

The wisewoman carried an armload of dirty laundry. "You may enter now, but be careful of the mess. We're still cleaning it up."

"We will." Hamal jumped from the bench and nearly collided with Astra as she carried two buckets of soapy water toward the front door.

She grinned. "Wisewoman Yasif has taken me on as her apprentice."

"Congratulations." He grinned back. "Would you like some help with the buckets?"

"I've got them. I'll be finished cleaning shortly. Then maybe we can talk for a short bit?"

"Maybe." Hamal ducked into his mother's room and the strong scent of honey and Dryzzian mint greeted him. Spread over the bed was the purple blanket Ehsan had received from the innkeeper in Todros. How did that get here?

Astra returned. He heard her speaking with his father.

Hamal stepped away from his sleeping mother and peeked through the crack of the partially opened door.

Father gave her a brass bell with a wooden handle, the bell Hamal had made for Astra.

"Thank you, sir." Astra tucked the bell in her pocket. "I have a couple of questions to ask you."

"All right." Kaseem set aside his cards.

"How did you steal my bell?"

"I found it poking out of the back of your little tent."

Astra nodded, her cheeks a light shade of pink. "I think I already know the answer to my next question, but I want to be sure. Why did you steal Sonji and my bell?"

"I stole the bell because I'd seen you use it to call the mare, and I stole the mare because I thought she was the key to a treasure my father had asked me to retrieve." Father tapped his pants pocket holding the note from Uncle Willard. "I recently learned the horse was not literally the key and that my father has died. I no longer have to grant his final wish."

"I'm sorry for your loss." She bit her lip and released. "And I forgive you for stealing Sonji and my bell."

"Thank you for your condolences and your forgiveness." Father headed for Mother's bedroom.

Hamal stepped out of the way for his father and Astra.

She sidled by him and into the room with her buckets. "I don't need long to finish cleaning."

"Uh-huh." Hamal moved his chair so he was out of the way.

Later, Astra led Hamal outside. "There's something I need to tell you—the sultan has dropped all charges against your father. All the riches he stole have been paid back, and he's never killed anyone in Dryzza ... so, as long as he stays here, he's a free man."

Hamal scooped Astra in his arms and kissed her. He set her down. "I don't know why or what you did to free him, but thank you."

"What if I wasn't the one responsible for helping Kaseem?" Her cheeks were bright red.

Hamal laughed. "No one is kinder than you, Astra."

"You're sweet to say that." Her eyes glittered gold and emerald-green.

Three days had passed since Fatima left. Wisewoman Yasif and Astra tended to his mother. Sometimes Astra worked on the piles of mending or her needlepoint of a tiny Sonji stealing a key for Princess Gefen. Ehsan visited and made deliveries. Jabir, his wife's uncle, and other neighbors stopped by with food or news of the outside world or just to say hello.

Knock. Knock.

Hamal answered.

David and his donkey waited. "You'd mentioned you'd wanted to help with Jabir's delivery."

"I do." Hamal hesitated.

Astra looked up from her needlepoint at the kitchen table. "I'll stay here, and let Kaseem know you stepped out for a short while." She tied off her thread and lifted her needlework. The tiny Sonji glittered in silver thread. Gold decorated the sultan's room and outlined the key the horse stole. The lifelike detail was amazing.

"Thank you, Astra. And beautiful work." He gestured to her mini-tapestry.

"You're stalling. Go." Her cheeks flushed pink.

Hamal joined David, and they walked to Jabir's new shop.

His hand shielding his eyes, Jabir stood outside his shop and faced the desert.

Hamal followed Jabir's gaze.

Fatima rode Sonji, and Mo flew ahead of her.

Jabir ran toward them. "Fatima! Thank the Creator! Fatima!"

Ehsan poked her head out of the shop. "Mama?" She raced after her father. "Mama."

Fatima dismounted and ran into her husband's arms. She reached out an arm and caught her daughter. "Where's Astra?"

"At Omaira's," said Jabir.

"We must go there quickly." Fatima ran for the village.

Sonji, Mo, Jabir and Ehsan chased her.

David elbowed Hamal. "You may go. I can unload by myself. And Jabir can pay me another time."

"But ..."

"I think you should go. You can help me by returning to work when you are a focused apprentice."

"Yes, sir." Hamal chased after the Paksim family. He followed them through Nahrot and right to his front door.

Sonji stood by the window. Mo flew inside behind Ehsan, Fatima, and Jabir.

Hamal ran after them.

The door to his mother's room was pushed wide open.

Fatima stopped beside Mother and uncorked a slender, glass vial of clear liquid tinted silver and purple. She helped Mother drink every last drop.

A silvery light emanated from within Mother. Her pale skin brightened. Her skeletal form filled in. The shadows beneath her eyes melted. The unhealthy dullness of her hair faded. She stirred.

"Hello, my loves."

Hamal's heart swelled. *Thank you, Creator.*

Astra smiled big as the moon next to him.

Mother hugged Hamal and kissed Father. "My generous Creator, thank you." She grabbed Fatima's hand. "And thank you, my friend."

Mo zipped about Mother's room.

Astra's great-uncle Trev huffed and puffed his way through the front door and to Mother's room. "I guess Fatima didn't pick a plant as her gift for answering her summons." He leaned against the doorframe. "And someone other than the blacksmith could have informed me of Fatima's triumphant return."

The house filled with laughter and cheer.

EPILOGUE

Astra handed the reins for Sonji to Omaira. "Are you sure you have to go now? You've hardly been well for more than a day."

Omaira mounted the white mare. "If we are to keep the Destroyers from finishing off the Veil, I must get to the palace and return the last piece of the machine to the Creator."

Astra nodded. "Yes, but why must you go? I could take the cog."

Omaira leaned in the saddle, resting her hand on Astra's shoulder. "The Creator asked me to bring it to him." From a leather cord about her neck glittered a cog the size of a winkll with an etching of a flower bearing three petals.

"I know, but …." Astra struggled for a good reason that would keep Omaira from leaving, but stopping the most stubborn woman in Nahrot was harder than stopping Hamal.

Omaira squeezed her shoulder and straightened in the saddle. "Keep an eye on Hamal and Kaseem for me … and pray I reach the palace in time."

"I will," Astra promised.

As Omaira clicked her tongue and tapped the mare's sides, Mo peeked from inside the satchel she carried and waved a clawed little hand.

Astra waved back, and her free hand strayed to the flower pendant hanging from her neck. Her stomach sank as she realized she'd forgotten to give Omaira the pendant.

ABOUT THE AUTHOR

When Jessica A. Tanner isn't writing stories full of vivid characters and creatures, she enjoys a view of the Rocky Mountains, takes long walks, and hangs with her many critters. Jessica is a member of the American Christian Fiction Writers (ACFW), Realm Makers, and Wolf Creek Christian Writers Network (WCCWN). She has a testimony in *Twenty-Three Journeys to Christ* compiled by Gregg Heid, three true-life stories in *A Book of Remembrance: A Collection of Everyday Miracles* compiled by Lynn Moffett, several pieces published under the Matter of Faith Column of the *Pagosa Sun's Preview*, and a piece and a short story in *Looking at Life* compiled by WCCWN. *Sonji* is her first novel. You can contact her at www.jessicaatannerauthor.com.

Made in the USA
Columbia, SC
16 August 2023

21708608R00224